SLIP OF A FISH

Amy Arnold, based in Windermere, Cumbria, was announced in June 2018 as the winner of the inaugural Northern Book Prize for her unpublished first novel *Slip of a Fish*.

The Northern Book Prize is an annual prize to celebrate an unpublished book-length work of ambitious literary fiction and a writer who lives in the North of England. When And Other Stories relocated to the city of Sheffield, we conceived of the Prize to demonstrate our commitment to finding and publishing great Northern writers. In 2018, we were thrilled to work in partnership with New Writing North and the Prize was part of the 2018 Northern Writers Awards.

Going forward, the winner of the Northern Book Prize will receive a prize advance (currently £5,000), as well as editorial support, publication, distribution and representation by And Other Stories. We would be delighted to hear from potential supporters and partners to enable us to increase the prize money and the Prize's reach.

You can read more about the Prize, including submissions deadlines and criteria, here:

andotherstories.org/northern-book-prize/

Northern Book Prize

SLIP OF A FISH

Amy Arnold

SHEFFIELD – LONDON – NEW YORK

This edition first published in 2018 by And Other Stories
Sheffield – London – New York
www.andotherstories.org

9 8 7 6 5 4 3 2 1

This book is a work of fiction. Any resemblance to actual persons, living or dead, events or places is entirely coincidental.

ISBN: 978-1-911508-52-6
eBook ISBN: 978-1-911508-53-3

Editor: Anna Glendenning; Proofreader: Sarah Terry; Typesetter: Tetragon, London; Typefaces: Linotype Neue Swift and Verlag; Cover Image: '10 am is When You Come to Me' by Louise Bourgeois, © The Easton Foundation/VAGA at ARS, NY and DACS, London 2018; Cover Design: Ronaldo Alves. Printed and bound by the CPI Group (UK) Ltd, Croydon, CRO 4YY.

A catalogue record for this book is available from the British Library.

And Other Stories is supported by public funding from Arts Council England. The author would like to acknowledge the financial support of New Writing North, supported by Northumbria University and Arts Council England, through the awarding of the 2018 Northern Book Prize.

Supported using public funding by
**ARTS COUNCIL
ENGLAND**

MIX
Paper from
responsible sources
FSC® C020471

The first time we went out together, Abbott took me to see a film about a man who didn't want his wife to get pregnant. The film was set in Utsjoki, in northern Finland. Utsjoki was dark. That's to say the sun didn't come up for the whole ninety-seven minutes. The actors were floating around, or rather, seemed to be floating around on backgrounds of greys and blues. Blues so deep it wasn't easy to be sure they really were blue.

Abbott spent the entire time shifting in his seat, tilting his head at different angles. I could tell he thought there was a problem with his eyes or his glasses. He kept taking them off and putting them back on again, wiping the lenses on his shirt, on his jeans, then holding them up to the light. There wasn't much light to hold them up to. All the disruption was making it difficult to concentrate on reading the subtitles, so I tapped him on the shoulder. I was planning to tell him a bit about the polar night. I thought it would help, I thought an explanation would reassure him.

The sun sits below the horizon in winter. For weeks. That's why everything's dark.

That's what I planned to say, and I was ready to say it. I must have been. I think what I actually said was that it wasn't unusual for small cinemas to have problems with their screens, and I gestured into the darkness. Whatever I said must have had an effect, because his fiddling and shuffling stopped after that. When I tapped him on the shoulder again, although I can't remember why now, he said there was no need to tap, there was no need to whisper either.

'Look around, Ash,' he said. 'We've got the cinema to ourselves.'

I wanted to add Utsjoki to my word collection. I wasn't sure whether it would count. I didn't have any other proper nouns, or foreign words for that matter, although I'd wanted ingénue for a long time.

'It's your collection,' Abbott said on the drive home. 'You decide.'

I couldn't decide.

'I don't know,' I said.

'Well, what are the rules?' he said.

And whilst I was thinking he said, 'That was really off, having a vasectomy without telling her, don't you think?'

'There's only one rule,' I said. 'I have to hear someone say the word.'

I took a deep breath. I waited for him to speak, and when he didn't, I went on.

'Finding the right word is like finding the right pebble,' I said.

What I meant was, finding the right pebble on a whole beach of pebbles. Thinking about it now, I'm glad I stopped there. I was getting carried away, flinging analogies around like that.

'So, shall I put it in?' I said.

He thought for a while. I thought for a while. We thought for the time it took the traffic lights to turn green. I was thinking about the time Papa and I were looking for the right pebble.

'But how will we know it when we see it?' I said.

Twice I asked him, maybe three times.

Abbott let the handbrake off.

'Put it in. Utsjoki,' he said. 'Why not?'

He let go of the wheel and made a sort of flicking gesture with his hand to show how laid-back he was about it. I put Utsjoki in. I didn't have many words beginning with u and it was the only one where t, s and j ran into each other.

'You can't get bored of it, can you?' I said.

Abbott checked the rear-view mirror, then signalled.

'Uts, Utsjo, Utsjoki,' I said.

He looked over his shoulder and pulled onto the dual carriageway. He breathed out.

'It's the sound of the o after the j that makes it. Like box, or socks, but more Nordic. Don't you think?' I said.

I spoke a lot in those days. I was always speaking.

I managed to get hold of a book called *Towns and Villages Inside the Arctic Circle* after that. The book had a whole chapter devoted to Utsjoki. 'Utsjoki: Finland's Most Northerly Municipality'. Yes, I still liked the sound of the o after the j, because that's what got me started, and you should never forget the things that get you started, but what I really liked, perhaps even more, was the idea of endless daylight.

In summer, the sun stays above the horizon for seventy-one days. Endless daylight.

Those were the words in the book. Endless daylight had a whole sentence to itself. The author, Jari, and I think his surname was Joki, must have known how good it sounded. He must have felt brave letting it stand on its own like that. Endless daylight, full stop. Yes.

I kept the book on the coffee table. Displayed it, you could say, although Abbott was the only one who ever came over. Still, when he did, he picked it up and read the back cover.

'Utsjoki's in there,' I said, leaning into the jo to help him remember. Utsjoki from the film.

I don't think he heard me because he said he hadn't known there was a series of *Towns Inside* books when he'd treated himself to a copy of *Towns Inside the M25* on his last birthday.

'It's been so useful to have all the London commute times and prices in one place,' he said.

'But Tilstoke's almost a hundred and fifty miles north of the M25,' I said.

'Well,' he said. 'You never know.'

I took the book up to my bedroom. Summer was on its way, and it felt right to have it beside my bed, where I could dip into it before sleeping. Seventy-one days of endless daylight. Endless daylight. Full stop. One thousand, seven hundred and four consecutive hours of it. Enough hours to warrant telling Abbott, but I had the impression he didn't want to know much more about Utsjoki, and I wasn't ready to hear him say something about how it would even out in the end.

All that daylight.

I went on reading about towns and villages inside the Arctic Circle anyway. To be honest, I couldn't stop reading, and the thing about endless daylight was true, because on page fifty-seven there was a photo of people swimming in a lake after midnight.

Swimming in Kevojärvi after midnight.

That was the caption. It didn't look like daytime in the photo. It didn't look much like night-time either. I suppose it might have looked like twilight if I'd known how twilight looked. Still, it started something inside me, that photo, a sort of tug north you could say. It could have been the light, or the two people wading, the ones nearest the camera. Whatever it was, I couldn't stop thinking about swimming in Kevojärvi at night. I thought about it when everyone inside the M25 was sleeping. When they were sleeping or worrying, because darkness brings both. And maybe that's what it was about Kevojärvi, about Utsjoki, about endless daylight. Seventy-one days without worry, although it probably all evens out in the end.

I thought about Utsjoki again after Charlie was born. Especially after Charlie was born. I decided it couldn't hurt to bring up the subject with Abbott again. After all, it had been a long time since we'd seen the film and he might have forgotten the things I'd mentioned before. We were tucked up in bed reading, and Charlie was sleeping. It seemed like a good time to begin.

'In summer, the locals swim in the lake at night,' I said. 'It's warm enough. That's where they swim, in the lake. In Kevojärvi.'

I had the book ready to show him. I'd folded the page with the photo of Kevojärvi and I had my thumb in the page I'd folded. There were seven people in the water. Two of them were wading and the others were swimming. The ones who were swimming were quite far out. The pair who were wading were close to the camera, but I couldn't tell whether they were men or women. It was one of the things I wanted to ask Abbott. Look at these two wading, I'd planned to say. Do you think they're men or women? Boys, perhaps?

I'd told him the lake was called Kevojärvi. I'd taken the time to learn how to pronounce it properly and I was about to show him the photo. I had the book in my hand, I was moving it towards him. I had the page folded over ready, my thumb in the page.

'Kevojärvi?' he said.

'Yes,' I said. I crossed my fingers under the duvet.

'I thought you loved Tilstoke Baths.'

'Yes,' I said. 'Yes.'

Charlie loves swimming in here. The lake off the Toll Estate. The only other people who swim here come on a Tuesday morning, it's a club or something. There are *Private* signs on the banks. There are signs on poles in the water. One says *No Swimming Unsupervised*, the other has a figure swimming in a red circle with a line through it, and you can't tell whether the swimmer's a boy or a girl, but Charlie says it doesn't matter.

'It just means no swimming, that's all,' she says.

You can swim here though, unless it's a Tuesday. It's fine to swim, and nobody checks.

And now Charlie's on the rock. She's thirty metres out. Fifteen strokes, if you're good. If you know how to breathe underwater.

There she is. Charlie, light of my life, fire of my heart.

I know. Of course I know, but it's fun, it's a game. Whatever Papa said about taking lines. Lines from stories, from poetry, from fables, myths, yarns, histories, speeches.

'It's like plucking feathers from a bird,' he said. 'You can't just – '

'But you aren't. Not if you take them and change them a bit. You aren't plucking, you're playing.'

'Come on, come on in,' Charlie says.

And I will. First though, I'll open my arms. To the lake, to the sky, to the beginning-of-summer sun. I'll gather them in.

'Are you swimming? Ash, are you swimming?'

Swimming, of course, and look at the water with the sun on it. Brown or green or yellow, all three colours, some other colour, dappled, maybe, but I've never known what to do with adjectives. I told Kate too, I said it straight out. But still. She wanted me to choose. Happy, sad, angry, confused? She said it would help her understand.

And what is the word? There probably isn't a word for the colour of lake water under the sun. There doesn't have to be a word, although it feels as though there should be. Most people think Eskimos have fifty words for snow, but they don't. It's myth, a hoax, that's what it is. Some things, a lot of things I suppose, are untranslatable. Anyway. It's May. It's a sun-through-the-leaves-on-the-water kind of day, and warm enough to swim at last.

'Are you coming or what? Ash?'

She's crouching on the rock. She's gripping the rock with bare feet, and the water beneath is brown or green or yellow. Dappled, probably.

'Come on, I'm getting cold. Just swim.'

'I'm keeping my T-shirt on,' I say, although nobody ever comes, except on a Tuesday, and it isn't a Tuesday today. We always swim with T-shirts on anyway, because Charlie once thought she heard some boys. She thought they might have come down from the Toll Estate. She thought they might have left their bikes on the bank, rolled up their jeans, paddled in, taken pebbles, stones, thrown them, watched them disappear. But we'd swum far out, too far out to be sure.

'Listen. Boys,' Charlie said, turning onto her back.

We listened. We stopped swimming to listen, but they weren't boys, they were gulls.

'Ash. Are you coming? Are you coming, or staying?' she says.

'Coming, stay where you are.'

Brown, green, yellow, one arm then the other, swum it so many times I know where to come up, fifteen strokes, one breath, to end up here, right here, in front of the rock. See.

'Without goggles,' she says. 'How do you always know?'

'You shouldn't swim in there,' Abbott says. 'Especially not with Charlie.'

He's fiddling with the skylight.

'It's not even clean, that lake, and anyway, you're not supposed to. It's private. There are signs.'

He pulls the bar to open it, then pushes. Pushes twice to get it to shut.

'Ash. There are signs, you know. She'd be better off at the baths,' he says, opening, then shutting. Taking two pushes.

'I thought so,' he says, adjusting his glasses. 'We're going to need a new striking plate.'

The day he decided on the skylight he came home from work with a pile of brochures tucked under his arm.

'What do you think to these?' he said, putting them on the kitchen table with emphasis. I say with emphasis, because that's how he did it. He did it with so much emphasis that two of the Play-Doh cows Charlie and I had been making wobbled, then fell over.

I'd always wanted a bedroom in the roof. I must have said something like that before he came home with the brochures, although I can't remember saying anything.

'It's for you Ash, for you,' he kept saying as he flicked through the pages. 'People go for skylights these days. And if we ever move . . . '

I wondered if he was still thinking about towns inside the M25. I kissed him. I wanted to. He was being kind. He was being kind, but his brochures took up space on the table.

So I stacked them up and put Charlie's cows back when he wasn't looking.

He was so happy the day the skylight men came. I swear I saw him take a little skip when the van saying *Whole-Lite Windows* pulled up outside our house.

'They're here, they're here,' he called out, and ran downstairs.

That's when I saw him take a little skip. Charlie saw it too, she said so later when we were sitting by the lake. He drank tea with the men from the van and nodded his approval of hinges and ventilation flaps. He said it was like having old friends over, although we didn't have any old friends.

The men worked on the skylight for two days. On the second day, Joan from number four came over to see what all the fuss was about. Abbott made her a cup of tea.

'You need to see it from outside and in, if you really want to get a feel for what a skylight brings to a home,' he said to her.

Joan said it was exactly what she wanted, to get a feel for it, and she followed him upstairs even though her knees were playing up.

'The things I do,' she said, and winked at Charlie.

Charlie and I went out. We walked down our hill to the lake. The swallows had already left. We sat on our coats on the bank and waited for the geese to come in. It was the best sort of autumn day. The right sort of day for geese. I remember the sky, shocked blue by the low sun, there would've been a tailwind too. Charlie talked and I listened. Charlie talked on, the way she does, and when there wasn't enough light to see across the lake we picked up our coats and walked home. The geese hadn't come. We agreed they probably wouldn't.

'Not today, anyway,' Charlie said, and squeezed my hand. 'Probably tomorrow.'

When we got to the top of our hill Joan was there, sitting on her front step smoking. She stubbed out her cigarette when she saw us. She sent the last puff of smoke into the air and watched it go. She was always sending puffs of smoke into the air.

'People go for skylights these days,' she said, getting up and rubbing her knees. 'Bespoke too. Adds value, should you ever want to move. Go down south.'

She called it commuter country, and she went on talking, and whilst she was talking Charlie was pulling at my hand, pulling it away from Joan, towards our house. She was saying, come on, come on, but how was I supposed to come on when Joan was talking, talking, and anyway, it was Joan who put a stop to it in the end.

'Ash,' she said. 'Your little 'un wants to get back.'

When we got home the front door was open, wide open, and Abbott was swinging in and out of it like a Newton's cradle ball. He went in and out, checking on the skylight, inside and outside. Inside, then outside. When the van finally pulled away he called us all together.

'Put Charlie's coat on,' he said. 'We're going outside.'

We went outside and stood in the street. Abbott hoisted Charlie onto his shoulders and looked up into the sky. I looked up too. I wondered if Abbott knew something about geese that I didn't. He was looking up and nodding as if he knew, as if he'd heard from 1,500 miles the first flap of wings, as if he'd held on to it all the way across the Norwegian Sea. That's how he looked.

'Well,' he said.

I held my breath and counted to three. I thought we were all expecting the same thing. He got hold of my sleeve and pulled me towards him. He pointed to the skylight.

'What do you think of that then?' he said.

Charlie's swimming six.

It's the number of strokes she has to hold on without breathing in. It's all about holding on, and Charlie wants to go to ten, she always wants to go to ten, but you have to start at two. That's the only rule, start easy and work up. Although it isn't always easy to swim properly in here. Sometimes, you have to wait for whoever's in front of you to touch the wall. Sometimes, whoever it is swims towards the wall, then stops swimming and starts gliding, with an arm outstretched, two arms sometimes, reaching, ready to touch the wall, ready to tag it. Everyone tags the wall, and almost everyone slows before tagging, because they're stretching and gliding, and sinking a bit. Sinking, instead of swimming, even though the thing they want most of all is to get to the wall. People stack up behind them, but they keep on, arms outstretched and sinking a bit. And people are waiting. Sometimes quite a few people are waiting. Abbott says you have to. Wait, he means.

'At least you're safe in there though,' he says.

But, now.

Charlie's swimming. Six strokes then she turns to breathe, six more and all the way to the end of the length. She's a swimmer, Charlie. She's a bit of a fish, a slip of a fish. I can hardly think of her without thinking of water. There she is in my mind's eye, half submerged. There she is, sliding away under skins of brown or green or yellow or blue. An arm here, a leg there, a torso, a head, appearing then disappearing.

There. Charlie, light of my life, swimming six, down the lane, towards me.

At least Abbott can stop worrying.

'At least it's clean. At least you know where you are with the baths,' he says.

And he's right. We're not far from the bottom of our hill. The red sign, the revolving door, the changing cubicles with yellow curtains. We know where we are.

We know where we are with the lake too, but sometimes you get lucky. I mean, sometimes it's possible to swim far enough out so the light catches, or doesn't catch. Sometimes it's possible. Really. Sometimes you're swimming and you look across the water, the water you've looked across so many times before. You look for the grassy bank running up into scrub, for the rock, for the spot where you went in, where you almost always go in, and you think the light must have caught, or maybe it didn't catch, and it must be the light, because it can't be anything else, because you're looking across the water for the bank, you're looking for the alder trees, the spot where you went in, where you always go in and you don't know. You're looking, and you don't know what you're looking at. You don't know where you are, although you know you're far enough out, you know you've been swimming for a while, and you like it. You like looking, looking across the water you've looked across so many times before and not knowing, and you keep on looking and not knowing, and you say to yourself, you say out loud, 'If only I could hold on, lost like this, at least until the light comes back.'

But wait, it's easy to get carried away. Abbott says I get carried away.

'All the time,' he says, and shakes his head.

I'll swim seven.

We'll swim seven.

You're supposed to swim in line in here, stay in lane, keep left, keep clear. We'll swim seven, Charlie and I.

Swim eight.

Swim nine.

We tag the wall then Charlie stands up. She straightens her goggles. She looks towards the far end.

She says, 'I'll go after that man, the one with the magpie tattoo. When he's tagged the wall, that's when I'll go.'

She means she'll try ten. She'll try holding on to ten, although she's never held on that long before, and her face is already red.

'This time,' she says.

She holds her fingers up, presses all ten against the air. And perhaps this time will be the time, because the difference between nine and ten is only one, but it's always been too far.

Charlie's stopped. She's standing up, shaking her head.

She's swimming back towards me with her head above water.

'I can't do ten,' she says. 'I can't do it. I'll never do it and even Dad can do ten.'

'He can't,' I say.

'How many can he do then?' she says. 'How many? Ash, how many can Dad do?'

Abbott's never been taught to breathe. He used to come to the baths with us when Charlie was small and already going under. He said going under was something all babies do until they learn not to.

'They learn,' he said. 'She'll learn.'

And sometimes he'd go off and swim a length or two with his neck stiff, his legs down and his face clear of the surface.

But Charlie kept going under, and eventually Abbott stopped saying she'd learn.

Once, after he'd swum his lengths, I told him it was safe, perfectly safe, to put his face beneath the surface. I offered to show him how.

'You don't have to swim at first. You can stay where you are. All you have to do is put your face under and breathe out,' I said. 'I can hold your hand.'

I think I might have said something about a seahorse too, because that's what he reminded me of when he swam. Anyway, he shook his head.

He shook his head.

I remember, because his hair was dry.

And now Charlie wants to play the floating game. She wants to know if Abbott can float.

'Well, can he?' she says.

I don't know. I can't remember him coming down to the baths with us after I offered to show him how to breathe. I can only remember him saying, 'You two go on without me.' I only remember going on without him.

'Let's just play then,' she says.

We need waves. There are always waves in the baths. There are always people. It isn't like the lake, where the water can be still enough, sometimes, to catch the ripples from a dipping toe, a dragonfly. Yes, that's how it can be, the lake, although not often, only sometimes. But here, always, the thrashing of arms and legs, the twisting and writhing, don't disappear, but come back. Like the flapping of butterfly wings, I suppose. Almost.

'Come on,' Charlie says.

She holds onto the wall and stretches out her arms, so her body and legs come up behind her.

I hold the wall. I stretch out my arms, and on the count of three we have to put our faces in and let go. We can breathe if we want, when we want, but we have to let the waves carry us.

Charlie counts. Charlie's always the one who counts.

'One, two . . . '

You're on your own. That's the game. That's all there is to it.

And whatever happens next doesn't happen quickly. You have to be patient. You have to wait until you've given up trying. And that's the thing, that's the fly. It's all in the way you're not, and then you are. Floating. The way things float, the way boats float, and Charlie and I have never seen a boat on the lake off the Toll Estate. All the water, so much water and never a boat. You'd think there'd be someone who'd like to go out, to row out, someone who'd like to float. You'd think there'd be someone like the man in the book. The man who rows out on a fjord. Out in a storm, he rows. You'd think there'd be someone in Tilstoke who'd like to row.

The man in the book doesn't come back. His wife waits for him, but he doesn't come, stays out on the fjord, and doesn't come back.

The lifeguard blows his whistle. He blows twice, and we're floating, like things, like boats, like that boat. The little row-boat. Two sharp blows on his whistle, and Charlie tugs at my arm and I can feel in her tug, in the way she pulls, it's time to stop floating, it's time to breathe, although there's something about holding on, something about being pushed and pulled and Charlie pulls, tugs, and I need to breathe, but breathing, even though I need to, desperately need to, isn't at all like the first breath.

The lifeguard points at us from his tall chair. He points at me and Charlie, he points at us, and Charlie says, 'We should swim. Now.' And we swim. And maybe the lifeguard thinks something's happened, maybe he thinks we're dead. Maybe that's what lifeguards are trained to think when you float, the way things float, with faces turned into the water. We swim towards the shallow end, best front crawl, breathing every three strokes, the way we're supposed to, and when we get there Charlie stands up, and once she's standing the lifeguard stops looking, and on the way home she says she promises. She promises she won't tell Dad.

I went into Abbott's study to find that book, the one about the man who took his rowboat out in the storm. Charlie was at school and Abbott was at work, and the house was quiet. Thinking about it now, there was an air of anticipation about the place, as though something sleeping was about to be woken. It was quiet. Quiet enough for reading, so I went into Abbott's study to find the book.

I pulled it from the shelf. It was exactly as I'd remembered it; a small paperback, black, with a painted flame, one line each of yellow and red and white. I knelt down on the floor of Abbott's study and read.

Signe lies on a bench.

That's how the book begins. That's how it almost ends too.

Signe lies on a bench and sees herself. She sees herself and she sees her husband, Asle, before he went out on the fjord, twenty-three years in the past. It was more or less how I'd remembered it, Signe lying on the bench, seeing herself and Asle, already knowing Asle can't come back.

I hadn't really remembered much more of the story than that. I'd read it twice before and didn't have more than its bare bones rattling around inside my head. The bench, the boat, the waiting, that's what I had, the waiting. The waiting for something that had already happened. And yes, there was something else in my head. Perhaps it was the waves. I could remember the push and pull of the waves, but there was something else, something beneath the surface. I can't say, but there was something, about that book, about being inside that book.

I carried on reading. I'd read it twice before and still I didn't like it. I didn't like how light the book felt in my hand. I shook it, then told myself to stop shaking it. I suppose I'd wanted to jar the words a little. I suppose I'd wanted to unsettle them.

I told myself I didn't have to read another word. But I read, and I must have been reading for a while, because I was getting pins and needles from kneeling down for so long. I sat down, then laid on my back. I carried on reading like that, lying on my back, on the floor of Abbott's study.

I read as far as the part about the boy. I'd forgotten about the boy. I'd forgotten he'd drowned. I'd forgotten he was only seven, the same age as Charlie. I'd forgotten everything. I only had bare bones and sensations. But there he was, the boy, dead. Drowned in the same fjord as the man.

I didn't like it. I didn't like how heavy the book had become. I didn't like the way the words breathed, the way they pulsed. What I mean is I wanted full stops. I wanted something to put a stop to it. Endless daylight. That's what I wanted. Self-contained, endless daylight, but the words kept coming, one after the other, which was only the way they looked on the page, but wasn't the way they were.

I went on with it. I couldn't put it down. I was searching for something to hang on to, something to grasp and make everything else fall into place. I looked everywhere. I searched through those words, but there wasn't anything. All I could find was Signe lying on the bench, that was all I could find, and it wasn't enough. One woman, lying on a wooden bench. It wasn't enough.

My phone buzzed in my pocket. It was just like Abbott to be there when I needed him. I read on a bit. It was difficult to put the book down, and anyway, I was comfortable lying there on my back. The feeling of his buzzing had calmed me a bit. Here we are, I thought as I read. Two women, lying on our backs. Although I knew Signe couldn't lie down indefinitely.

My phone buzzed again. I took it out of my pocket and looked at the screen.

Can you get the lasagne out of the freezer? A.

I'd said before, there was no need to sign off with an A.

'I can already see your name,' I said. 'And it makes it feel like the beginning of something else.'

'Like what?' he said.

'A sentence beginning with A. Any sentence. Like that one.'

'Which one?' he said.

I closed the book. I put it on the floor and stood up. I wanted to get the lasagne out of the freezer but I couldn't get over the feeling that Signe was lying on the bench inside the book, that she would still be inside it if I walked away.

It happened before. The first time I read that book, or maybe it was the second, I woke in the night. I had to ask Abbott if he wouldn't mind taking the book, although I meant the words, away from the bedroom. I asked him politely. He said he was sleeping. He couldn't have been.

'It's the words,' I said.

He propped his head up with his elbow and laughed.

'It's a story,' he said. 'A small paperback. It's no big deal.'

Kate said it too. It's no big deal, Ash. It's not a big thing. But that was later.

I wanted to get the lasagne. I was standing in Abbott's study. The sun had taken over the whole room. Its fingers reached down into the space between the carpet and the door. I wanted to get out, go to the freezer, but I couldn't leave the book. I was looking down at the book, the sun on the book, and thinking about the words, one next to the other, spreading.

'It's only a small paperback,' I said out loud. 'It's no big deal, Ash.'

Then I opened the door and ran.

I had the feeling the words were following me, I thought I felt them brush around my neck, then tighten a little. But Abbott's always said I've got a fertile imagination.

Now we see it.

The old ash tree, our ash tree, Abbott's and mine, although it was just a thing we said.

You can see it from the lake. It's easy in winter when the hedgerows run clean across the fields. In summer, you have to swim out and climb up on the rock.

And Charlie's already under the ash tree, lying on her back. She's already there with her knees up and her arms angel-spread in the long grass. And the sun. Of course, the sun, strung out in its blue sky, is the thing that's making it difficult to imagine, to picture. A boy, in late November. A seven-year-old boy, being pulled from the fjord and pressed into his mama's chest. Difficult to imagine his arms hanging down, his head hanging down, his eyes open and empty.

But quiet now. Charlie's talking. Charlie's always talking.

She's lying in the long grass. Both of us, a pair, you could say, lying in the grass, and the sun strung so far out it's impossible to imagine.

'So you didn't swim in the lake today?' she says.

'It's Tuesday.'

'Oh, the club?'

She turns onto her stomach to pick grass.

She picks grass. She piles it, she blows it, we watch it. Rise and settle. And who was the child in the poem? The one who said, what is the grass?

Charlie, picking grass and talking on. Despite the sun, despite the power of the sun.

A strange day, today of all days, to be thinking about the day Signe was lying on the bench. It must've been cold, a day like the days Asle and the boy drowned. Cold days, and dark. Although I can't remember. I can't remember whether there's anything to remember.

Charlie, climbing our tree, Abbott's and mine. It was just a thing we said.

Charlie grabs the bottom branch with both hands. She hangs and swings. Swings her body so her feet come up and she turns herself until the branch that was over her is under her. Now she's balanced. Now she's standing. Seven-year-old hands up against the trunk, and Abbott would say I should watch her when she climbs. Just in case, he would say.

'Climb up,' she says, shooting out an arm and a leg to show how easy it all is.

The sun. Of course, the sun makes it nothing like it was that summer, our summer, although it was only me who called it that.

She says, 'Come up.'

I grab the bottom branch.

'Come up, come up.'

I said the same to Kate that summer. I shouted it down, but she didn't come. I remember. Her skirt, her knees, her feet firmly planted, and the rain collecting in the earth around them. She shook her head, she shouted back. She shouted through the rain, louder than she needed to, because she wasn't that far away. Not really.

'Be careful,' she shouted. 'You crazy girl, you crazy boy, whoever you are.'

I turned away from her then. It was something new, turning away.

She'll be there when I turn back, that's what I thought. As long as I keep climbing, she'll be there.

I didn't turn back. I went on up. The branches were thick with leaves and wet. I kept on, inching on up, the way Papa had shown me. I kept on until I was high. I must have been high, because the branches bowed, they creaked. I whispered into them. I spoke. It didn't matter. I was brave, brave, brave. I was high, I was higher. High as a kite, high as you like, because when you're high you have something. I had something.

I had her, up there, although the rain was coming down, although the branches were bending.

Still, I came down in the end. I had to. The rain wasn't stopping, and anyway, there was Abbott. There was Charlie.

I climbed down. I found Kate crouching up against the trunk, her skirt stuck to her thighs. We were wet. Both of us, soaked through, and cold.

'Are you ready now?' she said. 'Finished?'

We walked back across the meadow, we must've walked back across the meadow, although I can't really remember walking. All I remember is that I hadn't finished. I didn't say so. Instead I told myself I could go up another day, but I'd already gone as high as I could go. I mean, we'd probably already got to the point where there was nowhere higher.

And now we've finished climbing.

We're walking home, and Charlie's in front. Charlie's striding out, pushing back the grasses. Long, loose steps, high on being high.

'You should actually be watching me when I climb high,' Charlie says. 'You should actually be holding my hand as soon as we come off the footpath. As soon as. That's when you should hold my hand. But never mind. I wouldn't ever tell.'

She takes my hand. Skips, tips of her toes, should be coming down by now, both of us. It's the sun, at the backs of our knees, and chasing, chasing us home.

'We're probably late. It's probably eight!' Charlie says.

It's a story we both know, and is always the way of things when we go out, because Abbott's got a watch. A nice watch. He feels the weight of it in his hand every morning.

'A nice watch,' he says.

He stands up straight whilst he puts it on; I've seen him pulling back on his shoulders. It's called Second Core, his watch.

'Second, because of seconds, you know, from minutes and seconds,' he said, the day he first came home with it. 'Second Core, because really, you can only have one core.'

'Apart from caw and corps. You know, c-a-w, and c-o-r-p-s?' I said. 'There, three possible cores, at least.'

'But I'm not talking about homophones now,' he said.

He asked if I wanted a nice watch. He undid the strap and handed it to me, or rather, pressed it into the palm of my hand.

'Feel the weight of that,' he said. 'A nice watch.'

I said it was a nice watch. I wasn't sure whether it was the weight that was supposed to make it nice. I couldn't really think why someone would want to carry around something so heavy.

'So?' he said. 'They do a range for women too.'

'I'd probably forget to put a nice watch back on after swimming, if I had one,' I said.

'Yes,' he said, and I wondered for a moment if he might cry. He had that kind of look about him. But perhaps I was reading too much into that look because later, when I was thinking about it, I couldn't remember ever seeing him cry.

*

We were late. As soon as Charlie opened the front door Abbott walked into the hallway tapping the face of his Second Core. He was looking us up and down. I think he thought we'd been to the lake, but before he could say anything about it not being clean in there, Charlie said, 'Don't worry, Dad, we were at the tree, the ash tree,' and he went back to tapping, although less forcefully.

After dinner Abbott put his arms around my waist. The back door was open and sounds from our hill were drifting in. The usual kinds of sounds: voices, cars, a door shutting somewhere, a dog barking. I was scraping the last bits of lasagne off the plates into the bin and thinking about how sounds drift in when you can't see where they're coming from. Drift in and don't just arrive. It was soothing, scraping the plates, listening for sounds on the night air, and yes, I thought, this is the way things arrive, nothing happens suddenly. It was at that moment Abbott put his arms around my waist. I stood up straight, I must have done it quickly, because the back of my head caught his chin and I heard his mouth snap shut.

'Ash,' he said.

And when he'd composed himself he put his arms back around my waist. We stood there for a while, not moving.

'If you ever change your mind about having a nice watch,' he said. 'I could sort one out for you at the drop of a hat.'

'And if you ever want to, you can come to the tree,' I said.

He said it sounded like a fair deal, which is usually the way the watch–tree exchange ends, although sometimes I say one core's enough for one girl. Either way, it's the end, and Abbott never comes to the tree.

We used to call it our tree. It was just something we said, but at the beginning it felt that way. A few weeks after we'd seen the Utsjoki film Abbott turned up at my front door without warning, though he said it was more impromptu than without warning.

'Without warning makes it sound, well, you know,' he said.

I didn't know. But I took impromptu for my collection. The m, the p, the t. The way my mouth had to work to get them out, that's why I took it. Then, of course, the u. Unexpected, I thought. Completely unexpected.

Abbott had his shirtsleeves rolled up and was carrying a picnic. I could see he'd gone and bought a French baguette. He was standing on the doorstep and the end of it was sticking out of his bag. He wanted to take me out. Out of Tilstoke.

'To the country,' he said.

He swept into a low bow, pretending to hold a hat in his hand. His shirtsleeves were rolled up, rolled up perfectly, and he'd parted his hair down the middle, exactly down the middle. I remember thinking how much he looked like F Scott Fitzgerald. His hair, yes, but not only his hair, his smile, which was more of a smiling look than an actual smile. I almost said something. I almost went back inside to get the book with the photo of F Scott Fitzgerald on the inside back cover. I almost brought it out to show him.

'Are you coming, Ash?' he said. 'Grab whatever it is you women grab, and come on.'

We went out to his car. We were sitting in the two front seats ready to move off. It wasn't the first time we'd sat like that, no. We'd sat like that on the way back from the film. This was the second time, sitting side by side, and I thought, I'm sure I was thinking, that I was beginning to get used to it.

'*À la campagne,*' Abbott said, turning the key in the ignition. '*La belle campagne.* That OK with you, Ash?'

I said we could always go to the meadow instead, if he didn't feel like driving far. We could always sit under the old ash tree.

'What?' he said. 'Where?'

He said he'd never set eyes on a meadow in Tilstoke. How could a meadow just spring up? If he'd lived here his whole life, how could it? He smoothed his hair, once, twice, on either side.

'But it's you who's sprung up,' I said.

His dad though, his dad was born here, born and raised. His mum too. Aunts and uncles and cousins. He made circles with his hands as he explained. His family, spiralling, sprawling outwards.

'Never a word about a meadow between them all,' he said.

'Still, there is one,' I said.

We went to the meadow. We could have walked, but Abbott wanted to drive.

'Now we've got ourselves in the car,' he said. 'And the picnic and all.'

He parked in the lay-by at the bottom of Lot Road and we walked along the footpath towards the meadow. We carried his big picnic bag, we took one handle each. It was late May, it must have been. The hawthorn was heaped with white flowers, and the bees were in and out of it and buzzing. We walked alongside the hawthorn, and as we walked Abbott's face opened up. It was as open as I can ever remember seeing it.

The footpath too, opened. Opened into meadow.

'This way, if we want to go to the tree,' I said, and I gestured through the grass. Through the long grasses and the buttercups, as sprawling as Abbott's family.

'This way,' I said.

And Abbott's face. His face, his features, unfolding beneath the high sun.

Let me try to explain, although how can I explain?

It was that meadow, that day, the rush of early summer.

'This way,' I said, although what did I mean?

It was the air, the swallows, it was the grasses stretching.

'This way, this way,' I said, overcome by a sort of giddiness. I tugged at his arm. I pulled him down with me into the sticky warmth of the meadow, right down inside the drone of hoverflies. There was nowhere to go down there, but we weren't going anywhere, we weren't trying. And Abbott, his face lax, looked nothing like F Scott Fitzgerald, and everything like Abbott. Abbott the boy. That's what I thought, although I'd never even seen a photo of Abbott as a boy, but still, I must have been sure. I put my hand on his forearm, just below where his rolled sleeves fell. The bees, the heat. Rogue weather, they called it. Rogue weather, and grass prints on my bare legs. I held his forearm and moved towards him. I moved in, I was moving slowly enough to see the look on his face, which might have been a look of anticipation. I moved in, until I was as near as I could be without touching him.

'I too am not a bit tamed. I too am untranslatable,' I said into his ear.

I stole the words. There was no need to tell Abbott. Papa would have said, you can't just, but you can. One feather, and it starts you longing for the bird.

We ate our picnic in the shade of the ash tree. Abbott didn't say much, just watched the swallows skimming the grasses.

'Nice,' he said when I told him they were swallows. 'Nice birds.'

After we'd eaten he wanted to carve our initials into the ash tree, using the knife he'd brought to cut the baguette. He said it was destiny, the pair of us having names beginning with A, and that we should make our mark on the world. He said we should make our mark and come back.

'It damages the bark, cutting,' I said. We packed up our picnic and walked to his car after that.

'Leave nothing but footprints,' I said as we walked.

I turned back to check. There wasn't a trace of us. No footprints, nothing, not even a shape where the grasses had been laid flat.

We went to our tree one more time. It was January. Abbott had been saying he wanted to go ever since that time in May and he'd finally got some time off work. He said we should just do it. Put on our coats, grab the car keys and go. So we went. He drove us to the lay-by on Lot Road. He likes to drive, and anyway, it was cold.

We walked along the footpath towards the meadow. The sky had come right down, the way it sometimes does in winter. Still, we kept on, kept the hawthorn so close we scratched up against its skeleton.

I watched Abbott's face. I watched his features move closer together, as though relying on each other for something.

I thought perhaps I should speak.

There were redwings on the hawthorn. A small group of them, balancing on its bones, picking at its berries. At the scrub underneath too. I thought perhaps I should point out their red flanks, say something.

But we kept on. We kept the hawthorn close until the footpath opened into meadow, and when it did, the grass had mostly disappeared to mud and the sky was down, far down. Of course it was only fog, and nothing to worry about. It was January after all. Abbott stopped walking. He stopped in the place where the hawthorn ended and the footpath opened up. He stopped, and looked, although there was nothing to see but fog. He turned. He turned as if he was expecting something else, as if by shifting a few degrees he might still find what he was looking for.

'But,' he said.

That was the only word I remember him saying.

We walked across the meadow, in the direction of the tree. The sky lay heavy. I mean, the sky was down, and it was difficult to see, difficult even to see the ground in front of us, but we carried on towards the old ash anyway. I walked in front.

'This way,' I said, although I've got to admit I wasn't completely sure.

Abbott felt for my hand, then let go.

'This way, this way,' I said, but I don't think he heard.

There was nothing to do but carry on towards the ash, because that's what we'd come for. I told myself it was only the meadow, it was only Tilstoke. Abbott's relatives had been here for generations and not one of them had ever been swallowed up into fog. It was thick, without doubt, but the idea of it swallowing anything. Hyperbole. Yes. But I had to admit it was thick. Thicker than I'd ever seen it. So thick, it slid deep into my oesophagus every time I tried to speak.

We got to the ash tree. It came out from the fog without warning. It came out whole. I suppose what I mean is unviolated. There it was, it always had been. Abbott walked up to it. He took a branch in his hand. He held onto it for a while then let go and took a step back.

There were black buds rising from the ends. 'Black buds,' he said later. Black. Black.

When we were safely inside his car he said he could see why people only visit the countryside in summer.

'All that nakedness,' he said.

'Nakedness?' I said.

It wasn't the kind of word he usually used.

'Anyway,' he said. 'It might be good to watch a bit of sport when we get in, a bit of snooker or something.'

'Yes,' I said.

*

But now. Now it's June and it's been hot all night, and after we'd come down, Charlie and I, after we'd tidied up the lasagne, put the things in the dishwasher, Abbott said he was off upstairs to put a sheet on the bed.

'It's my feet. I like something over my feet,' he said.

Papa used to tell me to lie on top when the warm nights came. He'd pull off the covers and throw them onto the floor. He'd say it was my chance. Your chance to let the night find its way into you, he'd say.

He'd pat the bed and his hair would shake. His black curls. That's what he always did when the warm nights came, but they didn't always come.

Abbott likes something over his feet. He pulled the sheet right up to his chest, he folded it back and clamped it around his body with his arms.

'There,' he said.

Before long he was asleep, and as soon as he was I got out of bed, went over to the skylight and opened it up, just a crack, just enough to let some air in. There wasn't any air to let in, not really. The air on the outside was the same as the air on the inside. I stuck my arm out of the skylight as far as it would go. I stuck it out and brought it in a few times. Inside and outside felt the same, exactly the same. I couldn't remember a single day with heat like that that summer, and I suppose some summers it never gets hot.

I didn't shut the skylight. I didn't think it mattered, but as soon as I woke I could tell Abbott was working up to something. I could tell from the way he was flicking the strap of his Second Core that he was going to make an announcement of sorts, and it wasn't a surprise when he did.

'Leaving windows open overnight brings flying insects indoors,' he said.

He pulled his shoulders back and strapped on his Second Core.

'So. They're better off shut,' he said, and smoothed his hair down on both sides.

But now he seems to have forgotten about flying insects. Now he's running late, he's looking for the sunscreen and can't understand why people don't put things back where they belong.

Charlie brought home a letter yesterday.

Could all parents/guardians provide a hat and sunscreen for their child/children, due to the unremitting warmth? It was signed off, *with warm wishes.*

So now Abbott's looking. He's crawled inside the cupboard under the stairs, he's half inside, half swallowed.

'Did you read the letter?' I say. 'Did you see the joke?'

'What now, Ash?' he says, backing out a bit.

'Did you read the letter? Somebody's written, someone at the school has signed off, with warm wishes. That letter, the one about the sunscreen. With warm wishes.'

'What?' he says. 'Can you look upstairs for it? Try the bathroom cabinet.'

'It's a play on words. With warm wishes. You know, warm, and –'

'She'll have to do without. It's 8.30 already. She doesn't like them being late, Mrs McIntosh,' he says.

He reverses, goes on reversing and when he's out in the hallway he squints a bit. He looks very warm now, a bit flustered, now he's out in the open.

'Is it warmer in there?' I say.

'No Ash, not warmer. We need to go. Charlie! Let's go.'

I stand on the front step and wave them off.

Charlie's in her car seat. Her car seat, covered in clouds. All of them white, all of them cumulus, and behind them the sky, always blue, one blue, uniform blue. It's unrealistic. Abbott says it doesn't matter, he says it doesn't have to be realistic.

'It's for children, Ash. Young children.'

But look now, look at the sky above our house. It's been blue for days. I don't know how many days, but it's hard to look up and not be surprised. I mean, day after day, blue. Blue, like Charlie's car seat, blue and nothing but blue.

Look, there, the people from number five have brought their leather sofa out onto the pavement. Perhaps the council are coming to pick it up later. Abbott says twenty-five pounds is too much to pay the council to do something like that. He says it should be part of the service, although I don't know which service he means.

And just as I'm going in, at the moment I decide to go back in, the woman from number five, the one who's about the same age as Joan, probably a bit younger, comes out of the front door carrying a piece of toast on a plate. She walks out to the sofa and lowers herself down onto it. She sits on the sofa, the one outside on the pavement, and eats her toast. And there, look, a mug of coffee by her feet. It must have been there all along, whilst I was waving to Charlie, as Abbott drove her down our hill. And the woman looks so relaxed, so at home, she looks as if she always eats breakfast on the pavement on our hill, with the sky stretched out above her.

'Terry,' the woman on the sofa shouts.

She looks towards their front door.

'Terry,' she says.

And where's Joan? I mean, you'd think she'd come out. She likes to know what's going on in our street. She's been here thirty-six years and knows a thing or two about the way people work, or she should know, she says, by now.

And now a man, quite a big man, a wide man, at least, is coming out of number five. The woman taps the leather sofa with her free hand and the man sits down where she taps.

'Fuck, it's hot,' he says as he lowers himself.

'Terry,' she says. 'Mind your language.'

Terry sits next to the woman whilst she finishes her toast. He shuts his eyes and tilts his face towards the sun and it's only half past eight and already hot and above him, above the leather sofa, the swifts are screeching and circling.

The man splays his arms out.

'Mind yourself, Terry,' the woman says. 'Mind yourself.'

'Sorry, love,' he says.

And now. Here comes another man, a man in tracksuit bottoms and trainers. A man who looks a lot like Terry but much skinnier, and much younger. A man with a tattoo across his collarbone. He's standing facing Terry even though Terry's got his eyes closed. Still, he's standing facing him and from here on our front step I can just about make out the last word in his tattoo, which almost definitely says *Regrets*. Yes, I think that's what it says.

'Something wrong with us, hun?' the woman says.

She must be talking to me.

'I said is something wrong?'

And there isn't anything wrong, no, nothing wrong, I should probably say. I was looking, that's all, just trying to see.

'Keep your eyes to yourself then,' she says.

And I wish the man in the tracksuit bottoms would turn towards our front step, because what can it say before regrets, if it does say regrets, because I can't be sure.

Big regrets, my regrets, all regrets, perhaps? I'm trying to see what comes before, but I can't see, because he's facing Terry, even though Terry hasn't opened his eyes, and now I can't look too hard, can't stare, because the woman, the woman with the toast, wants me to keep my eyes to myself, which might be something she says to Terry too. But what can it say before regrets? It must say something, because how can you have regrets on your collarbone without anything else?

'Get on in,' she says, the woman on the sofa.

She flicks her hand, and the skinny man looks over at her and says, 'For fuck's sake. For fuck's sake you.'

I can still see her from up here in Abbott's study. She's lying on her back on the sofa. Terry and the skinny man have gone, and she, the woman who flicked her hand at me, is lying right back and stretching her legs out. She's a bit like Signe, lying there like that.

Lying, lying – one of my favourite homonyms. You have to hold on for the preposition. Lying on, lying next to, lying back, lying to, and if there isn't a preposition it isn't lying. Not in the way Signe or the woman from number five are lying. And there, see, she's on her back again now, the woman outside, and I can see from here the writing on her top says *Mon Amie*. And if the skinny man would come, if he'd just come out I'd be able to see the word. The word that comes before regrets.

I know. I'll put it into Google, *regrets*. Abbott would be pleased. He says you can put anything into Google and it always has answers. He says Google can suck you in. But I've never been sucked in. There's no reason to get sucked in. I can shut the lid. It's as easy as that. It's easy.

OK. Regrets. Regrets. And here, look.

The 10 Biggest Regrets.

Here we go. And they always start at number ten. Why do you have to read nine smaller regrets to get to the biggest regret when the biggest regret is really the one you want to get to?

I wish.

I wish, they begin. All the regrets begin with I wish, which, if you take it on its own, sounds like the opposite of regret. So, I'll type in *wish*, see. Synonyms: desire, longing, hope, yearning. Nothing like regret. Words with a future, that's what they are, yes, a wish, a thing of hope, of opportunity, or it would be if it wasn't followed by the past perfect.

Abbott says there's no need, absolutely no need, to obsess about words. A word is a word is a word, he says. He thinks it's funny.

You can find anyone you want to with Google. Abbott's found all his favourite sportsmen. He follows them, that's what he does. I could find anyone I want to from up here in Abbott's study. Although it's hot. Especially with the window shut. And the thing about flying insects, the thing is, that once they've flown, I mean, once they've flown inside, they don't usually find their way out, because they don't plan to come in. They fly in by chance, by mistake I suppose, and there's only one way out and they almost never find it. It could be their number one regret.

I wish I hadn't flown in through the window.

I could find anyone I want to through Google.

Abbott comes up when you type his name in. His photograph makes it look as if he's doing important work at his desk. It feels familiar to see him there on the screen inside his study. But.

Kate Quin. That's what I type.

And there she is. There's Kate Quin, practitioner at Naturally Yoga. She's sitting on a rock wearing a red scarf, a summer scarf. Behind and above her the sky is dark and light, the kind of sky that's sometimes called moody, and you can tell the wind's blowing, or was blowing. It will always blow, because things in photos never change. She didn't like the wind. She was scared of it.

'Call me a fool, but I'm scared,' she said.

She linked her arm through mine. She wouldn't let go.

Here. *Testimonials.*

I warmly recommend Naturally Yoga . . .
Kate offers something special.
I can't wait to return for my next session.
Thank you, Kate.

Abbott found her first. He put his knife and fork down on his plate whilst we were eating dinner, he made a point of it. He cleared his throat and said Naturally Yoga seemed like a welcoming place, good for beginners. He said I should give it a go.

'You'll meet people. You'll have fun,' he said.

And here.

Classes, Technique, News.

News.

Come back soon for details of our Summer Solstice event.

The woman from number five has gone.

It's impossible to lie down indefinitely. Nobody, not even Signe, can lie down ad infinitum. I wanted it in my collection, ad infinitum. Definite and infinite, that was the way it sounded. I wanted it, but I didn't have any other two-word phrases. It would've opened up a can of worms if I'd put it in. So I didn't. Abbott said there was always infinitely, if I wanted it, but it isn't the same, not nearly the same.

The blue skies and heat go on. Every evening at six thirty, the weatherman points to a map covered in oranges and reds and talks about high pressure and jet streams. And every evening Abbott leans towards the television and nods and checks the temperatures on the map against the ones on his phone and says, 'That'll be about right,' and nods again and stands up.

Charlie's been wearing her summer dress to school. She pushes her long socks down around her ankles and by the end of each day her hair's stuck to her forehead. She brought another letter home, more of a slip than a letter, I suppose.

We'd like to remind those who haven't brought in sunscreen for their children that the sun is very hot.

On Thursday morning Abbott came downstairs without a tie. This morning the same, but waving his phone.

'Hosepipes are out, that's what they're saying. National ban,' he said.

Terry probably doesn't care about the hosepipe ban. I can tell he doesn't care about flying insects because the windows at number five have been open all week.

Earlier this evening the skinny man came out. He put a speaker on the arm of the sofa and played music from his phone. I could see him from Abbott's study, sitting on the arm next to the speaker and nodding his head. He turned the volume up. Up and up until Terry stuck his head out of one of the top windows and said, 'Too loud, son.'

He almost stopped nodding after Terry said that, but he didn't turn it down, just went on nodding and once in a while turned his head towards the top window. It wasn't too long until Terry said it again.

'Too loud, son. Too loud, Jay.'

'It's not,' he said.

He scratched under his T-shirt at his tattoo.

Most of the time, during the day, it's her on the sofa. Terry and Jay never say her name. They only say you. Her name could be U, I suppose. U for Ursula, for Ulyana. U for Uta.

Sometimes she lies down and sometimes she sits. I heard her telling Terry she's trying to get an all-over tan before the weather breaks, but the weather's already broken. Day after day the same sky, the same sun, the sofa outside, the weather broken.

'Come on in, Ash,' Charlie says. 'Come on in.'

She's far out. She's standing beyond the rock, twenty metres, maybe more, and she shouldn't be able to stand out there beyond the rock, it should be too far, too dangerous, too deep. But it's been so hot. The sun's been sucking the lake up into the sky, slowly sucking, and I can see it now, can see what it's been doing, is doing right now. Can see it, pulling beads of water from Charlie's skin, plucking them, sucking them from her shoulders, and I'll have to walk on past the rock to get to her. It isn't that clean in here, Abbott's right, it isn't that clean.

I called to Kate from the rock that summer. She was standing on the bank and wouldn't come in. I was on the rock, on the high point of the rock. I was standing there and the water was up, was right up, was lapping around my feet, even up there it was lapping. Brushing up, right up around the top of the rock, and I couldn't stay long, that's why I was calling. I couldn't stay much longer.

Kate shook her head. Wouldn't come. She could see the water was up, was up around the rock, had crept right up past the alder trees too, up there, all those metres back. The rain had been coming down, had been coming down all summer. The weather was broken. It was broken then, too.

'Ash,' Charlie says. 'If you don't come.'

'I'm coming,' I say. 'I'm coming.'

I'm wading in, past the rock, quite a long way past the rock, and still wading.

'Shall we swim? Just swim?' I say.

And we wade out, further out, so much further than we usually go, and all the time, the sun on our heads, the sun on our shoulders, I can almost feel it plucking, snatching. Although. Under our feet, silt. And all the time, warm water.

Our waists, our chests, and we keep on wading, and we go on wading, and the swallows, yes, we go on wading until the bottom of the lake falls away, comes away, and after all, in the end, we lift our feet, because all of a sudden we're not where we were, but far out, far enough out, and the water's deep. Deep enough to swim.

Abbott knows.

Yes, as soon as we walk in he knows. He can tell just by looking, how far out we've been. He can see that Charlie can't come down. He can see the mud on our shins, across her cheek, can tell by her eyes that she hasn't come down, not yet. He looks at her and he looks at me and he says he doesn't like the lake. He's never liked it, in fact. And what is wrong with Tilstoke Baths, because everyone else in Tilstoke is fine with the baths. His mum, his dad, his whole family were always fine with the baths.

'OK,' we say. 'OK.'

And later, quite a while after dinner, Abbott comes to me. It's still warm when he comes, almost too warm still, and I'm sitting on my stool in the kitchen. I'm on my stool and Charlie's on the step that leads out from the kitchen to the back garden. Both of us are reading, the pair of us, and Abbott comes. He tousles my hair. He waits for me to put my book on the table and when I do he says he's sorry.

He says he can see Charlie likes the lake. He can see that much. He can see, yes, but he isn't sure, not completely sure whether it's clean in there, whether it's OK for seven-year-olds to swim far out like that.

'There are *No Swimming* signs, Ash,' he says. 'Quite a few signs.'

He looks at his Second Core, but swimming in the lake has got nothing to do with time. None of this has anything to do with time.

'We'll go to the baths,' I say.

He kisses my forehead. He tousles my hair again.

'Good. Good,' he says. 'You've always liked the baths.'

Joan caught me watering the wildflowers last night.

I went out there after ten because she's usually done for the day by then. She used to say it herself. I'm done for the day by ten, she'd say, and sometimes she'd look at her wrist as if she had a watch, but I never saw her wearing one. Still. She used to say all sorts of things when she popped round. That's what she called it. Popping round.

She'd stand at the front door and ask if we needed anything, because what are neighbours for? And she was on her way to the corner shop anyway.

She'd stand at the door. She'd stand there, and after a while she'd take a step inside and lean up against the wall. I liked it when she did that. I'd get comfortable. I'd sit down, sit in our hallway with my back against the opposite wall and listen, because she had a way with words, Joan. What I really mean is, she had *her* way with words.

'You're quiet,' she said once. 'Not like the rest of them around here. Not like them at number five. Can't stop themselves from hanging out their dirty washing, if you'll excuse the pun,' she said.

Then she stopped. She stopped popping round.

I don't know why she did. Perhaps we were so quiet she forgot about us, but how could she forget, because even though we didn't make a lot of noise, we'd wave. We'd always wave, Charlie and I. We'd wave when we saw her at her window and she must have seen us, because we were right there in front of her, in front of her window, but she'd look right through us, or look away. Yes, she'd look away like she'd spotted a bird or something and we'd look too, we'd turn to look where she was looking, but we never saw a thing.

Joan caught me watering.

It was after ten and her curtains were drawn. I could see there wasn't a light on in the whole house, so I got the hose out. The flowers had shot up. They'd shot up, the flowers, the grasses, almost overnight. It was as if they needed to grow before the rain came. But the rain hasn't come, not yet, and by the time I went out there last night they were bent over. All of them, bent over and withered, that's how they were, and they needed water.

I turned on the hose. I turned it on a bit, not too much, just enough for a small stream of water to come out. I didn't want to waste any. Abbott had told me about the ban, but the flowers needed water and the earth was hard and there wasn't any water left in it for the flowers. I turned on the hose and the moment I did, the light in the top bedroom at number four went on.

She pulled the curtains open. She was definitely done for the day because I could see what she was wearing and it must've been something she sleeps in, because I'd never seen her wearing anything like that before. It was almost see-through. See-through and loose and almost white and she was there in her bedroom with the light on and the curtains pulled open and I was in with the flowers, in with the hose, because the flowers needed water, they needed it.

I put the hose down. I put it down, then I slipped down myself, down into the grass. I stretched my hand out to the red campion and cradled it. I wanted to look like I was tending to it, like I wasn't giving it water at all, but singing or whispering to it there in the low light. I thought Joan would shut the curtains if I was tending, not watering. She didn't move. She was staring right out of the window into the night and I was in with the flowers, crouching down and it was warm out there, even though it was after ten and the water was trickling out from the hose.

I thought about waving. I thought that if I waved she'd turn away, the way she used to when Charlie and I waved at her. It was getting dark and she should've been done for the day and the water was still trickling, and was starting to pool, and I couldn't get up and turn off the hose, because she was there at the window staring. Staring and wearing something almost see-through.

I didn't wave. I didn't wave because I didn't like the way she was staring. She was looking right through me, her eyes glazed. She couldn't possibly have heard the trickling from up there, she definitely wouldn't have been able to hear, but maybe she could see the puddle of water at my feet, although I didn't know how she could, or how I would ever be able to get up. How could I just get up and turn the hose off, with her staring out at me from the window? And I still didn't know. Still don't know, why she stopped popping round. It was after that summer. She didn't say a thing and she was good at saying things, but she didn't say a thing, she just stopped popping round and even when Charlie and I waved at her she didn't wave back.

I've got into the habit. You only have to do something eighteen times to get into the habit. I read that somewhere. Every morning I watch Abbott and Charlie drive down our hill then I go upstairs. I head upstairs and look out from the window of Abbott's study.

And there she is now. U, that's what I call her, sitting on the sofa eating her toast. She's getting an all-over tan, I heard her telling Terry, and that's what's she's doing.

She's in a routine. Every morning, as soon as she's finished her toast, she lies on her back and sets her watch. She waits for it to beep and when it does she turns. She always turns the same way. Always ends up with her face up against the back of the sofa, against a wall of brown, waiting for her watch to beep. And there she is now. She's in a routine, we're in a routine. We're waiting for her watch to beep, and when it does, when she turns, that's when I open the laptop.

Kate Quin. Kate Quin of Naturally Yoga.

I usually click on Testimonials, then News, and usually there isn't any but most people probably don't check all that often and look, here, the details of the summer solstice celebration are up and somebody's chosen big letters, letters bigger than the other letters.

Open to All.

It's open to all, the summer solstice celebration on Cotters Hill. It's open to anyone who wants to embrace the light and *We'll stay and celebrate until the sun sets just after half past nine. Can you think of a more glorious way to celebrate the light?*

That's what it says and there isn't space to think of more glorious ways because beneath the question there are photos. Photos of last year's celebration and I know Cotters Hill so well, like the back of my hand, and there it is, up there on the screen in front of me on Midsummer's Day, and there they all are, all of them from Naturally Yoga, all the people who couldn't think of a more glorious way to celebrate the light. There they are, on the longest day of last year, on the very top of Cotters Hill and off to the side is the Crag and there aren't many crags around here, no, but there it is, the Crag, on the photo on the screen in front of me in Abbott's study and there they are, everyone from Naturally Yoga, celebrating the light and there she is, Kate, from Naturally Yoga, there she is, looking past the camera, and perhaps she didn't know the camera was there. She's looking beyond it, out towards the Crag, and I can't look out towards the Crag. Not without thinking of the time the wind took my words away.

And can you think of a more glorious way?

It isn't a bad question, because the world's a big place and there must be more glorious ways to celebrate midsummer than to sit on Cotters Hill, but I can't think of them, because I'm thinking of the way the light falls on the hill, when it's the last light. If I stop to think about the way the last light falls on the limestone, the way it falls on the limestone and the grass so their colours become parts of the same colour, when I think about that, and the way the colours become rich, because that's the way they become when they come together in the late evening light. When I think about that, it's difficult to think of a more glorious thing.

Maybe Abbott would think it was a good idea to give yoga a try again, because he was the one who was always asking me why I'd stopped and he was the one who wanted me to start in the first place. He was the one. I'd told him it wasn't for me.

'But something must be for you,' he said.

'You go,' Abbott said, when I told him about the celebration on Cotters Hill. 'Charlie and I will find something to do. You go and enjoy yourself.'

I told Charlie I was going. We were at the baths when I told her. We'd swum up and down, let go and floated, and we were getting changed. I was rubbing her back with the towel. I said I was going up to Cotters Hill to celebrate the summer solstice, because it's open to all.

'If it's open to all you can take me,' she said.

'But there weren't any children in the photos,' I said.

'All means all. Every one. Every single one,' she said.

'No,' I said.

On the way home she ran ahead and when I held my hand out for her to take it she shook her head.

It's the longest day of the year.

I'm going to Cotters Hill. I'm ready to go. I was looking for the car keys a moment ago. I went upstairs to Abbott's study.

'Look out of the window,' Charlie said. 'The people from number five.'

I'd seen U out there earlier, but she's gone now. Now it's Jay. Jay and two other girls, or women I suppose. They're dressed up, all dressed up and Jay's drinking from a can and he's keeping a spare one in the back pocket of his jeans, and the girls are talking, leaning in and talking to each other and here comes another man. Skinny, but not as skinny as Jay.

He takes the can out of his pocket, Jay, and throws it to the other man, who is somewhere between a boy and a man, and he throws it to him and the other man catches it and looks at it and says, 'What the fuck is this?' And Jay says he can chuck it back if he doesn't want it but he does want it, because he opens the can and starts to drink from it and Jay walks over to one of the women, the one who's lying back on the sofa now, who's all dressed up in a little black dress, an LBD, that's what they call them, LBDs, I read it in a magazine once, and he walks over to her and he stands over her and she says, 'Go on with you, Jay.'

And he puts one leg either side of her and there isn't much room, but Jay's skinny and he puts his right knee in, squeezes it between the back of the sofa and the girl's waist, and he puts his other leg over her and he's over her and she's under him and you can see she's fat. You can see that from here.

'I said go on with you, Jay,' she says.

And he comes down onto her and he hasn't got a top on and you can see how skinny he is. She says it again, she says go on, but her hands are on his bum and she's got his bum and she's holding onto his bum saying go on and he lowers himself down and puts his hands on her breasts, he puts one hand on each breast and he holds onto them and he looks over at the other man and he says, 'Ryan. Ryan.' But Ryan's on his phone and the other girl's on the arm of the sofa and she's holding one of her shoes and she's doing something with it, something with the heel of the shoe, and Jay's pressing down, and the girl in the little black dress is under him and he's got his hands on her breasts and he shouts again, 'Ryan, over here, you fucking cunt.' And Ryan looks up from his phone and the girl's got Jay's bum and she says, 'You're the cunt' and she's holding his bum and he's come down onto her and she's a lot fatter than U, and Jay's skinny, but he's got hold of her breasts and he's come right down onto her and he says, 'I'll have these', and he keeps hold of her breasts and he moves them in circles, and she says, 'You've had one too many, Jay' and she laughs. She laughs and she's got hold of his bum and the other girl's put her shoe back on and she's got her phone out and Ryan passes her his can and she takes it and drinks from it and the girl under Jay is laughing and he's got her. He's got his hands on her breasts and you can see the muscles in his arms from here, and Abbott shouts from downstairs.

'I thought you were on your way.'

And Jay moves the girl's breasts up and down and he pushes his whole body down on her and her black dress has come up around her thighs. Ridden up, that's what it's done. And ridden is one of those words. He's riding, that's what he's doing with his knees pressing in at her waist. He's riding her, and he wipes the sweat away from his face using his shoulder, he does it twice and he doesn't look at her but he doesn't take his hands from her breasts and she's got her hands on his bum and the swifts are above them, high above them, and Abbott shouts up from downstairs.

'Ash!'

And he'll be looking at his Second Core and everyone from Naturally Yoga will be on Cotters Hill now and they'll be there and they'll be doing breath work and thinking about the light.

Her dress has ridden up around her thighs and Jay's come right down onto her.

Ryan turns around and says, 'For fuck's sake, Jay' and Jay laughs and the girl under him laughs and the other girl doesn't look up from her phone. And Jay is pressing down hard and the girl has stopped laughing and he presses down on her, harder, and I can see his muscles and she isn't laughing now and she says, 'Jay. Stop it, Jay.'

And he goes on pressing down, you can see that from here, you can see him pressing down and there's something in her voice and she's let go of his bum and she's pushing up at his chest but he goes on pressing down.

It's the longest day of the year. In Finland they celebrate by lighting bonfires. They light them on the shores of the lakes. There's a sign on Cotters Hill that says *No camping, No fires, No littering*. Kate said no one would know, if we lit a fire, no one would know.

'We shouldn't,' I said. 'Stop it,' I said.

'Stop it, Jay,' the girl says.

'Come on, mate,' Ryan says, and puts his hands on Jay's shoulders and pulls at him. 'Come on, leave off of her,' he says.

Jay says, 'Look at her, mate. Take one look at her, she likes it.' And he presses down onto her, he presses down hard and the other girl's on her phone. She's tapping on her phone.

'Ash,' says Abbott.

He pushes the door of his study open.

'Won't they have started? The yoga?' he says, and smooths his hair down.

'But look,' I say, and point to the window and Abbott walks to the window and looks out. He looks over at number five and he turns around and walks back across the room and says, 'Shall I drive you?'

And I go to the window and the two girls are sitting on the sofa and one of the girls is on her phone and the girl in the black dress is sitting next to her, and Jay and Ryan are standing and Ryan's holding out a lighter for Jay and you can see from here, you can see from here his tattoo says *No Regrets*.

'Will it help if I drive you, Ash?'

He's standing at the door to his study holding the car keys.

'Let me drive you. Cotters Hill, right?' he says.

And it isn't far, but he likes to drive and he's ready to drive. He's standing there holding the car keys. And we go downstairs, and we go out onto our hill and Abbott says the car's down here, that's where he's parked it, so we go on down and we pass them, Jay and Ryan and the girls, the one with the black dress too, we walk right past, and they don't look. No need to look, to see.

'Cotters Hill. Right, right,' Abbott says. 'I'll get the air con on. You'll cool down in a minute, you wait.' That's what he says, and I want to say, I think about saying, can you remember when we took Charlie up Cotters Hill just after she was born? But he's there with the air con, trying to get it just right, and I'm looking back, looking back towards number five.

'You'll be just right in a moment,' he says.

We walked up Cotters Hill. She was ten days old.

The midwife had said to take things slowly. Start with stairs, that's what she'd said, but I wanted to go to the top. I took it slowly. I held onto Abbott's hand as I walked and Charlie was strapped to my chest, sleeping. I looked down at her whilst I walked. I kept looking down, and every time I looked down and saw her there on my chest I couldn't believe she'd arrived.

'Charlie,' I said. I said it again.

I kept saying Charlie. I kept looking down at her whilst I walked, and I kept saying, I kept on saying, Charlie. Summer was over and the swifts had long gone, but Charlie, baby Charlie was strapped to my chest.

The midwife had said to start with stairs, so we didn't go up the steep way. It hurt to walk. It hurt so much, but I wasn't thinking about that, all I was thinking was Charlie, Charlee, Charlea. That was all I could think. We walked up Cotters Hill. There was pain between my legs, but I wanted to walk up. There was pain where the doctor had stitched. She asked me to slip my feet into stirrups whilst she stitched. That's what the doctor said. Slip your feet in here.

I didn't mind that much. I didn't mind being stitched up with my feet in stirrups. I was lying in the bed with Charlie on my chest and I could feel her little body moving up and down on mine, and I liked the feel of it, I liked it so much I didn't mind about the stitching.

Later it hurt. It hurt walking up Cotters Hill too, but I wanted to get to the top with Charlie. Abbott held my hand all the way. He asked me if I needed to go down, he said the midwife had suggested I start with stairs, and I said I wanted to go up. I wanted things to start well. That's what I was thinking. I want this thing with Charlie to start well.

We stood on the top of Cotters Hill. The wind was blowing up there and Charlie was strapped to my chest. We stood and we looked out over Tilstoke, and across to the Toll Estate. We stood for a long time. I was thinking about Charlie. I was thinking about the wind too. I was thinking how the wind made me restless. I wanted it for my collection, restless. I hadn't added anything to my collection for a long time.

'Restless, restless, restless.' I said it into the wind. It sounded a bit like the wind.

'Ash,' Abbott said. 'Not now.'

He pointed to our hill, to our house.

'There. There we are,' he said.

He stopped talking for a while after that. I could feel the throbbing between my legs but I didn't mind that much.

'A new beginning,' Abbott said, and kissed Charlie on the head.

Whenever there's an ending, look for the beginning. It was something Papa said the day I cut off my hair. The day I stood outside his shed with my long hair in the grass and his scissors in my hand. I was wearing the blue dress. He bent down, and when he stood up he had some of my hair. He held it up. He draped it across both of his hands.

'You'll always find a beginning with an end.' That's what he said.

After we'd stood for a while, we walked down. It hurt, walking down Cotters Hill, but all I could think about was Charlie and how she'd begun. I looked down at her. I kept looking down at her. I kept saying 'Charlie', I couldn't stop saying it.

I thought about the ending. I thought about the ending of Abbott's new beginning. Because why would he say new beginning when all beginnings are new. I thought about the ending, all possible endings, even though looking for the ending from a beginning wasn't what Papa had said.

A week later I walked up Cotters Hill again. Abbott had gone back to work. He'd started kissing both of us on the head before he left. Charlie first, then me.

He called us his girls and he kissed us.

That day, I strapped Charlie to my chest myself. The sun was out but it was cold, so I put Charlie's hat on. I put my hat on too. We went up Cotters Hill, the pair of us, wearing our hats.

I walked up the steep way. I'd almost forgotten about the pain between my legs. I walked with Charlie strapped to my chest. She had her eyes open, they were open all the way up and around the Crag. That was the way I walked, around the Crag. The steep way. And when we stood at the top we looked out across Tilstoke, and the wind was blowing.

I looked out and the trees were tired and the grass was tired and it felt like the end of something, because everything was tired, the way it's always tired when summer's long done and the wind blows. I looked out across Tilstoke.

I looked and I said, 'A new beginning.'

I don't know why I said it, but I did. It just came out. It was almost as if I'd planned to walk up there and say it. But I hadn't. I wouldn't have done that. I was so tired because Charlie was small. I was too tired to have done anything like that.

I always go up the steep way these days. I'm going that way now, even though I'm late. I'm going up Cotters Hill via Crag. By way of the Crag and it's hot, but I always go this way, and it's the best way to walk when the grasses are up, and it's been so hot but the grasses are still up.

No one from Naturally Yoga will go this way. Everyone goes up the other way, the way the families walk. It's the way the old people walk. They walk around the hill and up. They carry their poles and you can hear them clicking on the rock, you can hear them clicking away, but nobody cares about the clicking. Nobody minds the click, click, click. They like to go up and they can't go via the Crag, so they have to go up the other way. That was the way we went up when Charlie was a baby; when the midwife said I should start with stairs, but it's better going this way, although I lost my words around here that summer. It's difficult not to think of my words, the way they disappeared, but I like going this way, especially when the grasses are up. Especially when there's so much light.

They won't have come up this way, but why does it matter which way they go up when all they're thinking about is the top, the top, the top. But it isn't about the top, I said as much to Kate.

But they'll be there already. At the top. Celebrating the light. Doing breath work. That's what they do before they start and I know I'm late because I was looking out the window. That's why I'm late.

And can you think of a more glorious way?

It's too late for thinking about that now. About whether there would be a more glorious way to celebrate, because the longest day of the year has come. It's not worth thinking about the hours that have gone, because it's only the longest day once a year and there's no point in thinking about anything apart from the thing that's happening right now.

The here and now. That's what Abbott calls it.

And why is it called the longest day, when all days are the same length and only the hours of daylight are different? That's what they say though. That's what I say too. I say, it's the longest day, and everyone knows what I mean. I can imagine Abbott. I can imagine him saying Ash, not now. He always says. Ash, not now. You'll drive yourself mad. But if it is the longest day. If it is. And what Abbott really means is stop, not not now, but who says stop? Nobody really says stop.

But if it's the longest day. If it is, think of Utsjoki up there inside the Arctic Circle. Think of the endless daylight. Think about what happens if seventy-one days of daylight are only one day. And what about the polar night? Twenty-eight days when the sun doesn't rise. Twenty-eight days that never begin. Lost days, I suppose you could say. Ninety-eight of them, because that's what they mean. That's what we mean when we say the longest day. The rising and setting of the sun. That's what we're talking about. Two hundred and sixty-seven days in a year, that's all they get in Utsjoki, only two hundred and sixty-seven days.

Going up around the Crag is the best way to go.

It's evening on the longest day of the year and it's hot. It's still hot. And I'm only late because Charlie said I should look out of the window at number five.

'Look out of the window, Ash,' she said. And I looked out and the swifts were there and Jay was there with his hands on her breasts. I'm talking about the girl in the little black dress, although she wasn't a girl, she was almost a woman. He had his hands on her breasts and I'd never seen anyone take someone else's breasts the way he took hers and she didn't say a thing, not to begin with, she didn't say anything when he took her breasts.

I'm late. I'm late, but it doesn't take long to get up Cotters Hill and it isn't the same as the first day I came up this way with Charlie, or when I came up with Kate, because it rained almost every day that summer. The grasses were up then too, but it wasn't the same. We walked via the Crag and the grasses were up and she was wearing a skirt and I was in my shorts and there we were with our bare knees, the wet grasses against our legs. That's how it was. The grasses were wet against our legs and it was us two only.

Here I am, just below the Crag, and all I have to do now is scramble up. You can scramble up this way. I've done it before. You just have to get a good hold right here, then you can scramble up, so you can see the top of the hill. You can see the top from the Crag and if you're careful, nobody can see you.

And it isn't dangerous, scrambling up the Crag. As long as you know where the best holds are, it isn't dangerous. The climbers do it all the time. They do it without thinking, but it's too hot for the climbers today. I haven't seen a single one.

And here. I can see the top from here. It's a vantage point, that's what it is. And there they are, there's everyone from Naturally Yoga, on the top of the hill. And I've got to say, why not say, I'm looking out for her.

I'm looking out for her.

I'll wait here. Yes, I'll stay here until I see her, because it's always easier to join in when there's someone you know, and I can always sense when she's around. I mean, I can usually tell when she's around. But it's hot tonight. It's the longest day of the year and I'm not thinking about the lost hours, or the hours left. I'm not thinking about time. It's important to be present in the here and now, and it's so hot, even though it's evening. It's almost too hot to be waiting here on the Crag.

I can't see her. I can see the others. I can see them, but I can't see Kate. Kate.

It sounds like an echo, her name, when there's no one to hear me say it, but it can't be an echo because there's nothing but space behind me, and at the bottom of the Crag the grasses are up, the way they're always up in June. And maybe I should just wait, go on waiting. Wait until she comes. I can celebrate the light from the Crag, at least until I see her, and there's a good view from here. It's easy enough to see the top.

I heard one of them say she isn't coming. I heard the one with the flower band in her hair say she isn't coming. She said it to Jay. I heard her call him over and tell him. She called him Jay although he didn't look anything like Jay from number five. There are too many Jays.

'Kate can't make it.' That's what she said.

We'd saved the cake for the top, Kate and I. I was wearing shorts and she was wearing a skirt and there we were with our bare knees on the top of Cotters Hill.

'She isn't coming.' That's what the one with the flower band in her hair said.

It isn't about the top. That's what I said back then.

She didn't want me to run. She linked her arm through mine and said, 'No, don't, Ash.'

She isn't coming. Behind me is space, all that emptiness and nothing and no one to stop me running down.

I ran down the hill.

I climbed down the Crag, then I ran. I ran down the steep way. I ran down the way I came up, and if you've never run down, you won't know.

I wanted to run. She wasn't coming, she wasn't going to come. That's what the one with the flower band in her hair said. I heard her say it, so I ran down. It isn't about the top. I'd told her that before. She wasn't coming so I ran. I ran, and she wasn't there to stop me. Wasn't there to link her arm through mine, so I ran down the steep way. Through the grasses. I was running so fast all I could hear was breath and feet. I heard my feet on the grass, I heard my feet on the stones. I heard myself breathe. I heard my breath come out from my chest, out from my mouth and into my ears and back out again. I heard it making circles, out and in. There was nothing else to hear. There was nothing apart from my breath going out and in, and feet.

And I was running down, running down, and I was thinking about my feet. I was thinking about my feet and the sounds they made, over grass and over stones, and I wasn't thinking about anything else. I wasn't thinking about the hours that had gone. I wasn't thinking about how soon the days would get shorter, the swifts would leave, the house martins would leave, and wouldn't come back for months.

I was in the here and now, I was centred. I remember thinking, yes, my feet and the way my breathing sounds when it hits the air. I remember thinking, yes, I'm in the here and now, and I was running fast and I was thinking about my feet. I was listening to them.

I was listening for them.

I was listening, listening. I couldn't hear them any more, my feet on grass, on stones. I was listening, but there was nothing to hear. I was listening, but there was only breath, coming out from my chest, and Papa.

Papa saying, 'Apus apus, Ash.' Papa using all those As, all that alliteration.

'As if you had no feet, Ash. Run as if you had no feet.'

And I ran. I was running down. I was flying down and I had no feet. I couldn't hear my feet, although the ground was beneath them. And I wasn't thinking about time. I was making time. I wasn't thinking about it and I wasn't thinking about Kate. I wasn't thinking about her and I flew on past. I had no feet and I flew on past. I flew on, whilst she was walking up. Kate was walking up, in her dancing cornflower scarf, the one she hung at the foot of our stairs once.

I was flying down.

She was going up.

When I got back to our hill Jay was on the sofa alone. He had the music on loud but Terry wasn't there to tell him to turn it down. I waited. I stood outside the house and waited. I said to myself that I'd wait until Terry opened the window, I wanted to hear him say, Too loud, son. It would have helped. I wanted Terry to come, but he didn't come and it was too hot to wait.

We sit at the table next to the dog.

'Hello,' Charlie says to the dog. 'Hello, sir.'

The dog turns his head.

'Hello, sir, on this hot afternoon,' she says and he looks at her, the big dog, and she looks at me, and I nod my head and she goes on talking.

'Can't we just sit somewhere else?' Abbott says.

A quiet beer at the White Hart is all he asks, all he wants, it's a simple thing, but Charlie likes the dog, the one tied to the bench. She likes the big dog with the thick coat and she doesn't want to sit anywhere else. She says she doesn't care about anything else, she only cares about the dog and if Charlie's not moving then . . .

We sit at the table next to the dog.

Abbott holds his beer up to the light. There's been so much of it. Light, light, light. Nothing but light these past few weeks and he holds his beer up and the light comes through it.

'They do a good beer here,' he says.

And Charlie says, 'Dad's got a nice beer,' and she's talking to the dog but Abbott holds his beer up to the light one more time then takes a sip.

'A nice beer on a nice day,' he says.

'But whose dog is it?' Charlie says.

Because the dog is tied to the bench and there isn't anyone sitting with it. There are people sitting at tables, lots of people, but there isn't anyone sitting at the table with the dog. There should be someone with the dog, but there isn't, and Charlie's looking around and I'm looking around and there should be someone here to look after him.

Abbott says we should drink up, us two. Someone will come. 'People don't abandon dogs at pubs,' he says, but there are three other dogs at the tables and all the other dogs have people, but this dog doesn't have a person and he's tugging on his lead towards Charlie. He's so close to her, but Charlie's sitting on the bench and the dog is down there on the grass and the grass is yellow. It's been so hot the grass is yellow.

'This is the best dog, isn't it?' she says. 'Out of all the dogs, it's the best.'

It looks like a good dog, although all the other dogs have people with them.

'This is the best dog. Do you think it is?' she says.

She says, 'Do you think?'

And a man carrying a beer walks across the grass towards the bench, the table, where the dog is. The table next to our table. He puts his beer down on the table and he sits on the bench and he says, 'Mind out.' He says it to the dog.

'Mind out.'

That's what he says, although the dog's tied up on the other side of the bench. The dog's right next to our table and nowhere near the man, but still the man says mind out. And he's definitely saying it to the dog because he stretches his leg out under the table. He stretches it right out so he can reach the dog, so he can move the dog with his big boot. His big, brown boot. That's what he does. He hooks his boot under the dog's belly and he shifts the dog.

'Oh,' Charlie says.

'You see,' Abbott says. 'People don't leave their dogs.'

And the man takes his beer and holds it up to the light. He holds it up and the dog pulls on his lead. He pulls towards Charlie and Charlie says, 'Hello, sir' again, but quietly. And the dog pulls and the man says, 'Lie down,' to the dog. Lie down, boy. But the dog doesn't lie down, he wants to get to Charlie. He pulls on his lead towards Charlie, and Charlie goes to pat him, she puts her hand out, holds it out and the man hasn't seen her. No, the man isn't looking at Charlie. He's looking across the grass towards the car park.

'Over here, over here,' he says, and he stands up. He waves. 'Over here,' he says.

And someone's walking across the grass. Walking towards the table where the man with the dog is sitting. Walking slowly, or do I mean smoothly? Walking as though the yellow grass is water.

And it's hardly been a day. It was only last night. I was running down Cotters Hill and Kate was walking up. I was running so fast I missed her. She missed me. But here she is again, walking across the grass, sailing across the grass, towards the man with the dog.

Karma, that's what she would've said. Us two, meeting like that, two days in a row. And she's right. It has to be karma. We haven't seen each other for months, for years, now all of a sudden. Twice.

She's walking over. She's walking across the grass towards the man with the dog and he's waving his arm. A stubby arm. She can see where he is, but he's still waving.

And he gets up from the bench. He pushes it back with his thigh and stands up. He stands up and straddles the bench and he says hello and she's almost there.

'Hi. Hello. Hi,' he says. 'You made it.'

And he straddles the bench and he leans towards her. He leans over and he stretches out his arm. He holds it out, he holds it until she walks right into the space he's making with it. They move towards each other, the man and Kate, and Charlie says, 'The dog, look at the dog,' and the dog is panting, panting. He's panting and pulling, and Kate leans right in and he puts his arm around her shoulder and he pulls her. He pulls her in and kisses her.

'Everybody finished then?' Abbott says. 'Drink up, Ash,' he says.

And we get up. She's only just arrived and we're getting up to go, although Charlie doesn't want to. Doesn't want to leave the dog, but Abbott says, 'Come on, there are plenty more dogs where this dog came from.' And we have to go. We have to come on, but the man's got her hand. I can see from here, he's holding Kate's hand and I can see the hairs on his fingers, and Abbott doesn't have hairs on his fingers like that. Not thick, black hairs like that. I wouldn't like it if he had fingers like that, if he held my hand with fingers like that. But we have to go. We have to come on and walk back across the grass to the car park.

'They do good beer here,' Abbott says. 'They always do a good beer here, don't you think?'

'Yes,' I say. 'One moment.'

'What now? What, Ash?'

And I've stopped coming on. I've turned around. And there she is, sitting at the table, and it's been a while, it's been a long time, and I'm trying to remember and I can't remember. I can't remember her sitting with her back to me before. No, she wouldn't ever have faced away from me.

'Ash,' Abbott says. 'Ash.'

But where's the man? He must've gone. He can't have gone, because there's his dog. Lying down now. Given up on pulling. Given up on getting to Charlie. I suppose he's gone inside, the man, for chips, for beer, but she wouldn't drink beer. Wouldn't ever touch a beer.

'Ash,' Abbott says. 'We'll meet you at the car then.'

He takes Charlie's hand. He says, 'Come on,' and they go on walking across the grass towards the car.

They walk towards the car. Abbott stops and turns to look back at me and here I am, still standing here on the grass, looking at the table where Kate is.

'Ash,' he says. 'What are you doing?'

What am I doing standing here on the grass? What am I doing looking back across the grass? It's yellow now, after all that sun, it isn't even green. And Abbott's looking. He's waiting. Waiting for me to do something, and he doesn't go, he doesn't move until I do.

I walk back across the grass. I walk right up to the table where Kate is sitting, where the dog is lying. I walk right up and she's got her back to me. She's looking at her phone, she doesn't see, doesn't notice. And I could put out my hand, could touch her, but I can't. Can't just creep up and touch someone. It's different with dogs though. People do it all the time, reach out and touch dogs that don't belong to them. And Charlie's right, this dog is probably the best dog. He looks like a good dog, although he looks a bit sad. And I could put out my hand and touch him. There. He likes it. He doesn't mind at all. He seems like a good dog, a gentle dog, although he doesn't seem all that happy. Doesn't seem to like being tied up all that much. And she hasn't seen, hasn't looked up, and it wouldn't be right to touch her. Not here, not now. But the dog likes it. He likes having his head stroked. And why not, I think, if the man's not here, why not give the dog a chance? Why not unclip his lead? Give him a little chance. There. There you go.

'You can go if you want to,' I whisper. 'Go.'

And he turns his head towards me. It's a big head. He turns to look at me with his big head. He turns away, and then he goes. He crosses the grass. The big dog crosses the grass and his ears are up and his tail is up.

'The air con's on,' Abbott says. 'You'd never know we were having a heatwave. You'd never know, sitting in here, would you?' he says. 'Would you, Ash?'

'No,' I say.

And he lets the handbrake off.

'Let's go,' he says. 'Tilstoke bound.'

And it's nice to be able to think about homonyms again, to think of leaping strides.

'Stop, Dad,' Charlie says. And Abbott puts his foot on the brake and we lurch forward, we all lurch forward.

'The dog,' she says.

And there's the dog, standing in front of the car.

'Careful,' she says.

Abbott revs the engine. He revs the engine, but the dog doesn't mind, just stays where he is in front of the car, and he looks happy, the dog, he looks quite a lot happier now.

'Come on,' Abbott says. 'Move yourself, crazy canine.'

He reverses a bit, a tiny bit and he's about to drive around the dog but the dog walks a few steps and stands in front of the car again and Abbott can't go, he can't drive and he says, 'That man. He's let his bloody dog loose.'

And the dog is loose. He's loose and he's standing in front of the car and we can't pull out. We can't drive away. Abbott looks at his nice watch. He taps his Second Core and we look at the dog. We sit in the car and look at the dog.

'Get out,' he says to Charlie. 'Get out and move the dog.'

Charlie gets out. Charlie gets out and the dog is standing in front of the car and Charlie walks up to the dog and the dog turns his big head. Charlie puts out her hand. 'Hello,' she says. And the dog looks happy, so much happier.

'He likes her,' I say, and Abbott nods. He looks at his watch and he holds it up to the windscreen so Charlie can see it, but Charlie doesn't understand. She doesn't care about time. She's talking to the dog, saying something to him, and Abbott says he hasn't got all day. But it doesn't matter what he hasn't got because Charlie's coming now, walking back to the car with the dog beside her. She's walking with the dog beside her and when she gets back in the car the dog follows. He hops inside and she shuts the door.

'Ash,' Abbott says.

And what am I supposed to do?

'Ash,' he says. And the dog is there on the back seat with Charlie.

'Perhaps you should drive,' I say. 'Maybe just drive.'

And Charlie puts her arm around the dog. She rests her head against his chest. 'Papa,' she says. It isn't something she usually says. 'Papa, please.'

And Abbott says OK. He says, 'OK,' and he straightens his driving glasses and he puts the car into gear.

The dog gave himself to Charlie, just like that. He lay across the back seat with his head on her knee and he was sold on her, made up.

Nelson, that's his name.

'It's after Nelson Mandela,' she said. 'Have you heard of him?'

He follows her around. He walks behind her from room to room. Right behind her. And when they're walking she pats him. She pats him on his big head and says, 'Nelson.' She keeps saying Nelson. She keeps saying it the way I kept saying Charlie when she was brand new and I couldn't believe she'd arrived.

He follows her all the time. Every time she gets up, he follows her and when she can't be followed he lies down with his body over her feet like he's keeping her.

This morning I went into her room and asked her if she wanted a game of Bird Bingo.

'Nelson can come,' I said. 'He can come along.'

I was standing in her room with the cards in my hand.

I said, 'Do you want to play?' And I held the cards out towards her and on the top was the curlew.

'Come and play,' I said.

'We're busy,' she said. 'Busy, busy.'

So I took Bird Bingo to Abbott's study and paired the birds up myself, so at least they were sorted for the next time. I thought about putting them into alphabetical order, because we've always liked having the Arctic skua at the top.

I was going to sort them, but Jay was outside on the sofa and I wanted to see if the girl in the LBD would come back. There are plenty of things to do, I was thinking. If Charlie's busy, there are plenty of things I need to do. And I wanted to see if she was coming back, the girl in the LBD. I watched from the window for a while. I could hear Charlie talking to Nelson. I heard her laughing. They were thudding about, thumping about. They sounded busy. Busy, busy. I watched from the window. It didn't feel like the girl would come and she didn't. Nobody came.

I stood at the window. Charlie was busy and Jay was on the sofa with his phone. I stood there and thought about the words inside the book with the flame on the cover. They were right next to me, on the shelf.

I was standing next to the words. I wouldn't have minded. I wouldn't have minded at all if they'd started coming out of the book, one after the other. I wouldn't have minded watching them come out and multiply, proliferate, but they didn't.

They didn't do anything. I pulled the book off the shelf and started reading. I read out loud. I held the book out in front of me and I read the words, I let them out into the room, but they didn't do a thing. I was reading the words and all I could think about was Charlie. Charlie. I kept saying her name. I couldn't help it.

I said yes. Yes.

I said Nelson could sleep on her bed. Charlie hadn't come to me all day and I'd had to make the bird pairs myself and I'd almost started sorting them so that the Arctic skua was at the top. I said yes because I wanted her. That's why I said it.

So he slept on her bed. No, he sleeps on her bed. He sleeps there because I said yes and Charlie said thank you and skipped off, and when it came to bedtime, I was ready to say no, but it was too late because he was already on her bed and she was in her pyjamas with her arm wrapped around him and the swifts were screeching outside the window.

It was too late to say no, so I said, 'Come on, let's watch the swifts. Let's open the window wide. Let's throw open the window and sit on the sill and you can dangle your legs and I'll keep you safe. I'll hold onto you.'

Charlie looked towards the window.

'Come on,' I said.

She had her arm around Nelson and the swifts were screeching and I kept saying come on.

She looked towards the window. She's coming. That's what I thought. She'll come.

'You know Dad doesn't like flying insects.' That's what she said.

And she stayed where she was. So I went over to her window anyway. I opened it wide. I threw the window open and the swifts were there and I watched them for a while. I watched them turn in the sky and there wasn't a cloud. There wasn't a single cloud.

The flying insects came in. I didn't see them come, but there were so many of them. I didn't know what Charlie would think. I didn't want to think of Charlie. I shut the window. I shut it. Charlie was already sleeping.

I went to bed. I wanted to sleep. I wanted to slip away, to be slipping away. Sometimes you can catch yourself, feel yourself, slipping. And you're not thinking, you're not worrying, you're just noticing. Noticing yourself slipping.

He came back, the man from the pub. That's what I dreamt. I saw his hairy fingers pushing their way through our letter box. I saw them from inside our house. I was standing in our hallway and I could see his hairy fingers. He was rattling our letter box. He was calling through the letter box and Charlie and Nelson were sleeping.

'Open up, open up,' he said and I was looking at the wet on his lips and I wanted to look away, but I couldn't. He was calling through the letter box. He wanted the dog. He wanted his dog back. But Charlie and Nelson had come too far, they'd come so far together. Abbott said it too. It wasn't just something I'd thought. Abbott said it himself.

'Maybe that's what she needed all along. A friend,' he said.

But the man didn't go. He wanted his dog. He stayed outside our front door with his hand through our letter box. Abbott wasn't home and I hadn't put the bolt across the door. I didn't want to stay inside. I wanted to go out because the flowers needed water. It was hot. Even in the dream it was hot.

I wanted to go outside. I stood by the front door but I couldn't get out. His hairy fingers were coming through our letter box and when he called I saw the wet around his lips and I knew he'd swallow me if I tried to get past him.

He stayed outside with his hand through our letter box and Abbott was out and where was he, because he never sees. No, he didn't see the man put his hairy fingers on her breasts, Kate's. He placed them there. He let his hairy fingers fall into the shape of her breasts and he held them there. He didn't move. He let his hairy fingers feel the shape of her. I saw them taking the shape of her. Then he moved her breasts up and down, the way Jay moved that girl's breasts up and down, but Jay hasn't got fingers like that.

I called for Abbott. I called out. The man's fingers were crawling, crawling all over her breasts, and I wanted Abbott to see, to stop the crawling. I expected Kate to turn, all along I expected it, because I was standing right there and he had her breasts and his hand in our letter box and he couldn't have it all, but he did.

Joan's started talking to us again. She knocked on our front door. I knew it was Joan before Charlie opened it. I knew it would be, and there she was, standing on our front step the way she always used to. There she was, wearing elasticated trousers and holding a bone wrapped in paper.

'What's that?' Charlie said.

'Thought I'd buy that dog of yours a little something,' she said. She was craning her neck, she was looking down the hallway, but Nelson wasn't there.

'Doesn't hurt to have a little treat now and then, does it?' she said.

There she was, standing on our doorstep with the bone in her hand. The grease was coming through the paper. Her thumb was shining with it, her thumb and down to the thin skin of her wrist.

'I was passing the butcher's anyway. The one on the estate,' she said. 'I was passing the butcher's anyway, and I thought why not? Can't hurt now, can it, a little bit of brisket bone?'

I liked her talking. I'd forgotten how much I liked her talking. It'd been a long time since she'd stood on our doorstep talking, it'd been almost three years. Go on, I was thinking. Go on, go on. Keep talking, keep talking the way you're talking. That's what I was thinking.

'It's for after his dinner if your mum doesn't mind,' Joan said.

'OK,' Charlie said, and she held out her hand for the bone.

'If your mum doesn't mind,' Joan said again.

She looked behind Charlie to where I was standing and waved the bone, the paper and the bone, and Charlie held her hand out.

Joan kept hold of the bone.

She said, 'Does he do a trick, your dog? Bring him here and get him to give us all a trick.'

Charlie called for Nelson.

'He's ready for his trick,' Joan said as he trotted along the hallway towards us. 'See?' she said. 'Here he comes.' I'd forgotten how much I liked her way with words. Go on, I thought. Go on with your words.

'Let's see him do something then,' Joan said. And Charlie got Nelson to do a trick and when it was done Joan clapped, although it wasn't a proper clap because she had the bone and she didn't want to let go of it, so she had to clap against it, against the bone, against the greasy paper.

After she clapped she took a breath, a deliberate breath.

'You two should go on one of them talent shows. You know the ones, you know.'

I walked away. I left Charlie and Nelson with Joan. I left them at the front door and I walked along the hallway and sat on the bottom step of the stairs. It was stifling down there, the air was sticking to the insides of my lungs, I mean I'd taken air in and I was struggling to get it out, couldn't breathe it out. Couldn't breathe out all that well. And Joan. Joan was still talking, was still going on.

'Those shows,' she said. 'Did you see the one with the dog? Did you?'

And Charlie didn't say a thing. She didn't even shake her head, just held her hand out for the bone and waited.

78

'But he's so handsome,' Joan said. 'He nodded his head when I said that. Did you see that? I saw that. Wait till I tell Wilf. He loves a German shepherd, he does.'

I was sitting on the bottom step. Go on, I thought. Press on with your words, and I didn't have to carry on thinking like that for long.

'Always wanted one, a German shepherd, Wilf did, but I said there's not enough space in here, Wilf, and anyway you're hairy enough for the both of us, aren't you? No need for two hairy boys in the house.'

She stepped up, stepped inside our front door, leant against the wall, and went on talking.

I was on the bottom step. Here I am, I thought, although I knew I couldn't carry on sitting there in the heat. I knew Joan couldn't keep going on, not with the bone in her hand, not indefinitely, no. I was on the stairs. I shut my eyes but I could still hear. I heard Charlie ask Joan if she wanted to see Nelson do another trick and I heard Joan say, 'Yes.' I heard her clapping again. Clapping against the bone paper. I heard her go on. She went on. I thought, how can someone go on like that? Keep going on like that? And I wanted Charlie to come in.

I was sitting on the bottom step. I could hear Joan. I could smell the bone.

I wanted Charlie to come in. I wanted Charlie to shut the door on Joan and her bone and I didn't want them to rhyme but they did.

I was on the bottom step. I didn't like Joan talking. I'd forgotten how much I didn't like the way she went on and on, how I'd never much liked the way she went on, and I thought how useful it would be to have a nice watch. If I had a nice watch, I thought, I could say to Charlie:

Time to come in, dinner at six.

Five more minutes. Charlie, Charlie.

And Joan would have to stop. That's what I thought. If I had a nice watch, Joan would have to stop.

It felt like an emergency, with Charlie and Nelson in the hallway and me on the bottom step and Joan propped up against our wall going on and on without thinking. And the smell of the bone was hanging in the air and the air was too heavy down there at the end of the hallway and I wanted Charlie to come back in because Joan had her. She shouldn't have her.

In the end I got up.

I stood up. I walked towards the door. Charlie was sitting on the floor, Nelson's big head on her knee, and Joan was leaning where she always used to lean. She had her bone. Joan. Had her bone, had her bone.

'We need to shut the door,' I said. 'Abbott doesn't like flying insects in the house. I'm sorry.'

'I'm sorry,' I said again, and took another step towards her. I waited. Waited until Joan stopped leaning, until Joan stepped onto the doormat, and then I pushed.

I made sure she was on the other side and I pushed on the door. I pushed quite hard, and I heard her feet, her urgent steps. I heard her clearing her throat ready to speak, but I kept pushing, I went on pushing and I didn't look, didn't want to see, so I pushed. I went on pushing until the door was shut.

'Ash,' Charlie said. 'Ash.'

'You know how your dad feels about flying insects,' I said.

Charlie and Nelson went upstairs. I could hear her talking to him and I could smell the bone. I went into the kitchen. I opened the freezer door and stuck my hand in next to the cottage pie. I held it there. I held it next to the cottage pie and ran through the Fibonacci sequence. I didn't get far before something happened. I didn't get that far before Joan posted the bone through the letter box.

I waited. I waited with my hand in the freezer, with Charlie and Nelson upstairs. I waited until I heard Joan's front door slam shut.

I don't know why I didn't come down here on my own before.

I asked Charlie.

'Do you want to come to the lake?' I said, but Charlie was busy, too busy, and I asked three times. But three summer days.

Three summer days, with Kate. I'd almost wished we were butterflies.

And then I went under.

After that I couldn't hear her. I couldn't see anything but the bubbles I was breathing and the shapes the rain made on the surface of the water.

It rained all summer.

We wanted it to stop. We wanted to show our colours, fly a little, but the sky rolled on. The rain went on.

And now the earth is scorched, and the flowers in the garden are wilting and I can't water them because Joan's been watching. She's started watching. She's started coming round again.

And I'll keep my T-shirt on, in case somebody comes, but nobody ever comes.

Charlie once thought she heard some boys down here, but they weren't boys, they were gulls. We laughed at that. Boys and gulls. We said it a hundred times as we walked home.

I'm going in. There. Going in.

And I don't know why I didn't come down here on my own before. I don't always need to have Charlie with me, and

Abbott holds his breath underwater. He hasn't been taught how to breathe. That's what he says.

I like coming here alone. I've always liked being alone.

There. Going in. Wading in.

I'm glad I got here in time. There was no point in waiting for Charlie, because the lake's getting sucked up into the sky.

I'll wade out to the rock, I'll swim if I can, but it's shallow. Even at the rock, it's shallow.

And the water's been under the sun so long, it's warm. Warm water, it's soothing. That's the word.

I'll take my T-shirt off. I'll take it off and leave it on the rock and then I'll go deeper. I'll keep on wading until the bottom of the lake falls away from under my feet. And then I'll swim. I'll go further out than we've been before, I'll keep going further. And you have to breathe out when you go under. Breathe out. That's what I said to Abbott, but he never came swimming again.

I'll take my T-shirt off. And there. It's soothing when the water's warm like this. I like being alone. I've always liked being alone and I'm glad I came in time.

And you breathe like this. You lift your feet, you put your head under and you breathe like this.

Charlie knows. Charlie knows how to breathe underwater.

The photos of the solstice celebration are up on the Naturally Yoga website. There are twenty-seven of them in the photo stream.

I've got to number fourteen and where is she?

The woman with the flower band in her hair said she wasn't coming. But she wasn't right. She came. She was walking up whilst I was running down. The steep way. We were both going the steep way.

And there. In number nineteen. There, in her dancing cornflower scarf. She hung it on the end of our stairs. There's a woman in our house. That's what I thought when she hung it there. There's a woman in our house.

I was running down. I was flying down the steep way and she was walking up. We missed each other, but there she is in her cornflower scarf. In number twenty-one, too. She's pretty. It's not a bad word, pretty. It's not for boys though.

There she is.

There she is.

Dancing cornflowers. What's the difference between to want and to have? To want and to have had?

Ash, not now. That's what Abbott would say. But I'll tell you what the difference is.

I've got her. There she is. Numbers nineteen and twenty-one. There she is on the screen in front of me and it doesn't do anyone any harm to kiss her like this. On her lips, her glassy lips.

We're going to the lake. To the lake off the Toll Estate. We'll walk out of here, Charlie and I, and leave the swifts behind us. There'll be nobody there because it isn't Tuesday. I asked her four times. You might as well keep asking if you want the answer you want.

I've packed some things. I've packed a ball for Nelson. He likes to bring it back. He likes to be a good boy. Last week I threw the ball and Nelson went running after it. I threw it so hard it went over the roof of our house and carried on sailing. I followed its arc through the sky. I thought he'd find it. I thought he'd bring it back. That's what he likes to do.

I waited.

He came back empty-mouthed. I watched Charlie's face and waited for her disappointment to show. I wanted a change, that was all.

'You threw it too far,' she said. 'It wasn't him.'

She ruffled the hair around his neck and said, 'Good boy.' I hoped he was hot, too hot. I went on tending to the flowers.

I've packed our things. The sky is blue. Cerulean.

Kate always asked for adjectives. I never had any, but there's one. Cerulean, cerulean.

And now Charlie throws the ball out past the rock and Nelson brings it back. He swims.

'Good boy,' she says.

Good boy. She throws. He fetches. She throws. He fetches.

His tail floats just under the surface. The sun on it. The sun on his tail through the water. She throws again and yes, he'll be a good boy.

I was Kate's boy. Once or twice, I was her boy.

'Will you swim?' That's what I say.

The lake's getting sucked up into the sky and you never know whether you'll be able to swim again. And you never know when the day will come when you wade out further and further and you have to keep wading because the place where the bottom falls away has gone.

I'll ask again. I'll ask twice. Because two's the first prime.

'Will you swim?'

Twice I asked and now I'm going in. There. Going in. Wading in.

I'll wade out to the rock. I'll swim when I can but it's shallow. Look up above the place where the swallows fly, because the lake is being sucked into the cerulean sky. I didn't want a rhyme. Two is the only even prime. There, I said it and now I'm in and yes, the warm water is soothing.

I'll take my T-shirt off. Nobody ever comes here except on Tuesdays.

I'll leave it on the rock and then I'll go deeper and the bottom of the lake will fall away and I'll swim. Charlie should've swum. You never know when it'll be the last time and she knows how to breathe underwater. I do too. I stood on the rock, the high point of the rock. I called to Kate, but she wouldn't come in. No.

And Nelson is a good boy. He's better off with Charlie than the man with the hairy fingers. I had a bad feeling about him. So did Abbott. And now the bottom is falling away. I've caught it falling, the way you can catch yourself falling sometimes. Sometimes you catch things and you don't mind whether you keep hold of them.

I'll swim out. I'll swim right out. Charlie can stay there on the edge and throw the ball and I'll swim out away from the flies, because the flies have come and I don't know whether I'll get to swim in here again, if the sun goes on, plucking, snatching. And it is soothing, swimming in warm water. Swimming out, far out, wearing nothing but pants, and Abbott would call them knickers, but there isn't a good word and we're only just off the Toll Estate but nobody ever comes here. Except on Tuesdays. I should join the swimming club. They wear orange swim hats so they can spot each other, but nobody else ever comes.

I'm swimming now. I'm swimming, although Abbott would say I shouldn't swim because it isn't clean but I've got to get away from the flies and who knows when it'll be the last time.

Charlie's calling.

She says, 'Come in. Come in now, Ash.'

And I have swum quite far out.

I'm out quite far. But I know how to swim. I know how to swim and to breathe underwater.

'You're swimming away. Don't swim away.'

'Ash.'

Swimming away. Swimming a way. I'm quite far out and I'm still swimming and can I see the rock from here?

It was too shallow. It isn't always that way. I left my T-shirt and kept on wading. I left it there and it didn't matter because nobody ever comes and it isn't Tuesday. I kept on wading. I went on until I caught the bottom falling away. I felt it falling. The way you sometimes catch things falling.

And now I've swum out. I must've swum and swum. It's easy to keep going and it's warm. It's warmer than Tilstoke Baths in here and the sun's beating down on the back of my head but I could keep on swimming, I could go on swimming.

I am quite far out.

I might not hear Charlie from here. But I can't be that far out. It isn't Kevojärvi. I can't swim away in the lake off the Toll Estate. I couldn't swim away if I wanted to. And there might not be another chance to swim because the sun is sucking the lake up and I could keep on swimming and swimming and I wouldn't be able to swim away.

And now I'm on my back, yes, I'm under the sky. The water's soothing when it's warm like this and I had to swim out here, right out here, to get under the sky. I can float on my back and spread out my arms and my breasts are here under the yellow-brown sun water, but nobody ever comes. Not unless it's a Tuesday. I'm floating. I'm here on my back, under the sky and I'm like that boat, Asle's boat, but today is nothing like the day Asle didn't come back and you can't compare a Norwegian fjord to the lake off the Toll Estate. It isn't anywhere, the lake off the Toll Estate. It might not have a name.

I'm under the sky at least. It's a start.

And Charlie. And Nelson. And if I stay floating the sky will turn pink. It does these days.

I can swim away.

I couldn't if I wanted to.

But here under the sky it's calm. Asle was probably calm. That's why he didn't come back. It didn't matter what the weather was like. It didn't make any difference. He felt so calm there was no point in coming back. Because why would he come back to Signe? Why would he come back to a little house if he felt calmer out there on the fjord than in a little house with its stone walls pressing in, suffocating him? It doesn't matter what the weather was like. And if I had a nice watch I'd know how long I'd been gone, but I can see. I can see I'm quite far out.

I wouldn't have been able to swim away. Even if I'd wanted to. It was just a game. Swimming and swimming.

I'll swim in.

I'll wade in. I'll get my T-shirt from the rock and wade in and what's the opposite of falling away? I'll swim in. I'll keep swimming until my feet touch the bottom and now I'm swimming. Now I've got somewhere to swim to.

Charlie.

I didn't think she'd cry. I'll wade in. I'll wade right back in and I haven't got a nice watch, so I don't know how long I've been gone but Charlie's crying and I didn't think she'd cry because she's been all right with Nelson. They've been OK together. She threw the ball and he brought it back. I watched them do it over and over. They didn't mind the flies. They kept on throwing and fetching and there wasn't anything else for me to do.

I asked. I asked her twice.

'Will you swim?'

'Will you swim?'

She was waiting on his ball. That's all she was waiting for, so I waded out. She saw me go. She saw me wading out towards the rock, and she couldn't miss me and it didn't matter, me swimming away, but there was nowhere to swim to. I couldn't have swum away if I'd wanted to.

Charlie.

And it isn't far. I'll stop swimming and I'll start wading and I can feel the sun on the back of my head and I'm swimming in. I'm waiting to feel the bottom under my feet and then I'll wade.

The midwife said, 'Enjoy her.'

That was the last thing she said. And I have. I have. I walked to the top of Cotters Hill and that was the beginning. The new beginning.

I thought Nelson had changed things. Things changed so quickly.

But things don't change quickly.

And now I'm wading. Now I'm coming in.

'I left my T-shirt,' I say.

'On the rock,' she says.

I'll hold out my arms and if she wants to she can come. I'll hold them out.

This is the way I do it. I kneel down and hold them out. Things haven't changed. Nothing's changed. I hold them out so she can walk into them.

Papa said my mama knew how to hold me.

Papa knew how to hold me too, but there was no one there to tell him.

He held his arms out. He held them out so I could walk into them.

'Ash,' he said.

I was small.

I hold them out. Charlie's right there and my arms are too, stretched out towards her. I'll hold them here, if she wants to come, and a nice watch can't teach you anything about time.

And it's OK. It's OK.

I couldn't have swum away, even if I'd wanted to. It was calm. Calmer out there than in here. And there has to be a way to get your feet off the ground.

And it's OK. I know how to stay. I know to hold her like this. This is how I hold her.

Charlie. Charlie.

I didn't think she'd cry.

If you go far enough out it's calm. That's what I tell her. You have to keep swimming. You have to keep going until you're under the sky.

And I hold her. And it's OK. It's OK. And I say, 'Come down.' I say, 'Charlie, lie down, right here.'

And the flies have gone but the light keeps coming. And I didn't think she'd cry.

Charlie.

This is the way I hold her. And it's OK. It's OK. I didn't mean to keep on swimming. It was calmer out there. I didn't mean to leave my T-shirt on the rock and what am I supposed to do?

Almost naked then. You too. Both of us like this and it's OK. It doesn't hurt. It doesn't hurt if you don't mean it that way. And it's OK to be sorry after.

Kiss her then, like this.

Open her legs.

Kiss her, kiss her.

The swifts have gone.

Papa said you could never know for sure, but I knew. I always knew.

Charlie knew too.

That summer.

We were in the garden with the flowers. They'd grown so high. The petals were bright. The stems, the leaves were bright. Brighter than they should have been and they'd grown so tall they were stooping over themselves, the way tall people stoop over themselves when they know they shouldn't be as tall as they are. That's what the flowers were doing.

Charlie and I were in with the flowers. We were on our knees amongst the flowers and our knees were damp. They couldn't have been any other way. We were on our knees and the sky was thick with clouds and we couldn't see the swifts. We'd hardly seen them all summer but Charlie looked at the sky and said, 'Tomorrow. The swifts will go.'

The next morning the sky looked the same.

'All gone,' she said.

She said it before she'd eaten a mouthful of breakfast. I remember her saying it because she pronounced her gs like ds back then. All don. That's what she really said and I said it too. Don. And we nodded.

I knew.

That summer.

I lay on the bed whilst Kate dressed with her back to me. She was getting dressed and I knew. Or perhaps it was only later when I really knew, because if I'd known when she was getting dressed, why would I have been at the kitchen table a few days later, smiling, saying, 'Don?'

Charlie knew. That summer. This summer she's hardly looked up. She's hardly looked up although the sky's been blue, cerulean even. She would've seen swifts if she'd looked. She would've noticed them empty the sky.

For now there are swallows and house martins. They go too.

Kate said she'd come for the house martins, and for a while I believed her. I waited for her. Even though. I waited, but I knew.

The house martins left. They've left three times now. Three summer days. Don, don, don.

And now Abbott says I should rest.

'You haven't been yourself since.' That's what he said.

Nobody ends a sentence with since, but that's what he did.

He stuck his head around the door and said, 'You haven't been yourself since.'

So this is the third day of rest, three summer days, the sixty-third hour.

I've been watching the sky. I'm reading *Leaves of Grass*. And it is restful, watching the sky and reading.

I saw a woman on the train reading *Leaves of Grass* once. I was sitting up on Papa's knee. The woman who was reading had her hair tied up. I was only small. Not too small to be able to read, but small enough to sit on Papa's knee.

'Leaves of grass are impossible.' That's what I said in Papa's ear.

Papa laughed. The woman lowered the book. She smiled at him.

'It's poetry,' he said. Everything. No. He said, 'Anything's possible with poetry.'

The woman smiled again and my papa reached out and touched her. I don't remember where he touched her but that's what he did because I remember holding on to him. I had to hold on whilst he reached across the table towards the woman with her hair tied back.

Years later, but definitely before I met Abbott, I saw a woman reading it on the bus. The same book. She could've been the same woman as before. I asked her if the seat next to her was free. She nodded, but she looked across at the empty seats. There were plenty. I looked at them too.

I sat down next to her. I was sitting next to possibility. I told myself that was where I was sitting. I didn't mind waiting for the lights at the Ryland crossroads. Anything's possible. That's what I was thinking. Poetry, poet-tree. I almost went to the end of the line, and when the woman squeezed past me to get off the bus, she brushed me on the knee with it. With her copy of *Leaves of Grass*.

'Bye,' I said.

I waved. I got off the bus at the next stop and ran. I ran until I reached our front door.

Later, after I'd met Abbott, I told him about the woman on the train and the woman on the bus. I told him they might've been the same woman, I told him everything, every detail, and he listened all the way through. He nodded his head. He understood.

'Have you read it?' he said when I'd finished. *Leaves of Grass*. 'Have you read it?'

Two weeks later, after serving up risotto, he brought out a book from behind his back and put it on the table in front of me.

'*The Complete Poems*,' he said.

He said that *Leaves of Grass* was in there, but he thought I'd like them all.

'*The Complete Poems*. The whole lot,' he said.

He pushed the book across the table towards me.

I've been resting since.

Almost three whole days of rest. This is the seventieth hour, and it's a fitting thing to say, the seventieth hour, because here I am at 'To Think of Time'. It's a long poem. Most poems in *Leaves of Grass* are long poems, some are as long as a long short story. Abbott says he hasn't got time for long poems, but how does he know how much time he's got? That's the problem with his nice watch, it makes him think he knows.

He says things like, leaving in ten. You've got five minutes. He likes saying them and I've never seen him look back at the minutes after they've gone. No, the only time he ever looks over his shoulder is when he's driving. He never has the urge to stop the minutes from leaving because his watch goes round and round and it makes him think that time's chasing him, which is the opposite of the truth. That's what he thinks, time goes in circles, although he hasn't said so. Maybe I should get a nice watch. But I know this is the seventieth hour. I don't need a nice watch.

I've been watching the sky. It's empty. It's been blue for so long. Deep blue, azure, cerulean even. And look now, just when we were getting used to it. Yes, look up, look out of the window. There are clouds building.

There are clouds in our sky and I thought I'd seen U look up earlier, or was it yesterday? I thought I'd heard her say it was going to break. I thought I saw Terry nod, but I've been resting for a long time. This is the seventieth hour and I've been looking at the sky. I mean, I've been reading and looking at the sky and I've been resting, and I wasn't sure whether that's what she'd said, but yes, now the clouds are definitely building. They're building, that's the only way to describe it. The clouds are building. And perhaps I should call Charlie, but I haven't seen Charlie, not since I started resting and I suppose Abbott said, 'your mum's resting', and she went off with Nelson. I suppose that's what happened, but look at the sky. Everyone, no, anyone would want to look at the sky because the clouds are building, and who says nothing happens when you're resting, because something always happens and time can't move in circles, even though watches make you think they do.

Charlie would like this. The clouds are stacked in the sky, the sky's dark, getting darker, and yes, she'd like this because it feels like something's about to happen. Look. The sky's dark, the clouds are stacked and it looks, it definitely looks like it's going to rain.

The windows of heaven were opened.

Those were the words in the Bible. Papa said he didn't like me reading the Bible, he said he didn't know why we didn't get rid of that book, but nobody gets rid of their Bibles. I liked the Flood. I liked the part when God told Noah to get all the animals into the ark.

Every bird of every sort.

And every creeping thing that creepeth upon the earth.

Creepeth. That was the word I liked. I had to read it to myself, under my breath, because Papa didn't like the Bible. I wanted creepeth for my collection.

Charlie liked creepeth too. Abbott said he didn't mind one way or other about the Bible, but he didn't want creeping animals inside our house. It isn't anything to do with the house, it's to do with the ark. The arc. Two good words. Charlie would like them both. She'd like the sky right now. She'd like the way the clouds are building up and up and surely clouds are the only things that can keep on building, that can build up indefinitely, and Charlie would like it, she likes it when something's about to happen and why shouldn't I go downstairs, now the clouds are building? How can Abbott expect me to rest when something's about to happen? And the sky's dark, yes, the sky's got so dark it's difficult to read, so I'll go downstairs, and seventy hours of rest are enough hours of rest for anyone, and something's about to happen to the world. Something's about to happen.

It rained. Of course, it rained. I went downstairs and sat at the kitchen table on the wooden stool. The rain came down. Charlie opened the back door.

Rain pelteth.

That's what I was thinking. Rain pelteth. It came out of the sky and onto the patio, the shed roof, the grass, the flowers.

Pelteth, like creepeth. That's what I was thinking.

But what's the point in taking feathers from a bird when I don't know which bird I'm taking it from? Rain pelteth. Perhaps it was Keats. He was Papa's boy. Once or twice I was hers, although what did she mean, her boy, but you can't pluck lines from poems. You shouldn't. It isn't right.

Charlie and Nelson sat inside the back door, the rain was coming down. A wind was coming in and Charlie put her knees to her chest and her arm around Nelson.

'Dad doesn't care about flying insects when it rains,' she said to him.

There was a chill in the air. Abbott felt it too.

'Hot chocolate, anyone?' he said. 'Hot chocolate?'

That's what he said, and after he'd said it a sound came out from the throat of the earth itself. I swear, that's where it came from. It couldn't have come from anywhere else, a sound like that.

Nelson slunk off from under Charlie's arm. His eyes turned. They looked the way they looked that day at the White Hart. They looked the way they looked when he was pulling on the lead. Pulling and pulling towards Charlie.

'Hot chocolate?' Abbott said, and I swear the earth turned. The huge earth turned. Charlie stepped out onto the patio. She beckoned to Nelson. She said, 'Come on, come on out,' but Nelson didn't come. The rain was falling, and she was under it, she was out there on the patio, under its pelting.

Charlie got wet. Of course she got wet. She stood on the patio and the rain was coming down. She stood there without moving. She stood on the patio without moving and she looked like she was thinking about the rain. But it was me who was thinking about the rain, about the way it was pelting down. It wasn't Charlie.

Rain pelteth. That's what I was thinking and I could hear it hitting the window, the patio. Charlie was outside. She was standing on the patio and she wasn't moving. Rain was running down her arms, her face. Rain was coming off her nose. She stood there and the earth turned again and again and there was lightning too.

'Charlie,' Abbott said. 'Come in now, it's wet.'

And the sky was dark and the rain was coming down and Charlie was standing on the patio getting wet and I was wondering whether she could stay there indefinitely, but nobody stays anywhere indefinitely, not even Signe, even though she was lying down at the beginning and the end of the book with the flame on the cover. Even though she's lying there now, lying upstairs, in the present tense.

I knew Charlie had to come in. She couldn't stay. The rain was soaking into her T-shirt, her hair. She stood on the patio and let the rain run into her.

When she was done she came in. She stood on the mat by the back door. Rain was running off her.

'Don't take another step,' Abbott said. 'Take your wet things off right there, and Ash'll get you a towel.' She needed a towel. The rain was coming off her, it was running onto the mat.

'No,' Charlie said.

'Charlie,' Abbott said. 'Take your wet things off now.'

Charlie stood on the mat. The wind was coming into the kitchen. I was sitting on the stool and I could see her body shaking.

'Ash,' he said.

I got off the stool and went upstairs for a towel. Rain pelteth, that's what I was thinking. I was thinking about whether anything would come up if I put it into Google. I could type *rain pelteth*, or *Keats rain pelteth*, if I was feeling brave, and maybe something would come up.

I brought the towel downstairs to the kitchen. I held it out for Charlie, and she took it. Outside the rain was coming down. It was hammering, hammering against our kitchen window. I sat on my stool. Charlie was on the mat, holding the towel.

'Go and have a rest,' Abbott said.

I went upstairs. I didn't feel much like reading. I lay in bed and wondered whether I could get the laptop from Abbott's study and put *rain pelteth* into Google. I thought about it and I watched the sky rolling and listened to the sounds of the earth. They made me feel small, the sky and the sounds. I liked feeling small. I tried to think of other ways to feel small like that. I was lying there thinking about how small I really was and I was listening to the rain pelting on the skylight, that's what I was doing, and I wanted to put *rain pelteth* into Google, I was reminding myself to do it, I was reminding myself over and over but I must've fallen asleep. I didn't catch myself falling, the way you can sometimes catch yourself falling, I went from awake to asleep without noticing.

It was dark when I woke. I'm getting used to the dark. You can get used to unfamiliar things.

When Papa's hair turned grey he said exactly that:

'The trick is to get used to change.' That's what he said. But change isn't an unfamiliar thing, it's whatever's changed that's unfamiliar. You never know what's next, I mean. I must've said something like that to Papa, because he scooped me up. Yes, that's what he did. He scooped me up onto his knee and called me My Ash, and for a moment everything was the way it had always been, but when I looked up I could see how his hair was changing, how it was turning from black to grey and Papa was smiling at me and he knew the trick, I could see it in his eyes, I could see he was used to each grey hair, but I wasn't. I was looking at his hair and I could tell I didn't know the trick yet.

It was dark when I woke this morning. I watched the sky until the light came. The clouds were rolling. I tried making myself smaller again. I was getting so good at it I almost disappeared. I kept half an eye on Abbott's watch, it was on the stand on his bedside table and I could see the hands going round. They were going round slowly, but they were going round.

'I'm still here,' I said out loud. 'In the world,' I said.

Abbott didn't stir.

When he woke at seven thirty I tried being small again. Be small, be smaller, I said to myself as he was fiddling with his glasses, but I couldn't. And now they're downstairs and I'm supposed to be resting but I'm in Abbott's study. I'd been thinking about putting *rain pelteth* into Google. I couldn't stop thinking about it. Rain, rain. Rain pelteth. Round it went.

I waited until Abbott put the TV on and I went into his study. I'd decided to type *Keats rain pelteth*, instead of *rain pelteth*. I'd been thinking hard and I was almost sure the line was Keats. I went into his office and looked out of the window. You only have to do something eighteen times for it to become habit, so that's what I did. I looked out of the window. I looked out of the window and that's when I noticed it was gone. The sofa. The sofa from number five.

It's gone. They must've taken it inside last night, when they saw the rain clouds building. U, Terry and Jay.

Jay might've said, no regrets, as they carried it in and made the house smaller. Or feel smaller. And making the house feel smaller isn't the same as making yourself feel smaller. No. It already looks quite small, number five, but I've never been in. I've only ever walked past twice. I try to walk on our side of the street, which means I have to walk past Joan's. A lot. I've been in there once. Inside Joan's. She invited me in.

'No point us chatting on the doorstep. Come on through,' she said.

I went into her house. Joan's house. Number four. It was full of things. Things on shelves, things on the walls, things on little tables and a big table, things on the sofa, the armchairs. There were things on things, things piled up, and what were all her things, where had they come from? How had she got them there, how would she ever get them out?

She said, 'Come through.'

It was the right thing to say, because that's what I was doing, coming through. I was thinking come through, come through. I didn't want to think of all the things I was coming through, so I came through. Coming through, that's what I was thinking. That's all I was thinking.

I came through to her kitchen. There were things with faces in the kitchen. There were bears and dogs and kittens and other faces, and there they all were and Joan said she'd fix me a cup of tea and the faces were looking out, looking out from the things they were in. I stood with my back to a porcelain dog. It was waving its paw, the porcelain dog, and what was wrong with waving like that, a white porcelain dog with a bow in its hair, with its paw up, waving? I stood with my back to it, I tried to forget it. It would've been easier if it hadn't been waving, but it was. Joan stretched her arm around my side. She took me by surprise. She groaned a bit, and pulled the dog out from behind me. She held it up in the air. She held it up and it reminded me of the time Abbott won a trophy for playing ping-pong. Table tennis, not ping-pong.

'Isabella,' she said. That was the porcelain dog's name. She held it in front of my eyes, I scrunched them shut, but I could see behind them anyway. I could see a silhouette of the porcelain dog, the dog with the paw that was waving.

'Sit down here and have your cuppa,' she said.

She put the dog down. She pointed to a mug on the counter. 'Grab that.'

A sheep in a Christmas hat. The mug she pointed to. The sheep was looking out, looking out from the mug. Its eyes were glazed over, there was a sheen on them, a shiny film that might have meant something awful if the sheep had been real, but it wasn't real.

'Go on, grab it,' she said.

And the porcelain dog was there, right where I could see it and the sheep, the sheep on the mug too. I lifted it. I lifted the mug and the sheep sang. There was still a film over its eyes but it sang. It was singing from inside the mug.

All I want for Christmas is ewe. That's what it sang.

I put the mug down.

'What do you think of that then? He sings. He sings when you lift him.'

I sat at her table. There were faces all around her kitchen.

'They're all smiling,' I said, but I must've said it quietly, because Joan didn't hear me.

They were smiling, all the faces were smiling and looking out and there was the sheep inside the mug, the sheep with the film over its eyes, and it wasn't Christmas, it was almost April and the daisies on her lawn were up. They were turning their faces towards the sun.

'I prefer standing on the doorstep,' I said.

I thought I'd said it more clearly, but she didn't seem to hear.

I got up and walked outside. I waited for her on the doorstep, because I didn't mind her talking to me on the doorstep, or anywhere where there was sky above us. I liked it, I liked listening to her voice. But I couldn't breathe inside, not with the faces. The things and the faces. Because what were they looking at? What could they see inside her house?

It was better on the doorstep. So I waited there. I waited for her, but she didn't come. That was the only time I went in, and I've never been inside number five. Although sometimes it feels like I'm part of their family, U and Terry and Jay. Them, and me. You only have to do something eighteen times for it to become habit.

And now their sofa has gone and I suppose they have too, with or without their regrets, and the rain's coming down and we've got a stream, we've got our own little beck, running down our hill.

I'll open the window. Abbott doesn't care about flying insects when it's raining, so I'll open it. And why would he know what I'm doing up here if he's downstairs watching TV with Charlie?

And how would Abbott know if I went outside, if I stopped resting and went outside?

If he's watching TV with Charlie, if Nelson's sitting at their feet, if he's in the living room watching TV how would he know? I can write *rain pelteth*, with or without Keats. I won't forget. I've hardly been thinking about anything else.

It wasn't here yesterday, this stream, this little beck and now I'm standing in it. Here I am. Here, with water cutting around my ankles. And that's the trick, isn't it? Getting used to change. It had to change. It didn't change. Everything stayed the same. For days, for weeks, the sun was staring out of its sky. Blue, azure, cerulean.

The sun was staring, and people were asking when it would break. They were talking about the weather. They wanted to know when the weather would break and they looked up into the sky and everything was the same and everything went on being the same and I heard Joan say, 'Oh well, we'll just have to get on with it.'

Everyone got on with it and the leather on the sofa dried out. It dried out and it fissured. Deep lines fingered their way across the leather. Papa knew the trick, but I never got used to his grey hair.

It's impossible to rest ad infinitum, so here I am, standing in our own little beck. In our stream, our runnel, our brook, our creek, and the rain's coming down. Coming on down. We've got our own little stream and now we've got it, the cars have gone. We can't have it both ways, although Kate did. And I'm standing in our stream and water's cutting around my ankles and carrying things away. It's taken them up, ends of branches and wrappers and leaves. It's carrying them down and off they go and where were all these things before they were carried?

Two sticks.

I stopped two sticks on their way down our hill.

'One for Charlie, one for me.' That's what I said.

I said it out loud. One stick for Charlie and one stick for me.

And it's been a long time since we raced sticks, Charlie and I, because the sun's been staring out from its sky. It stared so long it made the leather sofa crack, and when Nelson arrived Charlie was busy, so we haven't had time. There hasn't been much time.

One for Charlie and one for me.

I'm taking them to the top of our hill. It isn't far, but you should start from the top, the very top, so I'm taking them up. I'm walking through our stream and the water's cutting around my ankles and carrying things, taking them away, and I've got two sticks. You can tell which is Charlie's and which is mine and we have to make it fair. You have to put them in at exactly the same time. You can't drop them, you have to crouch down to do it, you have to crouch before you place them in the water, and Charlie used to squat down like this when she was small and you have to make it fair. The sticks have to be side by side, like this, here. You have to count before letting them go.

One, two.

And maybe I let go of Charlie's a bit early. It's easily done. I crouched down, put the sticks side by side and counted and let go and off they went.

It's impossible to rest all the time.

There they go, our sticks, down our hill, going down, and is that Charlie's stick that's winning? Is that Charlie's or mine, the one in the lead? And where will they go now I've let go of them like that, let go of the sticks without thinking, because they can't both win. There isn't room for two winners.

And is that Charlie's stick, or is it mine, the one that's stopped now? Because they didn't look the same when I was carrying them up the hill, but now I'm not sure. Is it Charlie's that needs setting free or is it mine?

It's stuck. It's lodged itself there and I'll have to set it free, it's in the rules. You're allowed to set them free, if you can reach them, but is it Charlie's or is it mine that's lodged itself here, right here, amongst this black?

I knelt down. The water cut around my knees. It was flowing down our hill and taking things with it.

I'd guessed. I knew.

I knew it was a swift, the black thing the stick had lodged itself into. That's why I knelt down. That's why I didn't mind kneeling down. That's why I didn't mind the water cutting around my knees, or the way it took things, the way it was taking things. I was wet, I was soaked through. I didn't mind.

I was kneeling in the water and I'd forgotten about the sticks. I was thinking about the swift. I had it in my hand and I was thinking how heavy it was, how heavy it was now it was full of water. I had it in my hand. I had it against my cheek. Water was dripping down my sleeve, water was cutting around my knees and the sticks had gone, both of them, and they must've gone because they weren't there and they must've gone down, our sticks, Charlie's and mine, with all those things, and I couldn't let go. No. I had the swift against my cheek and I didn't mind the water around my knees. I didn't mind that everything had turned to water, because I had the swift against my cheek and it was heavy and it was dripping and I was thinking about the Bible and I was thinking of the Flood and how the waters prevailed upon the earth, and I was kneeling in the stream with the swift against my cheek and I could feel it dripping, and I was thinking how much I liked the word prevailed because I understood, I knew, prevailed, and the swift was dripping and the rain was coming down and I knew I could feel small again if I thought about the waters prevailing upon the earth.

I threw the ball. I threw it the way Charlie throws it. I threw it into the lake but Nelson won't go in.

'You like playing ball. Get the ball. Nelson.'

It's out there on the lake, the ball, Nelson's ball. It's sitting amongst the cattails, forgotten or lost, but which, but which is worse?

'In you go. The ball.'

He won't go in. Doesn't turn his big head, lies down and rests it on his paws and why won't he go in when he's been in before? Why doesn't he go in now when he likes to go in and out over and over? Why won't he go in? The ball's sitting. Sitting on the water and it can't sit there indefinitely. It looks like it can, but it can't. Even Signe. Even Charlie. In the end she came inside. I fetched her a towel but the rain went on dripping onto the mat. And now Nelson won't go in and maybe it's because I'm not Charlie, because Charlie isn't here. He likes playing ball with Charlie. He plays ball all the time.

Abbott asked her. Lynn. He said it might be an idea to get me some help.

'Help with Charlie, now the holidays are here, you know?' he said.

I didn't know.

'You haven't been the same since,' he said.

That's how he ends the sentence. Every time he ends it like that. He ends his sentence with since and he smooths his hair down on both sides.

'It's a lot for you,' he said. 'It's just an idea.'

But it isn't an idea, not just an idea, because Lynn's got Charlie. She'll bring her back at four, but things have changed. Things have changed since, and that's the trick, isn't it. Get used to it. And now Abbott says I need rest and he wants me to rest, but someone had to take Nelson out, that's why I came.

He wants me to rest. That's why he called Lynn. He'd seen her at the school gates and she's always been friendly. That's why he called her. And Charlie's always got on well with Sophie. That's what he said.

'She's nice. She's nice, Ash.'

Lynn walked to the car. She did seem nice. Friendly, at least. Charlie was holding her right hand and Sophie was holding her left hand and she was taking them to her car.

'I'll drop her back around four. Four at the latest. You go on and rest.'

I followed them. She had a lot of words, but she was nice.

'Now then, Sophie, if you get in first and mind Liam as you climb over. That's right, it's taken me all morning to get him off to sleep. All morning.'

It reminded me of Joan. The ease of it, I mean. I mean, the way the words slipped out one after the other. She was so used to words. She was bent over, she was doing something inside the car and the words were slipping out, one after the other.

'That's right, love. Well done. Just there, right, move over a tiny bit. Just a bit. Well done.'

She was bent over at the waist and words were slipping out. The top half of her was swallowed up in the cavern of the car. One of those big cars. She was bent over, and her T-shirt had ridden up. That's the word, ridden, the way that little black dress had ridden up. I never saw Jay's girl again. I looked, I expected her for a while, but I must have forgotten about her.

Her T-shirt had ridden up, Lynn's, I mean, and the top half of her was swallowed up in the cavern of the car. She was moving things, making space for Charlie.

'Now I'll shift this stuff so Charlie's got somewhere to sit. Have you got your booster seat, Charlie sweet?'

She leant in further. She was doing something inside the car and her T-shirt had ridden up and I could see where her jeans sat. I could see where they were sitting, on her hips, her jeans, that's where they sat, and her T-shirt had ridden up. It wasn't cold, she wouldn't have been cold with her T-shirt like that, although it was overcast. Overcast, but warm enough. I'd forgotten about the sun. I was watching Lynn put the children in the car. I'd forgotten about the way it had been staring out from its sky.

She had a lot of words, Lynn, but they weren't like Joan's. She isn't anything like Joan. Joan's probably old enough to be her mum, and I've never seen Joan wear jeans either. Polyester trousers. That's what Joan wears, that's what she wore when she came with the bone. She likes them with an elastic waist. She doesn't want anything too complicated at her age, that's what she said. But Lynn was wearing jeans, skinny jeans. They sat on her hips and I could see her skin where her T-shirt had ridden up, and she wasn't fat, not like Jay's girl, and she wasn't thin. She wasn't thin, like me.

'OK, OK. You can sit yourself here. That's right. Here. In you climb. OK, OK, are we ready?'

She came out from the car and straightened up.

She said, 'OK. Ready for the off?'

And she must have gone on talking when she got into the car, because I could see her mouth moving and I'm sure I saw Charlie and Sophie tip their heads back and laugh as she drove down our hill in her big car.

'You go on and rest.'

That was the last thing she said to me and Abbott would like it if I rested too. That's what he says all the time. That's all he says. And now Nelson won't go in.

He went in last time, but it's been a while since. Since Charlie was throwing the ball for him and he swam. Out and back, over and over. I saw him go. I saw his tail floating just under the surface. Charlie was throwing the ball and there was nothing else for me to do but swim. I asked her if she wanted to join me. I asked her twice, because two's the first prime.

And now he won't go in.

'Go in, go in. The ball. Go in.'

He won't. His big head is on his paws and I could go in. I'll go in. Wade out and get the ball then go on swimming right out past the rock and who would know, because it isn't Tuesday and nobody comes here except on Tuesdays and why wouldn't I swim right out, right now, whilst nobody knows. Why wouldn't I stand on the rock and shout and ask who's coming in, coming right in with Nelson and me?

Kate shook her head. She looked at the sky. The clouds were rolling across it and from where she was, from there on the bank, she would've seen the clouds on the water, rolling, as if the sky had somehow fallen in.

That's how it was that day. I can still remember. Over seven hundred skies since that sky, and I still remember.

And that's the trick, isn't it, because you can't keep skies from changing. You can't keep a single one, but you can practise. You should. Papa practised losing things every time we crossed the bridge in Nott's Wood. He'd lean over the side and spit into the beck. He'd spit into it and watch the water carry it away.

'Practise losing small things, so you're better at losing bigger things,' he said.

I asked him whether it would have been a big thing to lose all his spit at once.

'All of it. All the spit you've got.'

He won't go in. His big head resting between his paws, his eyes shut.

He wouldn't go in. He fell asleep. He was lying down with his head on his paws and he must've fallen asleep. I patted his nose, I stroked his fur in the wrong direction and he didn't move, so I pulled the swift out of my pocket. I pulled it out then threw it into the lake.

I should've answered the phone. I hadn't thought about time. Hadn't thought how four o'clock would come on so quickly. I didn't think. Didn't answer.

'It's gone half past four, Ash. We've all been outside for forty minutes and Charlie's a bit upset. She's had a lovely day, they've had a lovely day together, but. Call me back. I've got the baby. I've got Liam.'

I heard it hit the water. I swear I heard it sink, I mean I swear I heard it falling through the water.

I've never heard anything sink before and sinking or not sinking's the important part, more important than throwing and where's the ball now, the one I threw. I threw it. I threw them. Nelson lay there with his big head between his paws and the sky rolled over the water.

Lynn said they've been waiting. She said they've all been waiting. And she's got the baby. Liam.

I could go in. Perhaps I should go in. I could go on swimming past the rock to where the swift went in. I could dive down, go under, because I know how to breathe underwater and it can't have gone from the bottom yet. It won't have gone already, and if it isn't there I could go on swimming.

I'll swim far out and keep on swimming away. Swimming a way.

She'd been trying to get hold of me. She's got the baby and Charlie's upset.

And it wouldn't take long. I could wade out. I'd catch the bottom falling away. If I was lucky. I'd catch it falling away and once I got to the place where the swift went in, I could go under.

I went under. That day. That summer. I've been under before, more than once, and it isn't as deep as it looks. I could swim out. I could get the swift. I could swim under and bring it back.

'Didn't you feel vulnerable out there in the water?' Kate said.

She was wearing her dancing cornflower scarf.

Papa used the word vulnerable too, but it had three syllables when he said it. He only ever used it when he told me about birds, and once when he was talking about Mama, but he wasn't talking to me.

Kate used it all the time. Vul-ner-a-ble, vul-ner-a-ble. She used it the way most people use adjectives like good or nice.

'Let people know what's going on in that head of yours, Ash. Be vulnerable.'

But how do you do that? How do you make yourself into any adjective?

Now Charlie's upset. Lynn said so. I didn't think she'd cry. I waded in. I couldn't have swum away, even if I wanted to. I waded in towards the bank. I waded as quickly as I could and when I got to the edge I knelt down and held my arms out towards her. I didn't think she'd cry and I should get back. Yes, get going.

*

Lynn's got the baby. I can see her standing on the pavement outside our house. She's got the baby against her chest.

She's nice. She's nice, Ash.

She's got the baby. Liam. Liam, lee-am, lea-am, that's his name, and why does everything have to be like something?

I'll walk up to her. I'll have to walk up. Say sorry. Say, sorry I'm late, I haven't got a nice watch. Sorry I'm late. I'll have to walk up and say something, because there she is with the baby, and Charlie's upset. That's what she said. I'll have to say something.

Say something, Ash. Have you got anything to say?

There's Lynn with the baby. There's Charlie. She doesn't look upset. Lynn said she was upset, but she doesn't look upset. She isn't crying. She looks as though she's having a nice time and if I had a nice watch I'd know how late I am and I'm sorry I'm late. That's what I'll say. I'm sorry.

I walked up to her. Nelson and I walked up to her. She was standing in the street holding Liam against her chest. She was nice. She looked nice. Her hair was piled up on top of her head. I walked up to her. I walked right up with Nelson by my side.

'Could we please come in?' she said.

She was holding the baby against her chest. He was crying. Liam was crying. I didn't think he'd be crying, but he was crying and Lynn was saying please.

I let them in.

'You two run on upstairs,' said Lynn.

'Charlie,' I said.

She ran on upstairs. They thundered up the stairs. Eight legs thundering, that's what I was thinking. Charlie, Sophie, Nelson, eight legs. Eight legs, four arms, but it wasn't the arms doing the thundering. That's what I was thinking.

The baby was crying. He was still crying.

'Liam, lee-am, lea-am.'

She had him on her chest. She was rocking from one foot to the other.

'Liam, lee-am, lea-am.'

She asked where the kitchen was. I wanted to say come through. That's what Joan said when she invited me inside. She said come through and I walked through all her things, so many things, but there isn't anything to come through in our house. There isn't anything apart from the photograph of Abbott when he was the ping-pong king.

She came through. She sat on the kitchen stool. I almost said no, but before I could she said, 'I think everyone needs a drink.'

She had Liam against her shoulder. He was crying.

She kept saying Liam, Lee-am, Lea-am.

When Charlie was small I used to say Charlie, but it wasn't like that. Charlie, Char-lea, Char-lee. I didn't say that.

Charlie didn't cry that much. I can't remember her crying at all.

'Could I have some water, please?' Lynn said.

She was sitting on my stool. She was nice. She had her hair piled on top of her head. It wobbled a bit when she moved, but it didn't look like it would fall.

'They had a lovely day, the girls,' she said. 'They just got on with it. I hardly had to do a thing, they just got on with it, you know. All I had to do was feed and water them. It's lovely to watch them at this age, isn't it. All their little games.'

She was unbuttoning her top.

'I gave up on nursing tops with Sophie,' she said.

'Didn't see the point in having to buy more clothes after going through all those maternity outfits. But I tell you, it's one thing breastfeeding a girl. A little man is something else.'

114

He found her then. I watched his baby-bird gape coming for her, then the sound of suckling.

I got some water. She asked for water so I went to the tap and turned it on. Liam was sucking at her breast. I could hear the milk going down. I could hear it sinking. I let the water run, I let it run cold then filled a glass up.

'Thanks,' she said. 'I have to drink so much now I'm feeding him. It was awful when it was hot. I was drinking all the time.'

I opened the window. I could hear the sucking, the milk, I could hear it going down. I opened the window, but I couldn't get the pins through the holes on the stay. I was rattling it, trying to get them in. I had to rattle it. The baby was suckling.

'He likes his milk,' she said.

It's possessive.

I've heard Abbott say he likes his beer before. And whatever Abbott says about words, and whether or not they can drive you mad, people know what they're doing with them. She meant *his* milk. That's what she said. Possession means something, whatever Abbott says about words.

Papa said possession's an illusion.

'Even my black hair was only on loan,' he said.

He ruffled his hair with his big hand, the way my mama might have done. He didn't get to keep her either.

I got the pins through the holes on the stay. I had to rattle the window to do it. I could hear baby Liam.

'No wonder he's hungry,' she said. 'His feed's an hour overdue. I wanted to feed him earlier, but it was a bit, you know.'

She's nice, I thought. Her hair too. It's nice, the way she's put it up on her head like that. Kate never did her hair like that. She never put it up on her head.

She was nice, Lynn. She didn't say a thing about me being late, about not having a nice watch, and I could see she had one herself. It wasn't a Second Core, but it was a nice watch. I was thinking about her watch. I was thinking about whether I should ask Abbott to get me one after all. Perhaps it'll cheer him up, I thought. He'd like that. He'd like to ask Google about nice watches for women. For his wife. That's what he might put into Google. He knows how to optimise his searches, that's what he says and I was thinking about watches. I was thinking how children don't really wear watches, even if they can tell the time. I mean, you can only trick yourself that time goes round, in twelves, when you're older, because it's only when you're older that you need to trick yourself.

'Isn't it?' she said.

Liam had stopped his suckling. He was lying in the crook of her arm, sleeping.

'Isn't it, Ash?' she said.

I'd been thinking about time. About asking Abbott to get me a nice watch after all and I hadn't been listening. Normally I listen. Abbott calls me a listener. He used to call me *his* listener. He meant his listener. That's what he said.

'Strange. Isn't it strange? Imagining things like that,' Lynn said.

And I was wondering why it would be strange imagining things about time, and I was looking at Liam, lying in the crook of her arm. I was looking at the milk between his lips. Still between his lips.

'It's strange, the things they imagine at that age,' she said. 'I was just this minute saying that Charlie was worried you'd flown away. You know, when we were waiting for you just now.'

I'd managed to get the pins through the holes on the stay. I'd had to rattle it but I'd managed to get them through.

'Charlie,' Lynn said. 'Charlie said something about you being a bird, now, which bird was it? Anyway, she showed us them, up on your hill. She said her mum might fly away and she looked a bit upset. I thought she was having fun with us at first but she looked a bit, you know, upset.'

Lynn said I shouldn't worry. She said I shouldn't worry because little ones like to imagine things. She said she usually puts, no, she usually pops a few drops of lavender milk in Sophie's bath to help her sleep. She said there are usually no more flights of fancy after that.

She's nice. She seemed nice when she said that.

And now it's Grace's mum who's taking Charlie away.

'She'll ring you. She's nice,' Abbott said. 'You'll be able to get a bit more rest.'

I answered the phone when it rang. I wasn't going to make that mistake again. She said her name was Sashya, with a y.

'Sash-y-a,' I said. Sash-y-a.

Maybe she thought I was writing it down. Maybe I should've written it down. I've seen Abbott write things down when he's on the phone.

And now Sashya's here.

She's standing at our door with a bucket and spade. She's got a red bucket and red spade and she's holding them up, right up and she's swinging them.

'Sash-y-a,' she says.

She holds her hand out towards me.

'We spoke on the phone. Sash-y-a.'

The red bucket and spade are swinging. She looks at Charlie.

'Grace is waiting in the car, my lovely. But first, guess where we're going?'

She swings her hips. She swings the bucket and the spade and her hips and she's waiting for an answer but Charlie doesn't know where they're going and maybe Sashya wants one of us to say the beach, but there isn't a beach. There isn't a beach near Tilstoke.

'Guess, Charlie,' she says.

She swings the bucket and spade. She swings her hips and perhaps Charlie will say something. Something to stop the bucket and spade from swinging. Perhaps Charlie will say something. She knows she has to say the beach, even though she knows they're not going there. That's what she has to say if she wants the swinging to stop.

'The beach?' Charlie says. 'The beach?'

'The sandpit park,' says Sashya.

She lets the bucket and spade down by her side.

'Hurry up, hurry up. Grace is in the car, go on and join her.'

The next day it's Lynn again.

'Only me,' she says.

She pushes the front door open.

'I'll bring her back at three. I'll have the baby, so.'

At three o'clock she drives up the hill.

'Only me,' she says.

She pushes the front door open.

'I've got the baby, so.'

Now Saturday's come. Abbott made me peppermint tea to take back upstairs. He likes me to rest, although I don't know how long I've been resting. At first I counted. I counted the hours up to two hundred and fifty-three and I went part way to two hundred and fifty-four. After that I stopped. I let time go round and round the way it does when you've got a nice watch. It felt better. It felt better saying it's ten past two, it's quarter to four. I'd never really noticed the clock at the top of the stairs before. I can see it without leaving my bed, all I have to do is crane my neck and there it is, with its hands pointing somewhere between one and twelve.

Abbott's pleased I'm taking an interest in the time.

'You'll be asking for a nice watch soon,' he said.

He knows what he's doing with words, because there's a big difference between *time* and *the time*. I don't know how many hours I've been resting now. I stopped at two hundred and fifty-three and went seventeen minutes into the two-hundred-and-fifty-fourth hour. How would I know how many hours it's been when the hands on the clock go round and only ever point to numbers between one and twelve?

It feels like a lot of hours since I put *Keats rain pelteth,* into Google. It came up. 'Fancy', that's the title of the poem. 'Fancy', by John Keats. I found rain pelteth quickly. It was on the fourth line, but the poem wasn't really anything to do with rain. Papa was right about plucking lines from poems. It didn't make sense to say rain pelteth, the way I was saying it when the rain was coming down that afternoon. It didn't make any sense to say it like that. I was playing with feathers, not birds.

I was supposed to be resting but I went into Abbott's study and typed it in anyway. I had a lot of time. I was supposed to be resting, so I had enough time to learn the whole poem. The whole bird, that's what I was thinking as I learnt it. Soon I'll have the whole bird.

I learnt it. I learnt it line by line, feather by feather, I suppose. I added the feathers one by one until I had the bird. I'd been looking out of the window in Abbott's study, I didn't want feathers, I wanted the whole bird, and once I had it, as soon as I'd got the last line down, I'd shut the cage door.

I decided not to ask Google anything again.

I'd been looking out of the window in Abbott's study. I suppose I was waiting for Jay, or U, but they hadn't come out since it rained. They hadn't come out since. I was waiting. That's why I learnt the poem. I'd never wanted a bird before. I'd always been happy with feathers.

I didn't go back for the swift. I heard it sink. I heard it go down, and there wasn't time. There wasn't time to go diving under. Lynn said Charlie was upset. She was waiting outside and she had the baby and I didn't think he'd be crying, but when I got to our hill she was there with the baby against her chest and the baby was crying, and she was rocking him.

'Liam, Lee-am, Lea-am.' That's what she was saying.

Maybe I could have swum out for it. Maybe I should have. It would've been there on the bottom of the lake because I'd only just thrown it.

And look at the clock. The hands have been going round and soon they'll show six thirty and Abbott will call up the stairs because dinner will be ready. I'll come downstairs when he calls. He'll say something like, 'Tuck in. This should do you some good,' and I'll tuck in and so will Charlie, and Nelson's head will be resting on Charlie's knee and Abbott will say, 'He's been good for Charlie, that dog.' And she'll smile and I'll smile and Abbott will say, 'It's good to see you looking a bit brighter. You know, you haven't been the same since.'

I'm trying to trick myself into swimming forever.

I got the idea from the clock. The way it goes round and round and never shows more than twelve, because what would the time be now if it had gone beyond twelve and kept on going? Where would it go, I mean, where would it end, a clock like that? Because nobody wants to know the real time. Nobody wants to hear about their three hundred thousandth and first hour. No, they want to count to twelve then count again. That's what they want. That's what we want. Nobody wants a clock that scares them. They don't want to be scared, but they're looking for time. They keep looking for it everywhere.

Where did the time go? That's what people say.

That's what they say when they find themselves old. They find themselves old, people with nice watches, and they don't know where it came from, because they hadn't seen all their time, how could they see where the hours went when their watches go round and round?

It feels like only yesterday.

That's what Abbott's dad said, when time was running away from him. He was sitting at our kitchen table, said he was too old for the stool, too unsteady, said it felt like only yesterday watching Abbott ride his bike for the first time.

'Wobbling along the road to the Rec,' he said. 'Little red bike with orange flashes.'

He said, 'Do you still ride, son?'

'From time to time,' Abbott said.

He checked his Second Core after he said that. He went on checking it until his dad left.

I'd never seen Abbott on a bike. I couldn't imagine him with a helmet. I mean, with his hair, his smoothed-down hair, and a helmet on top of it. And glasses too.

Later he told me not to tell.

'Don't tell,' he said. 'About the bike.'

I'm trying to trick myself into swimming forever.

I got the idea from the clock going round and round. It was almost seven o'clock. It was almost time for Abbott to call me down to dinner. It'll be another thirteen hours until he calls me down for peppermint tea. That's what I was thinking. Eight o'clock, that's when he'll call. Thirteen hours from now. Thirteen. No, not thirteen hours. One hour. Think of it as one hour. The remainder after dividing thirteen by twelve. And that's when I got the idea. Because that's what you do. That's what you have to do, you have to go on dividing by twelve. You have to think in remainders.

I mean, take a lifetime. Take seventy-five years, take eighty years, take the exact moment at which you've lived for any number of years and there'll be no remainder, there'll be nothing left, and it only takes a few days before people stop counting hours, because who counts after seventy-two hours? Who knows the number of hours in five days without stopping to work it out?

Days and months too. Round and round they go, and nobody gets scared when it's a Tuesday, because there are always more Tuesdays until there aren't more Tuesdays, but nobody wants their hours. Nobody wants to listen to their hours ticking by.

I was thinking about the clock, I was thinking about the trick of twelve and that's when I thought of it, tricking myself into swimming forever.

Swim in fours, I thought. And why not four? Four, eight, twelve lengths, remainder zero. Forty, eighty, one hundred lengths. Remainder zero. Why not swim like that? I could swim on and on and I'd only ever have to swim up to four lengths and then I'd start again and all the time I'd be thinking I'm only just setting out. I'm only just starting out, I can go on and on. I can swim forever. And at least it's something to think about, swimming in fours. Because there isn't much worth thinking about when Charlie isn't here. Her costume's too small these days, that's what she said, and where did the time go? I mean it feels like only yesterday, Charlie putting on her costume and swimming in Tilstoke Baths with me.

I came here on my own. Abbott said it might do me some good. Light exercise. I wanted to swim so I'd never get tired, so I could swim on and on, even if I couldn't swim away, not in Tilstoke Baths, it's impossible to swim away when you're swimming in fours.

I am getting tired. I've been swimming round and round and I'm only at two but it isn't the first time. It's disorientating I mean, swimming in fours, because three's never enough. And that's the difference between swimming and hours. I mean, you want to know how far you've come. How far you've travelled. One hundred lengths, even twenty, are further than zero. Remainder zero.

I never get tired, I've never been tired, swimming in the lake, the one off the Toll Estate. I've swum far out, way out beyond the rock, and I didn't think once about getting tired, I didn't get tired, didn't feel a thing. I kept going, kept swimming out until I was under the sky. I told Charlie.

If you go far enough out it's calm.

You have to keep going until you're under the sky.

And I wanted to ask Abbott. I wanted to ask him about the photo of Kevojärvi, about the two people wading. The ones who weren't that far from the camera. I wanted to ask if he thought they were men or women. Boys, perhaps?

They were holding hands, the two who were wading, and it was difficult to tell.

I wanted Abbott to say that it was difficult to tell who they were.

I walked home from the baths. It felt good to be walking after all that resting. I walked up our hill. The house martins were still there.

Kate said she would come for them and I waited. The mornings came on with dew and a slow sun. Then spiders' webs. Before long they left. I never knew when they'd leave.

I walked up our hill. I opened the front door. Abbott called to me from the kitchen.

'Good swim?' he said. I went on through. I went on past the photo of him as ping-pong king.

'It'll build up your strength, swimming again,' he said.

'Hello, Ash,' she said.

'Lynn was just passing. She thought she'd drop in,' he said.

'It was nice of Lynn to drop in,' he said. He shut his book, clamped the sheet under his arms, then turned out the light.

It's nice when people drop in.

I don't know why I haven't come here before.

I rolled the log until it dead-thumped against the wall. I rolled it over so I could climb up onto it and here we go. I mean, here I am, standing on the log with a perfect view across the car park and through the windows of the yoga studio.

She'll come. She has to come if she's teaching a class. She has to. It won't be like the time I heard the woman with the flower band in her hair say she wasn't coming. And it must be almost eight. I checked the clock before I left, so it must be nearly eight and she always starts teaching at eight. Beginners class at eight. Begin at eight, don't be late.

There she is now. I knew she'd come if she was teaching a class. There she is, wearing a green top. She wears greens. She says she only wears things that blend with the earth, but what does that mean?

'What does that mean?'

'Not now,' she said.

She pulled me towards her and kissed the top of my head.

But what is not now, if it isn't stop? Nobody, not even Kate, says stop. And she says anything. She says everything.

There she is, in her shamrock-green top. I've got a good view from here, it's a vantage point, that's what it is, and I've brought hot chocolate in a flask.

'I get cold after swimming.' That's what I said when Abbott saw me making it.

'Let me pick you up from the baths then,' he said. 'I don't know why you like walking up our hill. It's rough.'

I'll make enough for two next time. It's a big enough flask. I'll make enough for two, in case I have to share, because that's how it started, this thing with Kate. It started with sharing. Abbott had put some granola in a pot for me to take to class. He'd bought it from the new health food shop on the high street.

'It's the sort of shop you yogis go to,' he said.

I took the granola. I took it, and I left the pot on top of my jacket at the side of the studio. I was going to wait before eating it. I mean, I'd planned to take the granola outside. I'd planned to sit on the wall and eat it after class. This wall. The wall I pushed the log up against.

That's what I'd planned to do, but I was hungry. She'd had us working hard. That's what she said:

'I've been working you all hard tonight.'

So I took a small handful, and I was planning to take the rest out to the wall, this wall. I was eating the granola. I was picking out some toasted seeds when she walked up behind me and put her chin on my shoulder. That's what she did. She put her chin on my shoulder and reached around me. She put her hand in my pot. She took some granola and ate it.

'Mmm, delicious,' she said.

Those were the first words she said to me.

I don't know why I haven't come here before. I could have come here any time. I've always known she'd be here. I've always known there was a copse on the other side of the wall. This side of the wall. I remember looking out at it. I remember looking out from the studio, across the car park, towards the copse.

'Focus on your spines. Deep focus,' she said.

We were sitting on our mats. Sitting in half lotus. I was looking out of the window towards the copse. The sky was blue.

Almost ultramarine. And under the blue sky was the copse, the trees. The following week, rain and wind. Weeks after too.

'Connect now. Deep in your core.'

I looked out across the car park. That's what I did every week.

Yes, I've always known there was a copse. Ever since I started yoga, I've known there was a copse.

And why not come here? Abbott wants me to find things to do. Well here I am, doing something, standing on my log. It's a vantage point here on the log and I can see right over the car park and into the studio. I can see her in her shamrock top. All I had to do was move the log. I only had to roll the log until it dead-thumped against the wall.

There were men here earlier. I thought I heard voices. And there she is, in her shamrock top. Because the beginners begin at eight.

Probably men walking dogs, that noise, those voices, but men walking dogs don't talk that much, and who would be talking in a small copse like this? What would they talk about? There's no reason to walk a dog in here, unless it's a cut through.

It's probably a cut through, so there's no need to worry, and I always liked her in green. I liked her in green before she put her hand into my pot of granola, it's just that I hadn't thought much about liking her until then and there isn't much point in thinking about whether you like what people wear or not, because people pass through. Most people pass on through.

I'll stay a while, if those men are men with dogs. They're probably using the cut through, so I could stay a while. I could stay until the end of the class. And I don't know why I haven't come here before, so I may as well stay. I may as well drink the hot chocolate, now I've made it, and it's probably fine to stay, if those men are using the cut through.

And look, Kate's walking towards the window. She's coming right over to the window. She's standing by the window and the only thing between us is the car park, which is hardly an insurmountable thing. A small patch of tarmac is hardly a thing at all. And perhaps she's seen me. She'd definitely be able to see me from where she's standing, but only if she was looking. I mean, people really only see the things they expect to see.

She's right by the window.

Her picture windows. That's what she called them. People know what they're doing with words, but Papa was right when he said possession is an illusion, and now she's right there by her window, doing the tree pose.

She taught me the tree. Vrksasana. She liked Sanskrit. She said it both ways.

'Ash. It's Ash, isn't it?' she said to me after class. 'With a name like that, we have to help you to get this one right.'

She nodded. It meant, go on. It meant, show me. Show me your tree.

'Tadasana first,' she said.

So I got into the mountain pose. That's how you start, with the mountain. I felt like a mountain, there in her studio. I felt the straight line of energy through the centre of my body.

'Good,' she said.

'Now, find your focus.'

But what did that mean, because once you start looking for focus you'll never find it.

Not now, Ash, I thought. Stop. I opened my eyes and looked out towards the copse.

'After focus, you'll find balance,' she said. 'It'll come.'

She stepped away and eyed me up. I kept my head straight, and I kept looking out towards the copse, and I could see the copse and I could see the way the wind was blowing at the trees and I was looking at it all through the glass, and the sky

was grey and it was dark enough for rain, but it wasn't raining, not whilst I was doing the tree pose, although it was dark
enough. It was definitely dark enough.

She looked at me.

'Yes,' she said. 'Yes.'

She stepped in.

'Find the pressure. Here,' she said. 'Like this,' she said.

There was nobody else in the studio. I found the pressure
of my foot against my thigh. At least, I thought I found it.

And perhaps I should go. I can hear those men again and
they might not have dogs. They might not be the same men I
heard when I was moving the log, because I haven't got a nice
watch and I can't be sure of the time, or how long I've been
here, although it's getting dark and it's got to be after eight,
and it's probably nearer to nine. And if I go, it doesn't mean
I can't come back.

I can come back. Now I've got a log, I can come back. And if
I go now I won't have to think about those men. I won't have
to think about whether there's a cut through, or what it meant
when she said she only wears colours that blend with the earth.

I came back to my log. To be honest, I couldn't wait. I thought
she might've seen me last time because why else would she
walk to the window? I thought about it hard and I couldn't
remember her walking to the window before. No, she hadn't
ever walked to the window. If she'd walked to the window I
would have remembered, because I was always looking out of
the window at the sky, at the copse beneath the sky.

So I came back. It must have been after eight when I got
here, because the beginners had already begun and there
wasn't much happening, although Kate was there in forest
green and she wasn't looking this way, she was teaching her

class. There wasn't much happening, so I decided to start on my hot chocolate. I poured some into the mug and when I looked up she was strolling towards the window.

And there she is, standing by the window, in forest green.

I expect she's noticed the crescent moon hanging over the car park, because she talked a lot about moon energies. She'd taken a course. She'd taken a course in the spring, which wasn't long before she put her hand in my pot of granola.

I expect she's noticed the moon between us.

'Is it waxing or waning, Ash? Tell me and I'll tell you about its energy,' she'd say.

She had a leaflet. She'd taken the course in the spring, so she still needed her leaflet.

'Waxing or waning?' she'd say.

And I'd tell her, and all the talk of moons made me think of a poem, an American poem, but she always said it wasn't as if I was American or anything, so I kept the poem to myself. I mean, I kept saying it to myself whilst she checked her leaflet, because it was only a short poem and there was time. There was enough time to say it over and over.

The moon was a thread of a thing that last day. She hadn't asked. I was waiting for her to ask.

Is it waxing or waning, Ash? That's what I wanted her to say. I wanted her to say the same things she'd always said. She looked out of the window. She looked up at the moon and I had my answer ready. Waning, I was going to say, but she didn't ask.

She looked up at the moon.

'Almost fallow,' she said.

She shook her head. She rattled the last of it from the sky. I swear that's what she did. She definitely liked moons. The week after she helped me with the pose she called me over after class to show me the crescent moon.

'Ash,' she said. 'Ash. Ash,' she said. 'It's easy to transition from the mountain to the crescent moon. From Tadasana to Ashta Chandrāsana.'

She liked to use the Sanskrit. She liked it both ways, that's what she said.

She jumped up from the floor. She was always sitting on the floor. She said my name and she leapt up from the floor. She started with the mountain. Then the crescent moon. She softened herself into its bow. That's what she did and she'd done it a thousand times before. She looked like she had. And when she relaxed she took a breath. A slow breath. A harmonising breath.

'You try,' she said, and I felt the shape of my waist with her hands on it.

'Gently,' she said. 'Slowly,' she said.

I opened my eyes. Abbott was looking at me through the glass in the top of the studio door. He was holding Charlie's hand.

'You said eight forty-five,' he said as I pushed it open.

He was looking at his Second Core. He was tightening his jaw muscles, he was clenching them.

'It's nearly nine,' he said.

I felt the shape of my waist where her hands had been.

'And you must be?' Kate said to him.

'Abbott,' he said. 'I'm Abbott, and this is Charlie.'

'Well, it's lovely to have you both here,' she said.

She put her hand out for Abbott to shake it, and after he had his jaw relaxed Kate went down on her haunches, crouched down to where Charlie was and whispered something in her ear, and whatever she said made Charlie grin. She was grinning. She was grinning about whatever it was, then Kate stood up. She pretended to zip her mouth shut, and Charlie copied her.

'Zip.' That's what they both said.

'She's nice, your teacher,' Abbott said as we walked towards the car.

Charlie zipped her mouth. She zipped it both ways, and more than once. Open and shut, open and shut, open and shut.

'She's nice,' he said.

But I was thinking about the crescent moon and how to transition into it from the mountain. I was thinking about the shape of my waist now her hands had been on it.

It's probably the moon that's made her walk to the window again. She probably knows about its energy without looking at her leaflet these days. But the moon wasn't visible last time, and she walked to the window then, even though she'd never done it before. No, there definitely wasn't a visible moon and was it waxing or waning? No, there wasn't a moon, but still. Still, she walked right over and I've never seen her walk over before. I can't remember her walking to the window, I can't remember seeing her do that, and I remember a lot of things. Abbott says I remember too many things.

She knows I'm here then. Here, on my log. It's perfectly possible, because I can't remember her walking to the window before. Call it serendipity, or karma, and that was her word. Karma.

I asked her to explain what it meant. I wanted it for my collection the moment she'd said it.

'What does it mean?' I said.

She took my hand. She told me.

Karma kept me awake that night. It was something to do with the letter k and the weight of responsibility behind it. I watched the sky through the skylight. I watched it roll on by. By the time morning came I was tired of thinking about karma and anyway, it didn't seem so ominous all spelled out in broad daylight, and the daylight was broad. It was summer. Even though it rained almost every day, it was summer.

I thought that top was forest green, but it isn't. Look at it now through the window. Look at it under the light of the moon. It's more dark moss than forest. I don't know why I thought it was forest. She was better with colours than me, but she shouldn't keep staring out of the window. She should walk away. Get back to teaching the beginners. She should stop looking through the window. It isn't nice watching people like that. Everyone always says you shouldn't stare.

She shouldn't.

Maybe she isn't. Maybe she's looking at the moon. Maybe she isn't staring at all, although she's never walked to the window before. I can't remember her walking to the window, and she liked moons back then. Yes, there must've been moons she could've looked at. She didn't. And I know a poem about the moon, but it's American, and after a while I had to think carefully, think twice about mentioning poems from America, because it's not as if I'm American or anything. No, it's just that some poems are better than others.

Lynn left a message on my phone.

She's planning to take the three of them bowling. Sophie, Charlie and Grace. It's a treat. She said she wanted to treat them. She called them *the girls*, like they belong together.

'Charlie might want to dress up. Wear something a little bit special,' she said.

And Charlie says she does, but there isn't anything to dress up in. She hasn't got anything a little bit special.

I had an idea. I waited. I waited until we'd put the plates in the dishwasher. I waited until Abbott sat on the sofa and patted the space next to him and said, what are we watching tonight, then? I waited until Charlie sat down next to him. I heard the TV. I heard them laughing, I heard her pat the sofa too. Telling Nelson to come up, come up, boy. I went out into the garden. I went into the garden to look for something to use, and there must be something, because it isn't that long since we made flower bracelets. Last year, the year before. We've made them every year since.

Every year since they'd grown too tall, the flowers. The petals, the leaves, the stems were brighter than they should have been. The sky was thick with clouds and we were kneeling, we were kneeling amongst the flowers, in amongst them, and the earth was damp, and before Charlie said the thing about the swifts going, before she said anything about them leaving, that's when we were making bracelets. We've made them every year since.

It isn't always wrong to end a sentence like that, with since, I mean, and there'll be something. Something I can use for a bracelet. Something a little bit special. Something for dressing up. Charlie might want to, after all, and I was sure it wasn't late, but Joan's curtains are closed and her lights are off, so it must be earlier than ten, but I didn't look at the clock before I came out, so I can't be sure, and I still haven't asked Abbott to get me a nice watch, but it can't be later than ten, so I don't know why Joan's done for the day. She said herself she's done for the day by ten, but what does she mean *by ten*? What does it mean if time goes round in circles? Because where is before, where is after when everything is before and after and everything comes around again, so when is Joan done for the day if she's done now and it isn't ten? I'm fairly sure it can't be anywhere near ten, it isn't long since dinner, and here, I'll use field scabious, because she's always looked good in blue. Looked good in cerulean. Under it. But it's been a long time since.

I swam out. I swam right out until I was under the sky. It was calm out there, so I had to swim right out. I kept on swimming and I didn't think she'd cry and it isn't that difficult to make something special. The stems are good for twisting, see. It isn't that hard, and I can take my time because Joan's done for the day and Charlie, Nelson and Abbott are watching TV. I waited until I heard her pat the sofa for him to come up, come up, boy. And I twist the stems like this, which is the way Papa showed me, and the way I showed Charlie, because this is the way you twist them to help them stay strong.

I never liked picking them, flowers, but Papa said it helps. Thinning them out.

But it didn't help with choosing. Because which ones stay? I mean, which ones go?

'Like this,' Papa said.

He held the twisted stems so I could see.

'Like this,' I said to Charlie.

I held them so she could see.

Kate said 'like this', too, but she was talking about yoga and Papa and I were talking about the way stems need to be twisted if you want to make something that lasts. And there must have been someone who said 'like this' to Papa, but he didn't tell me. He took the stems and held them out so I could see.

'Like this,' he said. 'Be careful with them. Be tender.'

And Lynn's taking the girls bowling, so a bracelet should be just the thing. Something a little bit special, because she's always looked good in blue.

'You have to take your time,' Papa said.

He was twisting the stems.

If you want to get it right, you have to take your time.

But possession is an illusion. He'd said that too. And I suppose if Papa stopped to think about it, he'd think that possessing time was the biggest illusion of all. Because he didn't have a nice watch, or any watch because he wasn't fooled the way most people are fooled.

And there, it's almost done. If you want to get it right, you have to take your time.

You have to take time. But where do you take it from?

The girls are standing at our front door. They're looking a little bit special.

They say 'ta-da!' when Charlie opens it. They say ta-da. Probably because they're wearing something a little bit special. Lynn says there's plenty of time.

'There's plenty of time, sweet,' she says to Charlie. 'If you want to pop upstairs and get changed.'

But there isn't anything for Charlie to get changed into and where can something a little bit special come from at the drop of a hat? But the girls are sparkling and Charlie isn't sparkling and I'm trying not to think of the day Mrs McIntosh said something about giving Charlie's hair a little wash.

'A little wash,' she said. 'It'll just help her be, you know. You know,' she said.

And why do people always say 'a little' when all they mean is the thing itself? Because people who say a little instead of the thing itself could save so much time, but they aren't thinking about time, even though most of them have nice watches, they aren't thinking about time, they're only thinking about saying the thing they want to say without saying the thing they want to say and Mrs McIntosh could have saved herself time. The bottom of her neck turned red when she said the words 'little wash'. I could tell she didn't want to say little wash and I didn't want her to say it either, but after she said it we gave Charlie's hair a little wash and after that her hair was as clean as the other girls' hair and Charlie hasn't popped upstairs, although there's plenty of time. She hasn't popped up because there isn't anything a little bit special to wear, and now there isn't plenty of time, even though there was, because Lynn's saying they should be off.

'We should be off then,' she says, and the plenty must have gone somewhere because it was here only a few minutes ago and where has it gone now, plenty? Where has it gone?

They're ready for the off and Charlie hasn't got anything a little bit special. She hasn't got the flower bracelet, although I took my time, and now they're ready, and now they're going, and maybe Lynn's taken plenty with her. Maybe she's stuffed it inside her hair on the top of her head because there's room for plenty in there. There's definitely room. And it looks nice like that, on top of her head. It does look nice, although Kate never put her hair up. No, she never put it up.

I told her I'd always had mine short. That's what I said when she asked me.

And come to think of it, I am tired. I need time to myself. I should shut the blinds and get some rest. Like Abbott said. Like Lynn and Sashya said, and thinning the flowers out helps. It helps the air circulate. It helps them breathe, and Charlie and I know how to breathe underwater, but Abbott doesn't. He says he's never been taught. And I'll probably rest. Thinning them out was the important thing. That was the thing that mattered, and now I'll rest. They all say I should rest. Go on up to bed and rest, in our bed. Abbott's and mine.

'Tiredness comes down on me like night,' Kate said. 'All of a sudden.'

She slept then, in our bed, after that first time. It was summer too. The height of summer, the height of day. The light was everywhere, but she slept. I didn't think it was possible to sleep in light like that.

'Why would anyone sleep?' Papa said. 'On nights like these?'

Sometimes he'd go. After he'd said something like that he'd go off into the night, except it wasn't really night and I didn't know where he was, but it wasn't dark and we both understood, because he was the first one to tell me about Arctic summers. I knew about them long before I found the book by Jari.

Kate slept. Right here. It's hard to believe. It's hard to forget. The light was coming in and it must have stopped raining for once, because the swifts were circling the rooftops. I could hear them. I could see them from where I was lying. I had time to watch them, there on our bed with her sleeping beside me.

She slept on her back with her arm flung out, although I didn't see her fling it and I didn't know if I'd get another chance. I was awake and she was sleeping, with her arm flung out, so I picked it up at the wrist, where it was heavy. I placed it across the slack of her stomach and waited a bit. I waited for a few moments, then I flung it back to where it had been just before. It made a noise, it played back into her body, but she didn't wake. She didn't even stir, and the light was coming in across the room and the swifts were circling the rooftops, and I didn't think about how long it would be until Abbott came home, although thinking about it now, I could've touched her. I should've at least looked at her some more but I couldn't, or I didn't, or I hadn't thought of it. All I did was shut my eyes and listen. I remember her. Full of noise. That's how she was after that first time.

As soon as she woke she folded her flung arm back into her body. Like a wing, that's what I thought. She folded her arm like a wing, and then rolled onto her side. There was so much skin. I mean, she had so much it took me by surprise. When she got up she dressed with her back to me. It was after the first time. All of this was after the first time. She dressed with her back to me, her breasts were facing the wall and the swifts were leaving soon.

'Are you coming to bed?' Abbott said that night. That summer. It was after the first time.

'To bed,' he said.

To our bed. That's what he meant. I'd never thought of it until. Until he said it, 'Are you coming to bed?' And it meant our bed and leaving out the possessive made it sound even more like ours. And it sounded naive. He sounded naive because he should have known. He should know possession is an illusion.

'Are you coming to bed?' he said.

'How can you sleep?' I said. 'How can anyone sleep on nights like these?'

'But you've slept in summer before,' he said.

I had.

It wasn't easy to sleep that night. Abbott rubbed his legs and chest up against where she'd been and all I could think was that he was hairy. I kept thinking about how hairy he was, I could hear his hairs brushing up against the sheets, and I'd never thought much about how hairy he was before but that night I couldn't think of anything but his hairs. I thought about her too. I tried not to, but I did. I tried to think about Abbott's hairs, the opposite thing to thinking about her. But I couldn't think about his hairs the whole time. I mean, I couldn't go on thinking about them without thinking about her. So I let Abbott hold me. I let him hold me whilst he slept. He held me, it helped me think about his hairs. I tried not to think about her. I listened. I strained to hear the sound of his hairs on the sheet and I almost forgot the way she'd got dressed, the way she turned her back on me.

In the morning Abbott asked what'd got into me. He said it was lovely sleeping together like that. Lovely was the word he used. He said he didn't care. He said he didn't care what'd got into me, he only cared that whatever it was had. He liked being close. That's what he said and I said OK and let him hold me every night that summer.

Now they all think I should rest, and here I am, in our bed, and when Charlie was small she said rets. It was one of the things she said, and it wasn't a word, rets, but we knew what it meant, Abbott and I. Everyone knew what it meant because it's the words around the word that make the word mean something, and not the word itself. It's true, but Abbott would say not now, Ash, and Kate would say not now, and maybe one of them or both would pull me in and kiss me to make me stop, or at least have a little rets. A little wrest. But what if I went on retsing? What if you always do what people want?

*

Abbott and Lynn and Sashya must've been right about needing some rest. I was thinking about homophones when I fell asleep, that must be what happened and now I'm awake and there are voices downstairs and the clock says three o'clock, which means there's plenty of time. Always plenty until there isn't plenty and if you've got hair piled on top of your head, that's where you can put it. Plenty of time. Bring it out when you need it. And there are voices downstairs and I'll roll over and tuck my arms like wings and I'll lie like this, because it isn't uncomfortable, I'll lie like this until the voices stop, because how can I go downstairs if there are voices, if there are people down there? How can I come down after my little rets, with homophones in my mouth and my ears when there are people sitting around, drinking tea and talking, talking. And there's plenty of time. I can wait. It isn't uncomfortable with my arms tucked in like this, the way Kate tucked her arm. The way she tucked it after the first time. Before she got dressed facing the wall, her back to me.

'Did you get some rest?' he says.

He's leaning against the sink, holding two empty mugs. He's standing with the mugs and he's almost swinging them and there's something about the way the light's coming through the window onto his face. There's something about it.

'You look a bit brighter,' he says. But it's him who looks brighter. There's something about the way the light's falling.

Lynn dropped Charlie home. 'It was on her way,' he says. 'So she popped in. Not for long. She wanted to drop Charlie home. She's a bit upset,' he says. Charlie.

'Charlie,' I say.

She's sitting cross-legged on the living room floor, Nelson by her side. His big head against her thigh. She's sitting next to the Bird Bingo box. She's sitting, and the cards are scattered around her, all the pairs that aren't pairs until the other half of the pair has been found. She's sitting cross-legged. She's sitting there, pushing the cards around the floor.

'Bird pairs?' I say.

'I'm not playing properly,' she says.

You can't play properly with one person. You need someone else, you need to be a pair, at least a pair, and the cards should be turned over, but they're not turned over and she's pushing them around the floor, which isn't the way you play if you are playing properly. But she isn't playing properly. She's pushing the cards around the floor, and she's made some pairs, although that's not how you play, but she's paired some up anyway. She's paired up the wrens and the tawny owls. The chaffinches, robins, song thrushes. She's done all that, but she isn't playing properly.

'I like the female blackbirds best,' I say. 'Because they're brown. They're not even black.'

She looks around. She looks at all the cards on the floor. She looks at the male blackbird lying there on the carpet. She puts her hand on him, she covers the orange of his beak with her hand and she pushes him across the floor towards me. And then I've got them. The male and the female blackbirds. I've got them both, and I put them together, I make them a pair and I put the female on top, because I like the females best, because they're brown and they're not even black and I didn't think she'd cry, but she might cry. She looks like she might cry again.

'Nobody else cares about male and female blackbirds,' she says. 'And everybody knows Bird Bingo's a game for babies. And everyone knows tractor shorts are for babies too. And nobody has them, nobody wears them when they're nearly eight. "Why did you have to wear your tractor shorts, Charlie?" That's what Sophie said. She said, "Why, Charlie?"'

And Charlie's right. Tractor shorts aren't a little bit special, not in the way Lynn meant a little bit special. Tractor shorts aren't special like that and neither are bracelets made of flowers even though you have to take your time. You can take all the time you want, you can make them to last and they're still not a little bit special.

'I hate my tractor shorts now. I hate them.'

She strokes Nelson's big head. She strokes him. She presses down on his head with her small hands. Presses and presses.

'Charlie,' I say.

She screws her face up. She picks up the pair of blackbirds. She picks them up and she throws them down and when they come down they land together. I mean almost together, the female and the male, and she might cry. She'll probably cry and she makes her hands into fists, she screws them up, her face and her hands and she holds her fists against her eyes to stop the wet that's coming, falling the way rain falls. She holds her fists there to dam the wet, but it's making its way over the folds of her hands and onto the insides of her wrists and won't stop, doesn't stop, not yet, the way rain won't stop when you want it to.

A ghyll, a rivulet, a beck, a rill. She's crying. She's crying as she shuffles on her knees through birds, through pairs of them. She's crying as she shuffles towards me and keeps on shuffling and puts herself, her whole self on the edge of my knee, her fists at her eyes, the tears coming down the way rain comes down.

'I'll hold you,' I say.

I could've held her.

Now Charlie's sleeping and here I am in bed again and Charlie isn't crying, no, she isn't crying now, she's sleeping. I went in to check on her and I could've held her. I could've.

143

But you can't do the things you could've done. That's the way grammar works. You can't mix tenses. You shouldn't. I could've held her and it wouldn't have meant a thing because I've been holding her since she was small and now bedtime has come and gone and Charlie's sleeping and I didn't think she'd cry but it isn't what you think that matters. It's what happens, what happened. Actions, not thoughts. Abbott said all my reading and thinking won't change a thing.

'Concrete action, that's what changes things,' he said.

Concrete actions.

'Think of Gandhi, think of Martin Luther King,' he said.

'I'm thinking,' I said.

He said I'd made my point.

Later he said, 'Nothing's changed though. See?'

But nothing changes without thinking first. I like it both ways. Thought and action. That's how I like it, both ways. Now Charlie's sleeping, Abbott too.

Abbott asked if I wanted to grab a little breath of fresh air today. I don't know where it came from. All this time he's been wanting me to rest. All this time since, I mean. He hasn't been keen on me going swimming. All this time he's been suggesting I stay in, rest a little, read a little. A little more. And each time I stood by the front door with my swimming kit over my shoulder he tapped at his Second Core.

'How many lengths, Ash? When can we expect you back?'

He's been wanting to drive me all this time. Down our hill, up our hill. It's rough. All this time since, I mean.

'How about grabbing a little breath?' he said today.

But I know about little. I've heard it before, I know the way its blacks come up against the surface. I know about them, all those littles, and Abbott might think I can't remember, but I can, I remember them all, starting with Asle. Starting with Asle in his little rowboat, that's where it started, with Asle in his little rowboat, and I could go on, I could go on. A little something, a little black dress, a little beck, little ghyll, little wash, little reads and rests, rets, another little rest. And don't think I can't remember more, because I know about little. I should've said. I should've told him to be careful.

You crazy boy. Tell me what you're doing. That's what I should've said. I mean, once you're in. Once you take the plunge.

I went outside. I stood outside in the street where he wanted me. I grabbed a little breath, I took in a little air and wondered if I'd been wrong about Abbott, using the word little I mean. I took a breath and in that breath autumn was creeping and I wondered if I'd been wrong, if all he'd wanted was for me to take a little breath, but when I went back inside he was whistling. Charlie and Nelson hadn't moved from in front of the TV, but Abbott was whistling and wiping at the surfaces, and whistling.

'I might rest,' I said.

He stopped wiping.

'I thought you might like to swim. Later. Tonight,' he said. He said he'd been thinking about rest. He'd been thinking about loosening the reins.

'You know?' he said. 'Relaxing things a little bit.'

He went back to his wiping, his whistling.

'OK,' I said.

'It'll be good for us,' he said. 'You'll see.'

It's been a long time since he used the future tense. Been so sure, I mean. So I took him at his tense and here I am, reins loosened, and look, there, the moon's grown so much it's fit for spawning. Look at it hanging over the car park. Hanging between us. Me on my log, Kate in her studio. A sinking, swollen thing between us. Parturient, almost. Yes, that's almost the word, and the problem with adjectives is always almost. I could never find the right one. Could never commit.

'Happy, sad, angry, confused? Tell me. Ash?'

But what was I supposed to do with all that choice? What was I supposed to say?

Mother Moon. That's what she called her. Our cosmic mother.

And look at Kate now, in her sky-blue top. Look at the moon hanging over the car park and between us. Beginners begin at eight. She was never late, not for yoga, and this evening I went out without Abbott tapping his nice watch.

Look at her, there in the studio, moving into the bridge in front of all those people. The beginners. Setu Bandhasana. She liked the Sanskrit. She liked it both ways. That's what she said.

We were in her bed and it wasn't the first time, no. It was after that. We were in her bed, she was lying on her back. She kept her feet planted, lifted her pelvis. She didn't have a stitch on.

'The bridge. Setu Bandhasana,' she said.

'It helps the sperm on its way,' she said. 'Go on little ones. Swim. Swim.'

She collapsed the bridge. She was laughing. I was looking at her.

'Ash,' she said.

I thought I might cry. I didn't know. It was her, you see. All of her.

'Don't look so worried,' she said. 'I like it both ways.'

We lay looking out of the window. Neither of us spoke and the rain was coming down. The sky was rolling too.

After a while she said, 'What did it feel like to be pregnant? I mean, how did it actually feel?'

I drew an arc above her bare stomach with my hand.

'Like this,' I said.

She laughed. I thought I might cry. She was somewhere inside me. I thought I might.

'No, really, Ash. What was it like? Was it rather beautiful?'

I wanted to tell her how it was. Truthfully, I mean.

It was the waiting I remembered most. The waiting. Summer crawled and I was heavy. I slept through the day. I slept all the time. I kept my hand on Charlie. Over her, I suppose. I kept it there whilst I slept, whilst we waited, and when I woke, in the moments after waking, Charlie would turn inside me and we were the only two who knew.

Us two only.

And how do you explain something like that?

She said, 'Ash? Was it rather beautiful?'

'No,' I said.

Her eyes filled up then. I didn't think she'd cry. I'd never thought she'd be the one to cry.

I touched her stomach. I touched it where a baby would've been if it'd had the chance, and when I moved my hand away there was a feather. A white one. It came out of her the way a bud comes from a branch.

'See, you're beautiful,' I said.

It wasn't like me to say a thing like that.

'Put it in my purse, Ash.'

I leant over her, my breasts were hanging down. Her sheet was as white as the feather in my hand. The feather that went to the top of Everest, that's what it reminded me of. I told her about that feather, there and then. I told her everything, but I don't think she heard.

'You're my guardian angel,' she said.

She reached for her lipstick.

But I need to concentrate because listen, here I am, I mean, there she is, and those men again. Those men. The ones walking their dogs. They come to this copse all the time. Every time. They could be looking for birds, for feathers. They're probably walking dogs. That's what most men do. Yes, they're probably only men walking dogs, although I haven't seen them, no, I haven't seen them with or without their dogs and now she's at the window again. There she is in her sky-blue top and Abbott's been thinking. It's time to loosen the rains. Maybe he decided it that summer too. It never stopped raining. It must've stopped. It only stopped after. Afterwards.

But for now he's decided. It's time to loosen them again.

There's a time for everything. Yes. But Papa didn't like the Bible. He didn't like plucking feathers from birds either. He didn't like the Bible at all. He never said why, although Sashya did. She said her name was Sashya with a y and she thought I was writing it down. Lynn with a y too, although she never said so. And she never used to go to the window back then. Kate, I mean, not Lynn. With two ns. Two ns and a y. It's time to loosen the rains. Abbott's decided. And she didn't go to the window back then.

I've racked my brains, I've been racking my brains, and why isn't there a difference between i and y.

Kate goes to the window, but only since I've been coming. Only since. Here she is, at the window, staring out over the car park without waving or smiling. She's staring out, past the moon, yes, beyond the moon, even though it's swollen, bloated, she's staring out beyond it.

She shouldn't. She shouldn't come to the window and stare like that, stare across the car park without smiling or waving.

And all of a sudden I'm tired. It's come down on me. Like night. It never matters y or i, no wonder Lynn didn't say Lynn with a y. She knew she'd sound the same and she seemed nice, Lynn, that first time. Friendly at least, and her hair. The way she piles it on top of her head. It looks pretty. I think Abbott would agree.

All of a sudden. That's what Kate said. She slept then, all of her, after that first time.

'What the eye doesn't see the heart can't grieve over,' Joan said.

It was the first thing she said when she saw me. I was taking a little breath of fresh air out the front just now, and I wondered if she'd forgotten about the bone, about posting the bone. How could she have forgotten? Altogether forgotten?

Lynn was there. I suppose that's why I was taking a little breather. She opened the front door herself.

'OK to come through?' she said. 'Ab?'

'Come through,' he said.

She didn't take her shoes off. They clicked on the tiles as she came through. She came through. She said only me, but it wasn't only her. She was carrying Liam in the car seat and Sophie was holding her hand. I was sitting on the stool in the kitchen listening to the sound of her shoes on the tiles. The girls went into the garden with Nelson. Abbott put the kettle on. I was sitting on the stool. I could hear the girls. I heard them throwing the ball for Nelson. Charlie was talking on. I used to tell her she talked on and here she was again, talking on, and some things don't change. I sat on the stool and listened.

'I'm afraid the little man needs a feed,' Lynn said.

She felt for the top button of her blouse.

'Of course,' Abbott said. 'Yes. Feed away.'

I went outside for a little breath of fresh air.

The reins have been loosened. Abbott loosened them. That's what I was thinking. I thought I could hear them flapping whilst I was out in the street, although there wasn't much of a wind. I turned towards the direction of the noise and as I turned Joan put her hand on my shoulder. I hadn't seen her coming.

'What the eye doesn't see the heart can't grieve over,' she said.

She kept her hand where it was. I could smell cigarette smoke, but I didn't mind that much. I was thinking of Lynn unbuttoning her blouse. I was thinking of her hair.

'Feed away,' he said and I think I saw his jaw relax, but I can't be sure and you only get to see everything once and you can't be sure. Not really.

'I'm heading down the hill for a few bits,' Joan said.

She said we could head down there together. She took her hand off my shoulder. It was the first time Joan had invited me anywhere since she'd invited me to come through to her kitchen. I knew I'd be all right walking down the hill with Joan. It was fresh air I'd needed when she'd invited me in that time. That's all I'd needed.

We walked down our hill side by side. Joan walked slowly. I was thinking about Abbott's jaw relaxing. I was thinking about Lynn undoing her buttons. I couldn't stop thinking, even though Joan was beside me. Even though the smell of cigarette smoke hung about her. I was thinking about Abbott walking towards Lynn. Stepping towards her, I mean, and Joan was saying it was high time she got Nelson another bone. She was going to drop by the butcher's anyway. High time, high noon, high seas. No. I was thinking about Abbott on his haunches. The girls were in the garden. Charlie, my Charlie. And Abbott was in the kitchen and I'm sure I saw his jaw relax and he must've stepped towards her, he must've crouched down, and Joan said, 'You're not vegetarians then?' And Abbott leant in towards Lynn and put his hands around her breasts. He had to spread his fingers. They were full with milk, her breasts. Parturient, almost. Yes. He touched them. He was tender like a boy. He was nothing like Jay.

'Ab,' Lynn said.

She spells it with two ns and a y, and Abbott was like a boy. He was taking care, taking air, a little breath, until Joan said, 'Where are you off first then?'

And I didn't know where I was off but there he was, crouching down and tenderly, and Joan probably said where she was off, and the girls were in the garden. He opened his mouth. He put the soft flesh of it around one of her nipples. He drank. He must've been drinking because milk was pooling under his bottom lip. Running down his chin. A ghyll, a rivulet, a beck, a rill. And he wasn't crying and neither was Lynn, but people cry when you least expect it and he went on drinking until he was full and it took a long time, we were walking down the hill, he must've been hungry, yes, and Lynn. I don't know what she did.

'Well, I've got to pop to the pharmacy,' Joan said. 'If you're only along for the walk. For the company. All those pills they give me. I rattle all the way back. Every time.'

And I don't know how it is when you're Joan's age, but I'm all right getting home and it can't be comfortable wearing your trousers like that.

I'm all right getting home. I've always been all right. And Abbott's loosened the rains.

I'll go back up the hill. I'll walk home. Joan walks slowly, but you get used to it. She rattles all the way back. That's what she said and there's nothing wrong with the way she walks. Why not walk slowly when the reins are loose because going home isn't the same.

And where am I off first. I could be off. I could do whatever I did, whatever we did. That summer. Under loose rains.

I'm going into the charity shop, and if Joan comes back, if she puts her hand on my shoulder again and says whatever it is she says about the eye and the heart, if she says it under her breath, that's what I'll say. I'll say, 'I'm going to have a quick browse in here. In the charity shop.' I've never been in and now I'm in and there are always people in the charity shop, I've seen them on my way to the baths. There are always people in here and in the baths, but there's never anyone in the lake, unless it's a Tuesday, and Abbott said his mum used to get him clothes from here and they were proud of him, the first day he went to work wearing a suit.

'We've got Lego, if you want Lego.'

They talk to you in here, Abbott was right. That's why they work here, because they like talking.

And now he's talking to me, the man behind the counter.

'Lego goes quickly,' he says.

'You'd be surprised,' he says. Surprised. But I've never known much about adjectives. I only had to choose one and I couldn't.

'Surprised, how quickly things go.'

Books too, four shelves of them. Abbott didn't say anything about books. He said the charity shop was full of people's hand-me-downs. Hand-me-downs. I wanted to say it again and again, but I knew Abbott wouldn't like it. I said it in my head. In my hand-me-down head. There are shelves of books, lots of books, and she calls him Ab.

It isn't his name.

Lots of books.

Abbott doesn't have hairy fingers. That's what she'll think when he touches her. And when he's full, after he's had his fill.

Books. Four shelves of books.

His parents were proud of his suit.

Lots of books. Pages and pages, ad infinitum.

'Not really a book man myself,' he says.

Abbott was right. They talk to you.

'Everything on that shelf's a pound. Anything you like.'

And I'm thinking of Abbott and I'm wondering whether I saw his jaw relax after all.

But that isn't the point now, no. All these books. Pages, ages. Papa wouldn't approve of playing with plucked feathers. No. The poem itself is the aphorism, and of course it is. Papa was right.

'Much of a book person, are you?'

And Charlie would like this book. *One Girl, One Dog.* That's her. Them, I mean. Charlie and Nelson. A girl and a dog. The *One* must be for emphasis. Writers do that.

If you can spot the subtleties, Papa said, and Abbott isn't the only one who leaves sentences hanging like reins, like rains.

One Girl, One Dog.

More adventures with Emily and her beloved dog, Scout.

Yes, Charlie will like this, Charlie can have this.

I slid *One Girl, One Dog* under my jumper. That's what I did.

A woman was tugging her pushchair, trying to get it up the step, into the shop. The man behind the counter jumped up to help her. She pulled and he lifted. I was looking at the book, I was reading the blurb. Emily and Scout. Her beloved Scout.

The man told her they had Lego. That she'd be surprised. Surprised how quickly it goes.

'Right,' she said, and whilst they were talking, and pushing and pulling, I slid the book under my jumper. Charlie can have this, I said to myself. She can have it. I was standing in the shop with the book under my jumper. I wanted to get out but the woman's buggy was blocking the door and I knew I had to ask. I knew I had to say something if I wanted her to move.

It's difficult to sleep.

One Girl, One Dog seems to have saved the day. Charlie sat next to me on the sofa and we read our books. She curled up. We read our books. That's how it was, that's how we were, reading, word by word, by word by whorl. The back of her head and mine look the same. Anticlockwise, that's the way we were. The way we were. Reading our books. Charlie had her legs tucked under her, holding the words in her hands. *One Girl, One Dog.* I slipped it under my jumper when he wasn't looking. They never look, people who talk. And it's difficult to sleep.

Charlie read her book. I read mine. We were sitting together. That's how we were. That's the way we were. And Charlie, Charlee, Charlea, smells nothing like Joan, and I almost got used to her on the way down our hill. The smoke, the slow walk. I almost stopped her from taking her hand off my shoulder. I'd got used to feeling cold, but I guess some things work out for the best, because Joan went off where she was off first, and after I checked the man in the shop was busy I slipped the book up my jumper. He didn't see. He'd come out from behind the counter for the pushchair. For a conversation. For some push and pull. You don't have to like words to like talking.

We read our books. I had *Haiku*. I held *Haiku* in my hands and I watched Charlie's face as the words went in and there isn't anything wrong with hand-me-downs. They read the same, like words, like whorls. The same. Anticlockwise, and you can only tell because my hair's short, it's always been short and Papa said my mama would've approved. And thinking of her, thinking. It's difficult to sleep.

I've read it three times now. *Haiku*. *Haiku*, translated by Kirsten Smith. I read it last night, with Charlie next to me, I breathed them out one by one. Whole haiku. Mists, mountains, mornings in the out breath. It was the third time I'd read it. I told myself that good things come in threes, although it was difficult to sleep after that. I couldn't sleep. And here we are again, curled up next to each other, reading. Abbott says *One Girl, One Dog* smells the way his clothes used to smell. Charlie put her nose right next to it but couldn't smell a thing.

'You will,' he said.

And here we are. Three times I've read it. Three times I asked her to come to the lake and it was calm out there under the cerulean sky, I had to go right out, I had to keep on swimming until it was calm and sometimes things turn out OK in the end, and it's all to do with words, although I wouldn't say that to Abbott, no, but here we are, side by side, curled up. Again, reading, again, and you'd think it'd be quiet but it isn't quiet now because Abbott's on the phone.

If he's talking. If she's talking. If they go on talking, Lynn and him, and if all these things stay the way they are, which isn't the way they should be. If you can explain away a mountain in seventeen syllables.

Charlie looks up.

'Are you actually reading, Ash?'

Charlie can't read when it's noisy either, that's what she says.

'All this noise,' we say, we almost always say, and we put our hands over our ears. Four ears, four hands. All our ears and hands, and all this noise and Charlie goes back to her words, her pages and if Abbott's talking. Yes.

But here, now, Charlie curled up on the sofa with her girl and her dog, her hand in her hair. My hand in Kate's hair. The greys were coming through, but what did it matter? We liked it both ways.

Noisy, noisy, noisy. And what can they say after seventeen syllables? Abbott. Lynn. All their words, all this time. Whole haiku in the out breath.

I already knew something was wrong, could already tell. We were curled up on the sofa, books in our hands, and I could see Charlie had almost reached the end of *One Girl, One Dog*. I could see there were only two or three leaves of paper left. I was looking at the leaves and thinking, when this is over, because I could tell it was almost over, and I hadn't seen any other books she would have liked in the charity shop. There weren't any. But there she was, reading the last pages, closing in on the end. Something was wrong. I could already tell, could already see she wasn't that comfortable. She was turning those last pages, turning them backwards and forwards as if something was missing. As if she was looking for something.

She uncurled her legs. Sat up straight.

'Why didn't you get me the end?' she said. 'This isn't the end. This isn't how it's supposed to end,' she said.

'Ash?'

She showed me the book. *One Girl, One Dog*. She put it at an angle so I could see clearly. She was pointing at the last page, the last word. I could see it was the end, the real end, the right end, but I saw her finger shaking. She couldn't keep it still.

'Why didn't you get me the end?'

'The end. Ash?'

I tried to listen. She was talking to me and I tried to listen, I was leaning towards her, leaning in like people do, to listen, to understand, to listen. And I'd seen the last word, she'd shown me the last word and I was trying, I was, but I didn't understand. And she was saying:

'Ash? Ash?'

There was a lot of noise.

There was a lot of talking, they were all talking, all at once. I was trying to understand and I couldn't understand, and I was holding *Haiku*, I was leaning in and Charlie said, Charlie kept saying, and I counted her syllables, I counted to seven, could have been eight, if she'd broken it down, and whether she had I didn't know, I was counting them out, counting out loud and Charlie shouted. She shouted.

The book was by my face, she held the words, waving them, waving them and all her noise, all the letters, all their noise.

'The end?' she said. 'Where's the end?'

The words were in my eyes and I was trying to understand. I couldn't understand, I was trying, but the noise.

'The noise, the noise, the noise, the noise.'

I said it, I said it. Noise with an i with a y, like Lynn, but I couldn't keep on because is and ys weren't enough and Charlie was shouting and Abbott was talking and maybe he'd stopped and we were walking down and after Joan took her hand from my shoulder Lynn's milk had pooled under his lip and he'd been so hungry, I'd been so cold, and there had never been so much chatter. So much din.

'Charlie!'

Abbott was standing in the door frame. He wasn't talking. Not talking, smoothing the hair on both sides. Once, twice. Smooth them three times. I wanted him to. I thought he might, good things come in threes and I thought he might, might cry. You can never tell. He didn't, stopped at two, but Charlie didn't, didn't stop, went on, stepped up on the sofa, up on its arm, waved the words above her head and threw *One Girl, One Dog*.

I saw it fly. I saw the earth bring it down, I saw the pages flapping, loose reins, everything loose, everything.

'Lost.' That's what she said.

And the words, the words, hold on, couldn't hold on, didn't hold on, so I had to get down, go down, kneel down, I had to put my hands out, catch the words, falling words, slipping through my fingers, now, slipping now, like haiku water.

Abbott came towards us. I thought perhaps he would help. All the words. The words, and Charlie on the sofa with her arms out. He shook his head.

'I'll fix it,' I said.

She said I couldn't fix anything. Yes, that's what she said, and I always remember the words people say.

So it's difficult to sleep now. You'll understand.

It won't be long before Lynn makes it into our bed, brings her y and her ns and lies them down indefinitely, yes, in our bed, and you can see why Asle stayed where he was, calmer on the waves, under the waves, than lying. On her back and waiting. Signe. U too, waiting until the weather broke and it did. Signe, always in the present tense and the blackberries are already good for eating. I saw them on the way back up our hill. I was all right getting home, all right, although the smell of autumn was in the air.

It's difficult to sleep. The nights are drawing in and Papa said, 'Spit and get used to it, spit over here and get used to it.'

Things were changing. Things are changing. The geese will come, the ones from Utsjoki and when they come they don't come quietly. It's difficult to sleep. The blackberries, the geese, the words on our carpet soaking in. Soaking in, probably, and it wouldn't hurt to clean them. Now Charlie's sleeping, now Abbott's sleeping.

'Blot first,' Abbott always says. 'It breaks up the fibres if you scrub.'

But he's never said anything about scraping. Scrape them up then sort them out. Everything can be put back, you can get used to change. You have to. Spit. Grey hair. Papa's, Kate's, I didn't mind, my fingers in at her roots. Caressing. She gave that word to me. She wanted it in my collection.

'Put it in?' she said. 'Will you?'

I didn't. I didn't tell.

I'll scrape. I'll sort the words out. I'll put them back where they belong, as long as they belong. And they must. *One Girl, One Dog*. They must belong. Belong, be long, be short. There must be a whole, a hole, the size of whatever, or this, or any word that belongs everywhere and somewhere and has crept in, crept up, like autumn, or dog. I'll sort them out, all these dogs. So many of them, falling through the fibres in front of me. Too late to blot, I'll have to scrape, although. Too many dogs and not many girls, and Emilys, so many Emilys. See here, three Emilys in this small patch, and two of them fallen next to dog which might be a coincidence but isn't, no, and if you take the words as only words, if you take carpet words, not book words, if they don't belong, don't have to belong, you can make sense, you can begin to make sense, piece together, and the problem with understanding or not understanding is hardly ever, or never, with the words themselves.

Emilys and dogs, and dogs, and fewer girls than there should be. But less talking, fewer girls, Ash, or you'll be up all night putting them back, you'll drive yourself mad making them all belong, be long, be short and trying them here and there like one of those jigsaws with a thousand pieces where you have to believe the picture on the box to believe the pieces all belong, but you know they do, but you know they did, and now. And now, you're holding a piece, another piece, a peace of sky, blue, cerulean, looks no different to all the others and you look at the piece and say to yourself, it can't be that difficult, can it? You say, it can.

And these are the same words, you realise, simple words, small words, you realise. Words are worse than jigsaw pieces when you're trying to fit them, you realise, they're a lot worse, so you have to keep fitting until they're as right as you know, which may or may not fit the picture inside the cover because there was only one picture, there wasn't a copy, and nobody thought, and it's simply not possible to see the hole, the whole thing, all the words, spun out, spinning out in every tense, all tense, and I knew. I knew. So you have to believe, have belief, you have to go blind, be blind, harder, a lot harder, than doing a jigsaw. But if you keep on, keep going, word by word, if you go anticlockwise, word by whorl, this, that, nowhere, stick, if you keep on with every word until, at last, at last, you're left with two words, two words there on the carpet, and you don't need me to tell you. No, you don't need me to spell them out.

The end. I'll say. The end.

And of course, yes, I can fix anything.

It's difficult to sleep. It's the log, my log. I went to my log and now I can't sleep.

I went to the copse to move it away from the wall. I wanted a different view. I mean, I'd been thinking about Kate walking to the window. It wasn't something she'd done before, I was sure, almost sure. I didn't like the idea of her staring. Staring without smiling, without waving either, so I decided to go back and move the log. To get a new perspective, to know what was going on with her, once and for all.

Once and for all, settle this thing, I said to myself as I walked through the copse. I went on walking towards the wall, towards the log. I was gaining momentum, yes, and when I got to the log I didn't stop, just walked around it and crouched down, all in one fluid movement. I crouched between the wall and the log, ready to push, and that's what I did. I pushed on the log as hard as I could. I pushed and used the wall to help me. I put my feet against it and pushed, but the log wouldn't budge. It wouldn't shift. I pushed again. I tried to do it quietly. I didn't want the men with dogs coming over. I was doing my best to keep quiet, but the log was stuck and I had to push hard, so hard I couldn't help grunting.

I stood up and looked across the car park towards the studio. Kate was standing at the window, staring, looking like she'd seen the whole affair. I mean the way I strode up, the heaving and pushing and. There she was anyway, with her mouth hung open, laughing. It wasn't the first time I'd seen it hanging open like that.

I didn't want to look into that thing. I pressed on with moving the log instead, got on the other side of it, crouched down and hung the weight of my body over it. I stuck my fingers into the grooves of the bark, I managed to get a good grip. Right, I thought, and dug my feet into the earth and tugged. I tugged. I heaved three times and on the third time I fell back, fell onto my back, but the log hadn't moved. It hadn't budged. I knew it was heavy, yes, but I'd moved it before. I'd rolled it until it dead-thumped against the wall.

I got up onto my knees after that. The men with dogs were talking. 'They aren't near,' I said out loud. But still. I decided to leave. I decided to head back through the copse and check for that cut through once and for all, yes, and just as I was getting up I remembered. I remembered putting a stone under the log to keep it in place. That's what I'd done after I rolled it against the wall. I laughed at myself. The stone's doing its job well. That's what I thought, and I laughed. It wasn't a loud laugh, I didn't want the men with dogs to come over, and it was getting quite dark in that copse, in the dark, beneath the sycamores.

I scraped at the soil under the log. Felt its damp. Felt it coming through the knees of my jeans. I was scraping with my hands and whilst I was scraping I felt her mouth too, the shadow of her unhinged mouth. Then her laugh. I thought I could hear it playing on the bones in my ears. I couldn't concentrate, not with that mouth, that laugh. I couldn't think, couldn't straighten my thoughts, couldn't be sure I'd put the stone there in the first place. In any case. I couldn't quite remember.

But just as I was about to give up my fingers got hold of something smooth. I held onto it, gripped on, I was trying not to listen, I was trying to ignore the shadow of her mouth, because I had the thing in my grasp, and that's almost what they say. I had the stone in my grasp, so I pulled.

I pulled. I pulled more than once, but whatever I'd got hold of wouldn't come out from under the log, so I got down further, put my cheek on the ground, my eye level with the base of the log, and that's when I saw it. The root.

As soon as I saw it I said, 'Not now.'

I said it twice. I said it out loud, but there it was, snaking out of the dead wood in front of me. I said not now again. I knew I had to stop. Kate was at the window with her mouth, laughing, and I had to stop, but she was the one who'd started this, she was the one who was always talking about being radical.

Yes, she was the one who started it. Her huge mouth gaping.

'Haven't you? Wouldn't you ever? Do something? Ash? Ash?' she said.

Radical, something radical. That's what she wanted, always wanted, and she said, 'What's wrong with you? The way you gawp.'

Yes, yes, she was pleased with gawp. She wasn't always kind, almost never tender, and I'd scraped up the words, a whole book, I'd been picking up the words one by one, none of them radical, and now her gape, my gawp, possession must be the opposite of radical, but nobody says, nobody mentions the words on the carpet. Must be harmless.

Dogs and Emilys especially.

Sticks, girls, gulls, boys, that's what they were, and Kate wanted me unlatched, that's what she wanted, she wanted me loose, loose, loose, like rains, the way they have to fall.

And how can I sleep now? How will I ever sleep?

To be honest I was scared kneeling down there under the sycamores, although it wasn't the first time she'd threatened to swallow me. It wasn't the first time I'd contemplated her

164

mouth and it was dark. I was getting quite cold. But there it was, her mouth, moist when I went in. And I knew when she left, I knew as soon as she left I'd have something, because I'd always known that doing and having were the same.

I forced myself. I forced myself to stand up, get up from where I was kneeling and look.

And how will I sleep? How will I ever sleep?

I looked. The moon had gone. It cheered me. I hoped she'd swallowed it. I hope it'd given her something to chew on. I laughed at my joke, laughed out loud, quite loud and I suppose it took me by surprise, the laugh. And what about the men, the men with the dogs? It was dark, yes, and I needed to get back, but there it was between us, the stickiness, the silence or whatever it was that was bigger than the car park. And that was when I decided. That was when I decided to climb up onto the wall.

I climbed up. Stood up, and made myself as tall as I could. I took a deep breath. I looked over towards the studio and there she was, yes.

'Kate,' I said.

I projected my voice.

'Kate,' I said.

I waited a moment. I waited until I could see down into the pit of her mouth, then gestured towards my log.

'Look, Kate. My log. It's grown a root.'

And now Abbott's taken *Leaves of Grass*. The moment I opened my eyes I knew. I'd had it here next to the bed, right on the floor by the bed, that's where it was before I went to sleep, and now it's gone.

He'd had it in him from the start. He'd always maintained that reading a fat book of poetry all the way through was weird.

'From cover to cover?' he said. 'Weird.'

He said you couldn't trust a man who celebrated himself. Do you know what that means, Ash? Do you? And what could I say, but I didn't have to. He picked up my book. He held the weight of the words in his hands.

Leaves. Leaves, leaves in his hands.

He held the book. Turned it without opening it.

'Walt. Short for Walter, or what?' he said, and when I didn't answer he put the book down.

'Always something of your dad in you,' he said then.

But Papa wasn't having any of that American stuff. Keats was his boy. I wore a blue dress, stopped short above my knees, I couldn't have been his boy if I'd wanted to.

Abbott's taken *Leaves of Grass*. He's done something radical, at last.

Radical, radicle, share the same root, although it had never crossed my mind until now, and anyway, in the end, she was first. It was all about downward-flowing energy, and she must have been right because they came from her feet, the roots.

166

Began with a radicle, it always does, but now I see it, now I see her. All square roots, cube roots, her great tap root, wherever it was going under the carpet. Under the carpet, and that's when I followed, that's when I came.

He's taken *Leaves of Grass*. He slipped that fat book from under my nose and I suppose I must have been sleeping. I suppose he must have been waiting, waiting until I was falling. He must have known I wouldn't catch myself the way you sometimes can. He must've known and taken it, slipped it from under my nose.

'Flabby stuff, Whitman,' Papa said, but Keats was flabby stuff too, or loose at least. He didn't know what kind of boys he liked, Papa, not really. And where is he now, with my book, my leaves, where has he taken it? I knew as soon as I woke he had.

And here he is now. Must've left me sleeping after he slipped that book from under my nose. And what does he want me to read, if I don't read *Leaves of Grass*? What will I read, because he's always asking, what can you do, Ash, what can you do to keep your spirits up?

Here he is. Listen, parking the car. Reverse parking on our hill, his revs too high and that's how I know him, but not the only way. I mean, that's how we know people, isn't it? He took *Leaves of Grass*. He had it in his hands whilst I was sleeping. Fat books shouldn't be read from cover to cover. Inside, poetry, inside, he celebrates himself, his man-root and I know what it means, always knew what it meant.

And it isn't nice, thinking of his man-root, Whitman's, I mean, and nobody said, but I think he liked it both ways. Still. I liked *Leaves of Grass*, all that optimism. I read it from cover to cover and more than once. It started on the train, on Papa's knee and Abbott knows. He knows all this. I told him the whole story, and he shouldn't have taken it, although reading and having are the same.

I can hear him reversing, his revs too high. Doesn't know which way to turn the wheel.

I heard him parking the car. I went to the window, pressed my face against it. I couldn't make out whether it was raining, I couldn't tell, but the pane was cold. Abbott was reversing, in and out, backwards and forwards, was turning the wheel and it wasn't right. Charlie and Nelson were sprawled across the back seat and he was turning the wheel and didn't know which way.

I went downstairs and stood in the hallway where she'd come through, only me, two ns and a y, although she'd never said, she'd never stressed the y. It was Sashya who did, and where was Sashya now there was only Lynn left?

I stood by our front door. I had things to say. I knew what I was going to say. I was standing near the front door because he had to come through, had to walk through, it was the only way in, so I knew. Stand here and wait, I thought, and I thought about the words I would say. I waited for the revving to stop. I had things to say. I knew about *Leaves of Grass*, I'd known as soon as I'd woken.

You shouldn't take things, I was going to say.

I was standing in the hallway and he'd never known how to reverse, although he liked driving. He said he did. Liked the feel of the keys in his pocket. The way they weighed him down. Never known how to reverse. Not instinctively. Not like birds, who know enough to know motion, and never, ever fly backwards.

Pull down on the left to send the back left, look in the mirror, look back. In and out like that, the wrong side of the wheel, and it'd been a long time since, and I didn't think she'd cry. I didn't think, and later. Thought I could make it OK, because it doesn't hurt if you don't mean it that way. I opened her legs. Tenderly. I promise. I promise you.

Papa was tender. Abbott too. His hands on my book, on Lynn's breasts, like a boy, he was, though you can tell by his hair he isn't. F Scott was receding too and Whitman liked to wear a hat, a smelly hat. His beard probably smelt too and Jay was different, he always looked quite clean and I saw the way he rode her. The way he wouldn't let her up. I heard Ryan say:

You cunt.

Abbott shouldn't have taken *Leaves of Grass*. If he'd wanted something he could've taken *Haiku*. But nobody wants *Haiku* now. It's easy to wash your hands of seventeen syllables, it's easy once you've seen how easily they slip downstream. I was ready to confront him. I was behind the door. I wanted my book. It was a step too far, taking it, slipping it. You shouldn't take something that's been read from cover to cover. You shouldn't stare without waving. I had to stand on the wall after that. I had to be the one to break the silence. I had to be the one to say.

And they always want words, they're always asking for them, but Abbott's forgotten. I had too many, enough to go on with. I mean, he used to say I went on, kept going on. I must have had words to be going on. Going on about that film, he said, but it wasn't the film, it was Utsjoki I was going on about, it was the lake, it was Kevojärvi, the photo.

Look at these two wading. Do you think they're men or women? Boys, perhaps? I'd wanted to say.

I'll tell you what I think but it doesn't count.

I was by the front door with something to say. It had been a long time since and I wasn't sure I'd remembered that photo properly. The pair wading, their arms around each other, or holding hands, I couldn't remember. I thought perhaps I should find the photo. I thought perhaps I should rest, but I wanted my book. I was ready to confront Abbott, I'd been waiting for the revving to stop and the revving had stopped and I was ready and they'd have to come through with or without. Only me. I needed a rest, yes, I thought perhaps a rest would help.

He found me sleeping. He told me I'd hardly moved an inch the whole time they'd been gone.

'Perhaps you should get up?' he said.

He was crouching down. He was holding onto my arm a little too tightly. Five thirty-five on his Second Core, up against my face.

'Ash,' he said.

And big watches are more dangerous than small ones.

'Ash.'

Charlie and Nelson were behind him.

Charlie and Nelson. It'd been a long time, and she must've noticed by now. I sorted the words, the whole book. *One Girl, One Dog.* I shut it when I was done. A hardback would've been more secure, but it was all for her. All of it for Charlie.

'Ash,' he said. 'Perhaps you should get out of bed before it's time to go back there again.'

I didn't see why. There are ways to be radical without moving. No need to get up and go back for the sake of a circle, for the sake of going round. I tried it before, going round, swimming in fours. Didn't get anywhere but tired. Swimming in the lake is different, there are bigger circles at play, but if you don't rest from sleeping it's difficult to sleep. Yes, I know that now.

I should've got out of bed before it was time to go back. Should've got out of bed when Abbott said get up. Get up. Charlie and Nelson were there, and I'm used to him, Big Head, I'm used to him now.

It's difficult.

It's difficult to sleep. Inside the tilt of the earth. And what kind of circle takes summer, brings autumn on? Ellipses are something else. You can't quite trust them. People are better with circles, are better with one to twelve, but it creeps more quickly, autumn.

All of a sudden. That's what Kate said, 'Have you noticed how it's getting dark early all of a sudden?'

It wasn't like her to talk about the dark. It wasn't like anyone to talk about the dark. Abbott never says a thing about it. She shivered when she spoke. She wasn't cold, she promised. She said it was more of a chill.

'Sends a shiver down your spine, the dark. Doesn't it?'

I didn't say.

I didn't say it's just the way the dark comes on. Didn't say I knew its momentum, liked it even, knew it would gather, knew it would slow, after the equinox, into the solstice, knew the tilt of the earth, polar nights, all these things, didn't say how much I really understood. Rhetorical questions aren't for answering.

Abbott never says anything about the dark, although once.

Once. He said I'd save myself a lot of grief if I stopped looking at the sky. I put grief in my collection after that. It should be a homophone but it isn't. It doesn't matter that much.

He's lying next to me right now. His mouth, his nose, our air rattling in and out of it. He doesn't know which way to turn the wheel. He sleeps as if nothing's changed and never says y although he said grief.

Once.

Better when it speaks, grief, isn't it? And if it doesn't it isn't, or it is. No one said, and you can't save yourself. You can't save yourself from grief unless you save yourself from love. Papa would know. He'd know where to start, which way to turn the wheel. He'd say, you might as well get up and figure it out, Ash.

See, Abbott never stirs. See.

He's always on his back, lying still. Signe was too, on her back. On the final page of that book she was still lying, lying on that bench, and then.

And then.

She felt for her breasts. I wasn't expecting it, Signe, I wasn't expecting, amidst all those words, to be woken up, roused, not on the final page.

Wake first then sleep. Love first then grief. After all, love ends in grief. All love ends in grief. It's too dark to get up and figure it out. I wasn't expecting to be aroused. I wasn't even sure how to pronounce her name. Signe, Signe, Signe.

I should get up. That's what you should do if you can't sleep. Get up. And look at Abbott and the way he lies and where has he put *Leaves of Grass*? Where has he put my *Leaves of Grass*? I should look. I shouldn't let something like the dark stop me. I've been watching, yes, and most people are more afraid of the light.

I knew what he'd done with it. All of a sudden I knew. I got out of bed and walked down to the landing in the dark. The way I walked, he wouldn't wake. I knew. I knew he'd be there, lying on his back when I crawled back in.

I walked away, crept I suppose, could hear the air moving in and out of his nose, could hear it as I walked down the landing, past the bathroom. Her door was on-the-jar. Charlie says Mrs McIntosh says, and I like it, on-the-jar. Who wouldn't?

I crept towards the door. Didn't want to wake her, she always slept lightly, she was always easily roused.

Don't go to her. Wait for her to settle, Abbott used to say. She was small, too small to settle, he'd say and I'd wait, I'd hover, and I couldn't see clearly until she had.

I was standing at her door. I knew where he'd put it, *Leaves of*

Grass, all of a sudden it had come to me. I couldn't see, but I heard her stir. And she always slept lightly, always leapt lightly, she knew when they'd go, the swifts, that summer, and I knew too. I knew where he'd put it, *Leaves of Grass*. I was sure. I was standing at her door, I was sure, was shore, and swam. I swam towards her as soon as I knew. I thought she was OK, and it doesn't hurt, it isn't meant to hurt if you don't mean it that way and who was it who said that? The first time, I mean.

I wanted to go in, to creep in. Her door was on-the-jar. I wanted the book, I knew where it was, I knew where he'd put it, but she sleeps lightly. These days. I wanted to go in but I waited. Big Head was on the end of her bed, making rhyme. Papa would know, would say, would definitely. Couldn't stay indefinitely and Signe, didn't think I'd be aroused. I put the book down, the book with the flame on the cover. I put it down and I looked around but where had it come from, arousal? There were only words after words, and everyone said, everyone says it's actions that matter. Actions count, not words, no, something to hold on to, and I had to get my *Leaves of Grass*, I knew where he'd put them, and it was dark, it was night, and Abbott was sleeping. I crawled into Charlie's room on my hands and knees, my hands and needs, and I must've been quiet because Big Head was sat on the end of the bed still. Still. I whispered in his ear, said, 'Don't stir, no need.'

I could see in his eyes, he understood. I crept in, slipped under her duvet, she always slept lightly, but this time. Things change. Papa said. I slipped in. Got to get used to losing things.

U left too, along with the sofa, Jay and Terry. All three. Don, don, don. Charlie always slept lightly, but this time, my hand in her hair and years to go until the greys come in.

I didn't think.

I didn't think I'd cry. It came from somewhere so far from my eyes I wasn't expecting it. Wasn't expecting her to feel so warm, so familiar. And why spit if you don't have to? Why take something so precious? He took *Leaves of Grass* and where did he put it? I wasn't sure. Wasn't all that sure. All my feathers, different birds, hardly a flock, touch has a memory and Keats is the boy, was his boy, and all along, all along I was pretend-ing to be hers.

I went back to the copse in the light, it was the first time I'd been down there in the light. I went waltzing on down there, the way you can when things have changed.

My log, with its root, and it isn't often you form attachments like that. That's what I was thinking as I walked to the copse. It was a joke. I said it a few times, to keep myself happy. I was happy. I was feeling upbeat, looking forward to standing on the log, to tracing the grooves of its bark with my fingers and feeling whatever it was. It gives back. I wasn't thinking about anything else. I wasn't thinking about the men and their dogs, the cut through. The whole place looked different in the light, and when I got to the copse I was still thinking about the joke.

It was light. I had all day. I had time. I walked through the copse, the sky rolled over the way it has been rolling. I walked through and under the sycamore trees all at once, I walked towards my wall, towards my log. I was trying out possession, waltzing up, whistling even. It looked a bit different, the copse. I suppose it must've been the light. I walked to the log, through the sycamores, under the sycamores, inside the sound of their leaves. I got to my wall and looked out across the car park. It was almost empty and the studio looked shut, but that wasn't it, no, that wasn't what was bothering me. It was the log. The log wasn't there.

I looked around, there wasn't anywhere to look but I looked anyway. I walked the length of the wall, in case, and I must've stopped whistling.

'Has anyone seen my log?' I said.

I thought, why not? If you don't ask. I said it again, again, I said it whilst I was walking the length of the wall. I walked it three times in total, and good things come in threes, yes, but the log wasn't there.

Of course, I knew. Abbott had taken it. He'd put it out of harm's way. He wouldn't want me climbing up, or falling down, or both. He wouldn't want anything to happen to me. He's kind. I knew the first time he touched me. I could see it in his hands. I could feel it in his hands, and tender was the night and F Scott Fitzgerald took feathers, made birds, and not everybody can, there aren't many people who can do a thing like that, make flight from nothing, from nothing but a pile of words. Keats was Fitzgerald's boy. Papa didn't know. I wanted to be Papa's. Boy, girl, boy, there wasn't any point. In looking, if he'd taken it, my log. What's the point if you have to spit first, if you always have to prepare and then. I mean afterwards, rest, rets, rets?

I walked home. I'd stopped waltzing. You have to stop at some point.

The sky was rolling and the wind was blowing and I was thinking about my log and how I'd wanted to run my fingers over its bark. How I'd wanted to do that one more time, taken time. Abbott had saved me from falling. I was thinking about his hands, how nobody likes hairy fingers, how tender must be a property, and couldn't really be an adjective. An imposter, tender, that's what I was thinking as I was walking, and had given up waltzing because nothing goes on and things especially don't go on if you want them to. That's the trick. That's what I was thinking whilst I was walking and the wind was blowing and the street was more or less empty, although it wasn't empty, because how was empty filled with houses one after the other and I couldn't see beyond, could only see houses until, merging with sky, but the sky was rolling and the street was still, was more or less empty and Kate was following me.

I heard her under the wind. There hadn't been a wind, there hadn't been a wind since. There hadn't been a wind when the rain came and spawned a stream, here on our hill, a stream to carry things away. We called it a beck. We called it a burn, a ghyll and there's no real way to say the h against the g naturally. But Kate was following me. I couldn't think why. Didn't want to think about y and then I remembered Kate was scared of the wind. She'd told me.

We were on Cotters Hill. When the wind blows up there it blows uninterrupted. That's when she told me, that's where she told me, on the top of the Crag. I was wearing shorts and she was wearing a skirt and we were on the top with our bare knees and I wanted to run, I was about to take off, take off running, because the wind was insistent, and I wanted to take off but she stopped me.

'No, don't, Ash,' she said.

She linked her arm through mine.

'I'm scared, darling. Call me a fool, but I'm scared.'

The wind was pushing, that's how it was, and I knew how it would feel if I went. I knew how it felt to open my wings, to feel the wind under them, but she was puffing and her mouth was filling, and air was weighing her down. It was weighing us both down.

'Don't go,' she said. I wanted to go, I wanted it so much I said.

I said:

'Does it have to be you who runs away? Does it always have to be you?'

The wind carried my words. It took them up in its teeth and I bent double and I spat, I spat, but still.

'Why does it have to be you?' I said.

She asked if she could tell me a story then and what could I say, but it didn't matter, she went on anyway, opened that mouth, told me the wind had blown her mum away.

'Clean away,' she said.

She let go of my arm and showed me. She showed me with vast sweeping movements, to help me imagine. I imagined where the wind had blown her, I could almost see, I could almost see how the grasses came down to where the river ran and if we went to look for her mum I could see us, yes, I could see us side by side and almost always lying down.

She wouldn't tell me if her mum had been found. She said, let's talk about something else, then asked about my mama. Let's talk about something else, I said, and we did, although I can't remember, I can't remember what we talked about, or what we were doing on Cotters Hill.

Kate followed me all the way home. I heard her footsteps under the wind and after a while, when I concentrated, I could hear the sound of her puffing too. I wanted to run, I couldn't run, and I knew Abbott had saved me from falling and why was I there in the street with Kate if it was Abbott who had saved me, who always saved me, and maybe the thing with *Leaves of Grass* wasn't the whole story and I wanted to run and I thought I should, because staring is one thing but following is another and I wanted to run, to run, to run, three times to keep myself, because she wanted my arm, to hold me down and I didn't. I tried. To run, but she held me, she linked her arm through mine, staked me almost, yes, then. Took the d from down and she did whatever she wanted, she always did, she tucked it where she wanted it, kept it until she owned me.

I put the bolt across the front door.

'Never thought I'd catch you doing that,' Abbott said.

He likes it bolted when the last person's in. He likes to keep us safe.

I slept easily knowing I'd put the bolt across the door. The wind was moaning, it was battering the windows. I knew nothing would get through the seal on the skylight. Abbott said I'd be grateful for a seal like that when winter comes, but it's turning September and I'm already grateful. He knows me. That's what I thought as I lay next to him, and I could think what I liked because I knew he wouldn't stir until morning, and when he did, he listened for my sleeping, he kissed me on the forehead and counted to three. He left his lips, one, two, and it might've been me who counted, but.

Not long after the kiss Lynn came.

She didn't knock. She opened the front door and shouted 'Only me' and came through carrying a few bits. It was the least she could do, she said. She said she knew I wouldn't want to be running around the supermarket if I was feeling under the weather. But we were under the weather. All of us. The wind was blowing but it was never going to get through, we've got eight years left on the guarantee.

She lifted the bags up onto the table and started unpacking them, putting things in cupboards. She knows her way around, I thought, and the girls ran on upstairs with Nelson. Charlie, Sophie, Nelson, eight legs, and Liam in his car seat chewing on a cardboard book.

'Might be teething,' that's what she said, perhaps she spells Liam with a y too, and does Ab want this in the freezer?

'Please. Yes please,' he said.

He wants to keep me from falling.

I should've told her, set the record straight, but she was busy with potato gratin, she rhymed it with satin, he only has to put it in the oven and pierce the film if he doesn't feel like cooking from scratch. We were in the kitchen, under the weather and I didn't know whether to rest or breathe, so I stayed on the stool until they told me which and I agree with Abbott, she's kind. She'd brought enough apples for Charlie to have one in her packed lunch each day. Although I was thinking about our apple tree, and wondered if anyone had even noticed its September branches, probably close to laden.

'Summer's gone so quickly,' Lynn said, looking out of the window, beyond, yes, probably beyond the apple tree.

Last week she cleaned.

I heard her tell Abbott she'd leave the master bedroom.

'If Ash is resting,' she said, under her breath, and under his, he said, 'thanks', and she didn't mind, she likes cleaning, she likes the, you know, feeling, when everything's the way it should be. She's probably so clean she squeaks when he touches her although they keep themselves quiet. I've got to say that. They keep whatever it is they're keeping under her hair, there's room for something big in there. For rhymes, for plenty, but at least they're quiet. At least. Which is more than can be said for Kate. She can't keep her mouth shut, and never could.

'What is it about her?' Abbott said. That summer. I'm sure it was.

'She doesn't stop talking. Doesn't know when to shut it.'

He moved his hand like a talking mouth. He was standing by the barbecue, pushing his fingers against his thumb.

'Ah, it's not big enough,' he said.

He moved away from the heat and snapped his crocodile arms, together and apart. Make a cavern instead, I thought. A place for getting lost.

'There are plenty more fish in the sea, Ash,' he said. 'In the river,' he said. 'Trout mouth.'

He laughed. He picked up the barbecue tongs.

I was sitting on the stool in the kitchen. Abbott and Lynn were putting away the bits she'd brought. I was sitting so still I'd almost disappeared, although Kate was there, Kate was wherever she was, could see me perched on that stool, and said, be still, which she must have lifted straight from the Bible, although it didn't seem like the wrong thing to say, so I tried to be still. I sat on the stool and imagined the lake, untouched. Without wind, I mean, or boys. With nobody wading or swimming.

And she must've got through the front door somehow, although I'd pulled the bolt across and checked it the way Abbott had shown me. She could see me though, from wherever she was hiding. Could see me trying to be still, and I was still, a statue almost, because. Lynn and Abbott, after a while, relaxed enough for him to say:

'Come here.'

And he said it twice, the second time softly, like the second wave, the gentle one, and I wondered whether, under the weather, she'd come when he said, but I knew the pull, the place where gravity takes over, and I stayed where I was on the stool, because Lynn was coming, and Abbott was asking, was more tender than I remember him, his edges smoother and I didn't want to think, though he took his glasses off and put them next to the coffee beans, and he hadn't said that we can't grind them, and it's usually me who doesn't tell, but Lynn was coming and Abbott was patient, as tender as.

They left and came back three times. House martins that don't come back are unheard of.

'Come and see them before they go,' I said to her. We were looking across the street, resting our elbows on her windowsill.

'Before they go?' she said. 'Why do they have to go?'

Not long after that they went.

Left and came back. Three times, but.

She's here now, hasn't had to come that far, although where's she hiding herself? Where?

They've flown seas, the house martins, flown in one fell swoop, and so many miles, and on wings that size. That size. But she hasn't asked. She never seemed to think to ask.

That day I told her anyway.

'When house martins go, they disappear,' I said. 'They might congregate high over the rainforests of the Congo basin. Nobody knows.' I was resting my elbows on her windowsill, two boys were passing, pushing their bikes along the pavement, but she had her phone. Her head in her phone.

'Nobody knows. Kate,' I said, and she lifted her head.

'They always come back though, right?' she said.

But coming back wasn't the mystery, and she had her phone, her head was in her phone, her thumb on the screen and I wanted to say, but I didn't say:

Don't you think? Losing twelve million of anything should raise suspicion. Or wonder?

Lynn washed and ironed Charlie's school uniform. She hung it on the back of her door in her bedroom and didn't see me creeping in behind her, standing behind her as she straightened it, as she breathed out.

'Yes,' she said. She brushed it down, and she likes the, you know, feeling, when everything's the way it should be. She took a step back, I was right behind her, I had to be quick, stepped back too. She didn't hear me, didn't notice, yet I was close enough to see. A white hair in the pile on her head was sticking out, out of place and I thought about touching, and I wouldn't have been the first person to think like that. I put my hand out, reached towards the hair, and she was standing, standing up straight, with posture. She was looking at Charlie's uniform, the way it hung, and she hadn't noticed, hadn't felt my breath, which must've been close enough to feel. But I had it, her hair between my thumb and forefinger, I was waiting for her to move.

'Do you mind the greys?' Kate said.

My hands were in her hair, I mean, her hair was over my fingers and later, sometime later, I found one and kept it until I let it go, and Abbott doesn't want to be late on Charlie's first day back at school. I heard him from the other side of the door this morning and I thought about getting out of bed to tell them, now it's September, the geese.

But they weren't thinking.

About geese, about grief, and Abbott wants me to stay, to rest, and doesn't want to think about geese. Instead, the first day back, and Charlie's going to write neatly this year, that's what she said, starting from today, she'll be neat, and especially if she gets a new book, and if nothing gets in through the window, it must come through the door.

Kate says. I agree. We haven't always agreed, but now we do. It's easier that way, when everyone's sharing such a small space, I mean.

And here, look, a long hair woven into the sheet. Auburn, I'd say.

Auburn.

It isn't ours. It isn't Kate's or mine. And now, pull on it, until it's free and I'm holding it like this. I'm holding it up so one end's loose and see, look carefully, this hair, so light it's found wind where there isn't wind. It isn't mine, almost a fathom too long and hangs in a curve, so can't be Kate's.

And didn't I say?

Didn't I think, at least, that it wouldn't be long until Lynn made it into our bed? And now here, at last, a thread of evidence, the hair, the auburn hair.

'Have you always had yours short?' Kate said.

I took the scissors from the drawer in Papa's shed. Three hot days in April and I'd been watching the sweat on his neck bead into real drops, the way of rain. I waited until Papa had gone, and I got the scissors. I didn't think, I tried not to, and took hold of my hair, pulled on it until it was straight, and chopped. I chopped until my neck was bare like his, completely bare. I took a little leap. And then I waited. In my blue dress, and I liked it short. My hair too. I already liked it short, short, short and I liked my neck, the skin on my neck where hair had been and wasn't. It was the change I liked. I stroked my neck and waited until Papa came back, and when he did he stood. He propped his spade against the shed and called me over to him, although he didn't say a word, just called with his huge hands, and I walked over, my blue dress up above my knees and when I got to him I leant my head into his waist and he tousled my hair. He wasn't rough. He was more like the way boys touch, when they touch, and it'd been a good thing, I already felt it, then knew for sure when he stepped back, his hands on his hips and said, 'your mama would've approved.'

'So have you?' she said, 'Always had yours short?'

'Always,' I said.

Although this hair. It isn't Kate's hair, or mine. This is auburn. Look at its length, the way it hangs in a curl as though it has memory and Papa said, I'm sure he said, grey or black, black or grey, hairs were dead anyway. But that only made it worse, the rhyme. It only stopped us pretending, left us getting used to change, and this hair, I'll only be able to lose it if I want it, but I don't want it, not this one. It could be auburn, or sorrel, and Abbott probably lost his fingers in it, in here, asked her if he could pull it down, her auburn tower, if he could look inside and find whatever plenty he needed, he probably asked, he's always been so polite, he wouldn't lose his hands, let them loose, without asking first and he wouldn't be used to cascading locks, or anything falling, and come to think of it cutting my hair off was radical. But radical's called endearing when you're small, and especially when you're wearing a blue dress. I wouldn't want endearing in my collection. Endear, oh dear, my dear, dear God, dear old Joan. No. Deer though, a completely different thing, with its sorrel coat and vanishing as soon, but where's the hair, I'm looking around and I can't see it, against our sheets, white, and the hair is auburn, or sorrel, fathom-long with a curve, as if it had memory, this hair.

Papa found my hair.

'Would you look at this?' he said.

It was woven into the thick of the nest as if it belonged there.

'A true bird-girl,' he said, though the way he tousled my hair was more like the way I'd seen with boys.

Bird-boy. Not girl. Your papa was wrong.

I'd put the bolt across, so she wouldn't, Kate. But she does, although where's she hiding? Where?

'Bird-boy,' she says. 'Aren't you? Hey?'

I didn't mind. I never minded what anyone called me. Boy, girl. Girl, boy, I couldn't see the point in being one or the other, and if I'd had the photo of Kevojärvi that summer I would've asked her about the wading pair. Do you think they're men or women? Boys, perhaps? I would've asked and she would've looked and if she'd said. It doesn't matter.

But it's difficult to hear what she says above the din, although Abbott would say it isn't a din, would say, he can't hear a thing and shake his head, but it's him. It's Abbott. He's the one who leaves things switched on. He plugs things in and leaves them with their lights flashing, he says they need charging, and I understand, I've told him I understand, but it's difficult to hear above all the din they make.

Now, that hair, the auburn one. Kate, look, it's wound its way around my toe with its curling end. Look, the hair, it's on my toe, it's wound its way around, and when I move my foot like this, up and down, it tightens, tugs on my toe. It's like a little root, see, and it's got a lot of give that hair, but be careful. Lest it snap, lest it become two.

I took the hair to the bin. I had to unwind it first. I took it to the bin and watched it float down and curl around the base. It lay there like a snake. I didn't want it escaping. I didn't like the way it had found my toe, wound itself around it, and I wondered for a moment if Abbott had put it there, in the bed, to stop me from falling somehow, but he wouldn't, I mean, it didn't add up and I was trying to remember whether I'd ever told him that wound is one of only a few serious homonyms.

Abbott found a hair. Kate's. He found it in his sock that summer, twenty-three days after the house martins left. But he didn't think. I mean, you don't think, you just think, he just thought, a hair, but he wouldn't have wanted me to find the auburn one, because a woman and a man. Do you know what that means? Do you?

He pulled on the hair he found. It came out of his sock, it kept coming out of his sock, he kept pulling. It couldn't have been his, or mine, or Charlie's, but what did it matter whose it was, if he was clean, although now he's cleaner, she likes everything, you know. He rubbed the hair between his thumb and forefinger so it would be gone the moment he let go and when he left the room I got down on my hands and knees and looked. I crawled across the bedroom floor and prayed it would find me. Somehow.

We saved the cake for the top.

Kate made it. She was as light as I'd ever seen her. She moved seamlessly between cupboards and surfaces, shaking and mixing and sprinkling.

'Taste this, Ash,' she said. 'Better now?' she said.

She was getting high. She was as high as I ever saw her, but it wasn't that high. I'd been higher, she said so herself, although she said it reluctantly.

She'd had to look up. I was climbing, I was going up, could see her looking, could see her eyes, her mascara. I liked it, I liked her, she liked me, she liked the way I went higher.

But wait, that day, the day Kate made the cake. We walked up Cotters Hill. I was wearing shorts and she was wearing a skirt and carrying that cake. She'd wrapped it in paper, put it in a tin, in a bag, a jute bag. The bag was suspended from the crook of her arm, and I wondered how long it would be until she said something about being vulnerable, because it was one of her words, vulnerable, and that's what I'd been thinking watching her, watching her tend to that cake. We walked up Cotters Hill. It wasn't cold and it wasn't raining, although it almost was. It might've been if we'd stopped, if we'd given ourselves time, to stop, to notice, I mean.

'The top isn't the best bit,' I said when we got there.

She linked her free arm through mine.

'What is, then?' she said.

She tightened her arm, she pulled it a bit tighter, and the wind was picking up. We were looking down at the grassy slope stretching out below us in every direction. Every way down was full of the kind of emptiness that calls you. I mean, it was calling, the way empty places do. I was about to go. I mean, I could hardly stay.

'No, don't, Ash,' she said and tightened her grip. 'I'm scared, darling. Call me a fool, but I'm scared,' she said.

I didn't go. I couldn't, although I could hardly stay. We walked to the Crag, we crouched down out of the wind and ate the cake. We walked down. She kept her arm through mine the whole way and told me about her mum.

'She left,' she said. 'She stopped loving my dad, so she left.'

The auburn hair found its way out of the bin. I put it there on Tuesday and now it's Thursday and here it is in the bed. It's sitting up in front of me, the top end of it in a loop, wound around itself, and thicker, much thicker than it was. I pinched it between my forefinger and thumb a moment ago and it lurched its pinhead towards me.

Kate laughed. She laughed when she saw me recoiling. We laughed. Went on laughing for a while and it wasn't the first time. It wasn't the first time we'd been in bed laughing, but where she is, and how she got in, she hasn't said, although it's broken the ice a bit, laughing like that, because I can't always hear what she says, not with all this din. It was easy to laugh, but you can't laugh, you have to practise losing.

We stopped laughing, although she went on longer, and I was about to say, but I didn't say because I caught sight of the auburn hair again. There it is, there, sitting up, feeling under our sheets with its roots. I'm glad. I'm glad I didn't know it'd escaped last night. I wouldn't have been able to sleep if I'd known. I suppose I should've checked the bin. I suppose I should start checking the bin as a matter of course, from now on. I won't sleep. How will I sleep, if I start thinking about the places it could wind itself, because the way it held my toe, that time. The way it tightened, the way people tighten, when they warn you. It's in their faces and hardly ever in their words and you shouldn't have to listen to distinguish between warn and warm, but you do.

But never mind the hair, I couldn't sleep anyway last night. For all the noise. I couldn't think straight for the sound of electricity. I ran through the Fibonacci sequence to drown it out. Papa always said, if you can get as far as, and I got as far as, but the buzzing, the crackling, seemed to be getting louder, so I kept on, got as far as seventy-five thousand and twenty-five, which sounds quite far, but isn't, isn't far at all, but everything was growing, numbers and noises, but maybe they weren't growing, or not as much as I thought because in the end I slept. I don't know how I did, but I did.

But now it's getting to me again. The buzzing and the hair, and I could go outside and take a little breath, but where would I take it when I'd taken it. And this buzzing, this electricity, not ours, probably Lynn's, and auburn can't be her natural colour. Kate was older, you were older, your greys were coming through. Even then. And now, you're all chatter, you never listen.

Listen.

When I tell you, the reason I can't hear everything you're saying.

It's the noise. The electricity. Abbott's electricity. And there's a master switch somewhere, a trip switch, I've heard him say, if you flick the trip switch it'll sort it, quite often, bring it all back. That's what Abbott does and comes back bounding, takes two stairs at a time, flicks the trip switch, two, four, master switcher. I never noticed, where he bounds from.

That hair, I should keep an eye, fucking thing, and who cares about the master, the switch, I'll turn them all off without it. I'll switch them all off, and nothing's radical unless it's seen, but anyway. People say mad, mad. That's what they say. And I liked the blue dress. I liked my knees, and now, now I know what I am. I'm gamine. That's what she said, Joan.

She stuck her head over the fence.

'You're gamine, that's what you are.'

The magnolia was hanging over her, its fleshy heads like mouths.

'It struck me, gamine, that's all, you know how things strike you sometimes?' she said.

She tapped her cigarette ash over our side of the fence and walked off. Strike and gamine. It wasn't like Joan to use words like that, the i, the eyes, the magnolia heads hanging heavy, her back door banged shut and all I've got to do is start. Start somewhere, flick one switch and the rest will follow. Get out of our bed. Get away from the hair. Take the stairs in twos, bound when I do.

Here, here. Soon I'll hear.

I'll switch them off. Switch everything off. On then off, on, off.

Abbott's study. The hub. All his precious buzzing things and now, think. Start with his laptop, hold my finger on the power button, keep my finger where it is and wait, yes, for its little light, its little light to disappear. His desktop too, why he needs two, but, here, the same, the little light, the sighing. His lamp, off at the wall and now I'm moving, now I'm getting the hang, and it's been a long time since. It's been a long time since I felt so alive, so effervescent, and where's his tablet, where are all his charging things, because if he can take *Leaves of Grass*, a log, if he can take stairs in two, four, six.

And now, downstairs. Off with the chattering TV at last, its eye, its sigh, listen, aah, and going down. The fridge, the freezer, the oven, the toaster. Their lights, their little electric selves, going down, going down. Now the phone, and yes, the phone, there's trickery in perception, there's trickery everywhere you listen and ears don't hear on their own, no, and dead magnolia heads fall. We heard them from our side of the fence, Charlie and I, and where did Joan go, where on earth? Knock down decibels, gain momentum, but. Momentum, inertia, resist change, both of us, so have a little rest and surprise yourself, save yourself, switch off. Off without the master, without the trick switch, turn off the cars, stop the bus from coming, stop Joan, her talking, the others too, Terry, U, the feet, the heads, stop the heads, the boat on the fjord, the waves, no, don't and still. Still, the song of myself.

Still the song of myself.

I couldn't have stumbled across a better homonym.

And now, sit in half lotus. Pull the blinds down. First. Then. Sit in half lotus.

She liked it both ways. She liked to fuck, she said that too. Her mouth opened and I was sure she was going to swallow me down, but. She laughed. I pinched my leg to check and I was still alive.

All this I swallow. I, swallow.

Ardha padmasana. Now. It opens the hips and calms the brain. She wasn't sure how. You weren't sure how and why did it matter?

Sit in half lotus and shut my eyes.

And where is she? Where are you? I've turned everything off. And of course. Of course you're not.

I've done the whole thing, one by one I've turned them off. Without the trick switch too, and you never showed up when you were supposed to. You didn't come, the house martins left three times and why didn't you marvel, why don't you marvel, why don't you sing their little bodies electric?

I'm going down now, look, look, my little light, my little life, going down, my head and legs coming together, meeting, and I'm perfectly folded. So. I'm a chip paper, a newspaper, a slip of a fish of a thing, and it's possible, it's perfectly possible to fall flat.

'What're you doing down there, Ash? The blinds are down. Ash?'

He's standing over me, they're standing over me, Abbott, Charlie and Nelson. Charlie in her school uniform, socks slack around her ankles and I'm down and I'm looking up and next to my head, Nelson's big head and. I'm used to it, now.

'Nelson was whining,' he says. 'We could hear him from the front step. Have you let him out? What are you doing down there?'

And what am I doing down here, Abbott wants to know, and I should be up, I can see in his face, I should be up, I shouldn't be down but I am down and why am I down, why are you down, that's what he wants to know.

'I'll let Nelson out,' he says. 'Come on, get up. Come and have a drink.'

I come through. We come through. Ten legs, more than eight, not thundering, only coming through, although Charlie should be talking, used to talk on, I used to tell her she talked on and she did, after school, she'd have a drink and something to eat and sit at the table and I'd have to say, Charlie, you're talking on, but.

'Tea?' Abbott says, holding up a mug. 'Two teas. Two teas and a glass of squash. Coming up.'

He adds water to the kettle. He says, 'Who's turned the kettle off at the wall?'

'Ash?' he says.

'Ash?'

'Ash?'

Ash. Which means why, not who, and he knows what he's saying. He knows.

'It was making a noise, a kind of buzzing,' I say.

'OK,' he says. 'Well. Maybe it's about to short circuit. You can't be too safe, but.'

He says he'll try it. The switch. He says we should stand back, Charlie, stand back, because he's going to turn the power on. And Charlie stands back and Abbott stands back. Stands back to the point where nothing but his fingertip could meet the switch, stands back and tightens his face and.

'Ready?' And we are.

'It seems all right,' he says. 'It seems all right now.'

He moves in. Flicks the switch off, on, off, on.

'Was it a buzzing or a crackling? I can't hear anything. Can you hear anything now? Ash? Charlie?'

And Charlie shakes her head, can't hear anything, and Abbott says, good, says, phew, as though. And reaches into the fridge for milk.

'Look,' he says. 'It's dark, the light's gone off,' he says.

And I'm thinking, tautology, yes, and he holds the door and gestures and yes, it's dark. Inside the fridge. The light's off.

'You might be right after all. About that crackling. And all that fresh food. The stuff Lynn brought over. What a waste,' he says.

He wonders how long the electricity's been off, he wants a time, I thought he was going to tap at his Second Core, but he hasn't. He wants to know. How long? And he's thinking about the potato gratin, thinking about losing his hands in her hair. And the way he asked, politely, the way he felt, urgently.

'What time was it? Ash?'

It was ever since. Ever since.

You followed me home, under the wind. There was no need to be scared. No need to hold me down. There wasn't anywhere for me to go. Listen though. I dreamt I was a feather. I dreamt I was a feather and at the same time, the wind. I didn't know whether I was free or trapped. I mean.

He says he could ask Joan.

'Pop round and ask whether they've had an outage too,' he says. And Charlie says yes and Nelson will come, because Joan likes Nelson and he hasn't been out, it looks like Ash hasn't taken him out, so we could, they could and then he says:

'Hang on.'

He points.

'You've turned it off at the wall. The fridge, look. Ash. The freezer, too.'

He says, 'Hang on.' He says, 'Hang bloody on.' And he looks around and he says, 'The dishwasher, the dryer, they're off, all of at the wall,' and he says, 'When did you do it? Ash?'

'Ash?'

And Nelson's gone back and Charlie's gone back and they can tell, Nelson can tell and Abbott opens the fridge door again as if to say. Then says:

'When?' he says. 'When, Ash?'

And Charlie's gone back and the fridge is black, the inside of the fridge and Charlie's gone back with her hands over her face and it's been a long time since she went on, since she sat at the table, or under the ash tree and I said. I said she went on and she was and now. Nobody's going on, nobody's talking, nobody dares. Abbott looks into the fridge and he doesn't say, but we can tell. He looks in and he pulls out. He pulls out a packet of chicken goujons, and he shakes it and he doesn't say, but we listen, until he stops shaking and pulls at the film lid, takes one, two, three tries and good things. Good things come in threes.

He holds one up. Dangles a goujon and doesn't say, but, dangles it, swings it and makes sure we're looking and where else could we look and he says:

'Use your eyes and fucking look at it.'

He says. He shouts. Then he crumples, yes, crumples onto the floor and curls up and holds his head in his hands and where's the goujon now because we're looking at Abbott and his hair and his hands in his hair which isn't smoothed down and I want him to, take his hand, I mean and tenderly, and.

Abbott put the food in the bin. I heard it fall. I heard him say, 'One, two, three things wasted, four, five, six things wasted.' Heard him in threes, and I guess he knows, and I thought about saying, thought about coming downstairs, standing in the kitchen and saying:

Omne trium perfectum.

He might've looked up, he might've said, he used to say, now where's that from? You've always got your nose stuck in a book. He might've smiled, he used to. He used to say, it couldn't be a bad thing absorbing everything you read and I would've. Said it again. Would've said, *omne trium perfectum*, and he might've tousled my hair, although he once said, suggested, I grow it out and would I ever? Would you ever like to look a bit more? And Kate said the same.

'Will you ever grow it?'

'I'd lose my strength,' I said. I'd be like Samson, but.

It was too late to go downstairs, to tell him, about good things, and I guess he knows. I guess he already knows.

I knew it was Kate, the breathing. It wasn't Abbott.

I watched his chest rise and fall and I counted. His sleeping breaths, his leaping breaths. I listened. I could hear he had a different way of keeping himself alive. She was deeper.

She was sleeping, somewhere close. I was sure his chest was rising and falling. Asynchronous, and, I thought perhaps, so.

I got out of bed. I walked down to the landing. The way I walked, Abbott wouldn't wake. I could already see Charlie's door was on-the-jar. I had to check it wasn't her. The breathing. I had to be responsible. I crawled in on my hands and knees, and I must've been quiet because Nelson was on the end of the bed and when I whispered he understood. He put his big head down. Went back to wherever dogs go. I had to check, to be sure. I had to press my ear to her chest, keep my head light and let it rise and fall. I had to check. I had to slip under her covers, put my arm around her, and she'd always slept lightly.

Charlie, Char-lea, Charlee.

She didn't cry that much when she was small. I can't remember her crying at all. I never thought she'd cry. I didn't think. I wanted to swim, to know whether the sky would swallow me up. If I let it. But it was calm out there. I wasn't expecting it to be calm, to be aroused. I wasn't thinking, just hoping. The cerulean sky. And Asle could've come back, if he'd wanted. He didn't have to go. Signe should've known there was no point. And when she felt for her breasts, at last. A relief, I thought. A relief.

They've laid orange cones along the inside lane of the dual carriageway.

Cones for miles, a line of cars, and dandelion seeds, escaping.

We're on our way to doing something about this, and Abbott likes to drive. It can't go on, he said. It mustn't. Enough is enough, because nobody can go on. Like this, the way we're going on. It has to stop. The way we're going on, yes. So. He's taking me to see someone. Dr Barns. He's putting an end to all this. Nonsense.

They're cutting the grass verges. I didn't say.

I didn't mention, because he's driving, that the dandelion seeds are falling like snow. Although.

I said instead:

'I don't like doctors.' Said: 'They read the wrong kind of books.' And Abbott said, 'Nonsense.' Although Papa knew. Said doctors were men in chairs, and you can't trust men in chairs. I didn't say. Thought Abbott would say 'nonsense' again, and shake his head. Instead, I said:

'Is this about the chicken goujons?'

'Not just the goujons,' he said, 'not just the bloody goujons.' And he wanted to know what had got into me. He wanted to know why the cat had given me back my tongue. All of a sudden.

'We are,' he said. 'Once and for all. Sorting this out.'

And now the traffic's backed up and we're crawling. The cones have been laid out and his Second Core is going round.

It's so good it'll never stop, it said so on the box, Abbott read it out, he read the whole thing. It'll never slow either, he said. and I can tell he wishes it would, wishes once and for all. And we're crawling, and dandelion seeds are blowing across the dual carriageway, falling, yes, like snow.

I say:

'The dandelion seeds are falling like snow.'

'Yes,' he says. 'Oh yes.'

Which can't mean nonsense, and sounds a bit like surprise.

And then he says, 'You'd better talk. When we get there.'

And yes, of course, Dr Barns will expect words, but snow and seeds are nothing like each other, and yet.

'Please stop the car,' I say.

Abbott looks straight ahead. He looks through the dandelion seeds, looks straight ahead, through the end of summer. The cars are backed up and we're not going anywhere, not quickly, although we can't stop. There's nowhere. To get off. They say. There's no way of getting off. You can't simply, all that easily, get off.

'Please,' I say. 'It's the thing about doctors. The thing about the books they read.'

'Come here,' Papa said. 'Come here and read me my last rites.'

I came over and read to him. All the right ones. Keats too. I read him Keats, but. Grey hair, black hair, black skin, grey, everything dies. Anyway.

Anyway. Perpetual motion is a myth.

'Please,' I say.

Dandelion seeds. Light like snow, like now, like no.

'Please,' I say.

'We need to do this,' he says. He looks ahead, keeps his hands on the wheel, crawls, perpetually, indefinitely, forwards.

And I'd better talk. Dr Barns will want words, that's what he'll want, so I'll give him haiku. Yes, haiku.

Barn's burnt down, I'll say. And it'll be a joke.

> *Barn's burnt down*
> *Now*
> *I can see the moon*

'Please,' I say.

And Abbott holds the wheel. He looks straight ahead, whilst we crawl.

'We could do something. Together?' I say. I look at him.

I say:

'What about going to the ash tree?'

I say:

'Remember when we almost carved our initials? Remember that winter, the fog?'

Orange cones for miles now. A gap in the clouds makes way for the sun. Dandelion seeds, lit up, moving across the dual carriageway, and falling.

'Please. Abbott.'

'It's been a long time since.'

I say:

'If you turn off. If you take the next left.'

I say:

'Trees. You know, trees.'

I'm getting ready to say: Their trunks get wider as they age. They have to get wide to support the tree as it grows and Charlie and I, the last time we tried, well, we couldn't get our arms around that ash, the old ash, ours, yours and mine, the one where we almost carved our initials. And what I'm trying to say is, we couldn't make them meet. Charlie and I couldn't get our fingertips to touch even though we stretched as far as we could, but if we tried, if you and I tried, I mean, to reach around her, we probably could.

I say it. And I wait. And I think of waiting. Of all the times I've waited.

'I could take you there,' I say.

And we're crawling. We're alongside the tractor with the yellow arm that reaches into the grasses. We're alongside the tractor and the man driving it, who isn't really a man, but a boy, although he's the size of a man, is as strong as a man, but isn't a man, until, and we can hear the tractor's engine, we can hear it turning over and we can hear the machine that cuts the grasses and at the end of the things we can hear. The grasses spitting, splitting.

The hogweed goes down, is slayed and September snow is escaping behind the light.

'Please,' I say. 'Turn left,' I say.

And he looks straight ahead and keeps his hands on the wheel and he sucks in air and looks straight ahead and we leave the man in the tractor with the long yellow arm behind and Abbott breathes out, adjusts his glasses, and pushes down on the indicator.

'There you go. There,' he says.

And I didn't think he'd cry, but. Now. Tears on his cheeks and coming down and it isn't the right time for indulging in words, in headwaters, headstreams, head starts and there might not be a way now to cut it off at its source, or say it's wrong or isn't wrong to name whatever falls from us.

And look behind. Look, at hogweed bodies, throats slit, slayed, laid, lying, indefinitely, yes, and at last I know, and we could, but we don't, we should've but we didn't. About turn. So behind is in front and in front is already. Look, in front. Orange cones and hogweed like sentries standing, the way they do before they're called up, and we haven't turned left, but soon, yes, if we keep moving, soon, the barn will burn and whatever falls, I said I'd catch whatever falls. I push my sleeve, into his cheek. So. It soaks up tears, gets heavier, gets darker and sticks to the inside of my wrist where underneath the skin small blue tracks travel, flow, run, like streams, like ghylls, around my body.

'Lynn.'

I say:

'Lynn would've brought a tissue.'

He pushes back against my sleeve and I push my arm back against him and one of us, either Abbott, or I, one of us has to be the first to move away.

We went to the ash tree.

Abbott held my hand as we walked, and when the footpath opened out into the meadow he put his arm around my waist. We walked through the long grasses towards the tree. I thought about Dr Barns. I thought about Charlie. I thought about the time we'd come here in winter. How the sky was dark, was down, the way it comes down in winter sometimes. I thought about how the grass had mostly disappeared to mud. How it would again. Before long.

He held a branch.

There were black buds rising from the ends. 'Black buds,' he said. I thought about how scared he looked then. How scared he looked now.

'But there's nothing to be scared of in September,' I said.

And yes, the sky was benign, bland almost.

'You're right,' he said.

He took one of the branches in his hand and held onto it for a while. Then he let go.

I said:

'Look out for geese, it isn't too early.'

And we looked, but there weren't any.

I said:

'Look out for swallows, it isn't too late.'

It wasn't too late.

The swallows were there, looping, writing overhead. September, I thought. Their last writes, that's what I thought but I didn't say, but thought about saying. I thought. The way I'd been talking on, the way I'd been, chatty, almost. I thought I might be able to say, might be able to explain. Rights, rites, writes, but where would I start and how could I be sure what Papa had meant because homophones turn on you. And what if a rose is a rose is a rose?

They didn't meet.

Our fingertips, I mean.

I said:

'You stand on this side.'

I said:

'Stretch. As far as you can.'

And I watched him stretch. I watched the way he pressed his chest against the trunk. To steady himself.

The clouds opened for a moment. Then shut.

They didn't meet, our fingertips, not quite.

So I picked up a small branch that must've snapped off in the wind. I waved it at him.

'Look,' I said, 'let's try again.'

And I watched him steady himself. Once more, I thought. Watch him once more, and then I stretched too, until I felt him on the other end of the branch. And I thought how high I'd been. That summer. How high we'd been, Abbott and I, which wasn't that high really. I thought. We hadn't ever been that high.

I said:

'We'll get a longer branch next time.'

I said:

'We can find a longer one each time we come.'

I didn't think he'd cry, but. The tears came back into his eyes and I thought how he must've been keeping them there, just behind the place where people can see and I thought it might be possible to keep tears in that place for a long time. Long enough to forget they were there. I wanted to think about that place and I didn't want to think another thought about streams or becks, although I could feel them running under the skin at my wrist and back towards my heart. I didn't want to think about runnels, or ghylls or rills or rhyme or rime even. I didn't want to think any more about words and the way they flip and turn and trick, so I said something. I had nothing to say but I said something anyway.

And when we went to bed he touched me.

He didn't come back for me this morning. I kissed him where his hair meets his forehead as he left for work. I waited. I thought he'd come back. I thought he'd be thinking about the ash tree, the way he touched me afterwards. You'd think he'd be thinking. You'd think he'd come back.

Last night when he touched me I held my breath. I held onto it, held it tightly, like it mattered.

'Ujjayi, oceanic breath,' Kate said.

She was sitting in padmasana.

'Listen carefully, Ash. It should sound like waves. Tell me if it does.'

I sat down next to her, pulled my knees up to my chin and listened to her oceanic breath. I listened to the rain on the window, to cars taking the crest of our hill. I listened to the swifts, to the crows, to openings and shuttings, to a ball kicked against a wall, a garage door perhaps. I listened to voices, children's, women's, to words surfacing here and there, finding their way up through the oceanic breath. I listened. I listened to her, I held my knees to my chin and listened. In and out, in and out, rain too, voices, birds, cars. I was listening, I was asking myself, what does this sound like? All of this together.

'It sounds like waves,' I said.

She smiled a little, not too much. Not enough to stop the ocean's swell.

I held onto my breath last night. It's the thing I've always done, so I don't know why I'm going over it now, the way I breathed in, kept hold of whatever it was in that air. He didn't come back for me this morning. I thought he would, and of course, his Second Core has been making its way around. It isn't going anywhere it hasn't been before, but now, it's one o'clock and they've gone, the house martins. The sky's fallow once and for all.

House martins that never leave are unheard of. I told them both that, Kate and Abbott. It was one of the things I told them both.

They always come back though, right? they said, although not at the same time.

It wasn't the point. Twelve million birds, far too many to disappear.

I keep coming back to it, last night. Last night when he touched me. I keep coming back to the way I held my breath.

'So many places, so many people, I can hardly remember them all. But I've never been with a girl,' Kate said. 'Not like this,' she said, and stretched her leg out under the table so it touched mine. 'You're so quiet you're like a boy. A boy, but tender.'

205

Like a steak, I thought, and I wanted to laugh. I couldn't laugh, could never laugh, because she was always looking. Thinking about it now, she was almost always inside me.

We went to her bed after that. The sheets smelt before we fucked. That's what she called it, fucking. It wasn't the right word. The sheets, they always smelt of bergamot, of something sweet I couldn't name. She touched me in so many places, I can remember them all. We fucked three times, although I wasn't counting, not until later.

I waited and he didn't come. I'd left my kiss where his hair meets his forehead. I held my breath and waited. At one o'clock I looked up into a fallow sky, although what was the point in looking up? What was the point in hanging out of the window like that and looking for birds that had already flown?

She told me to get back inside, stop leaning out, and at first I didn't think, just thought, there she is, Kate, telling me what to do again, telling me to come on in from the window. She was always telling me to do something. I used to say she was just like Charlie. You both talk on, the pair of you, both talk on and on, and by and large, there was a lot of talk that summer. Talk was almost all we had. But here she was, telling me to come on in, and yes, I came on in. I slid back in, I'd been hanging right out. I slid in and turned around expecting to see her standing in our bedroom, or at least I wasn't expecting not to see her and when she spoke again I looked around. And nothing.

He touched me.

Last night.

And I held my breath until he asked me to look which didn't take long it never does and when I did. Oh.

I looked at him.

Then Kate. Her too. Her jaw loose by my ear, so free, I had to pull back, jerk back. I wasn't expecting, although I wasn't surprised.

'What now?' Abbott said, although why he didn't look, I don't know.

'Look up.'

And over us larger than life. The weight of her, although I'd known. Known it'd happen before long, the way you know what'll happen before long.

The way you know. No.

Know. And do nothing to stop it.

I turned back. I looked in his eyes but they'd gone. I mean, he'd turned his head, but. She was there, her too, and I remembered how she smelt and I remembered it all, the way she'd always been, no, and I looked. Looked when he asked me to look and I touched him where he wanted when I couldn't find his eyes. I thought.

I thought I should. I thought.

'What is it with you?' he said.

I laid my head on his chest.

'Are you crying? What is it with you, Ash?'

'What is it with you?' she said.

My head was on her breast. I wanted to hold on, I mean, I didn't want to let go, I mean, I'd never wanted to let go. I probably shouldn't have.

'You like me, don't you?' she said. She turned on her side. One arm around me. One leg.

I almost fell asleep with my head on his chest. He didn't move, tried not to and the effort of him being. Still. The roll of his eyes through his chest. The roll down towards the crown of my head where my boy hair goes on sprouting, and then.

Towards my breasts, and only to ask. Were they rising and falling slowly enough? And I felt him hoping, asking, is she sleeping, sleeping, sleeping?

Kate slept. That summer. Always sleeping. Amatory sleep. Almost pernicious. I watched her, I listened, I dreamt up more adjectives but none that would do so I threw them away, was left with her sleeping. In her skin, warm. I was left with her sleeping.

'I dreamt of you,' she said. At the beginning. Around the time she put her hand in my granola pot. I searched for a word that meant only existing in dreams. There wasn't one. I wanted to stop searching for words, even at the beginning I did.

And now it's dark again. It comes around.
   These days he sleeps with his hands between his legs.
   'Do you like a bit of cock?' Kate said.
   She said she did. Liked to be fucked from behind, she said. She said you can't beat a big, fat cock filling you up from behind.

The little beck was running down our hill and when the worst of the rain had stopped I put on my wellies and went out. I took sticks, two sticks and walked to the top of our hill. I took one for Charlie. And anyway.
   The stream dried up. For a while, in its place, twigs, leaves, a trail of earth.

'Do you?' Kate said. She was asking whether I liked being fucked from behind.
   'Well? Ash?'

*

And now it's dark again and the wind's back. It runs up our hill, it groans, groans. Low places, and rattles loose. Almost anyone would think of launching themselves from the top of our hill on a night like tonight.

Almost everyone. Would think of stretching their arms out to hollow bones and skin-sprouting feathers, they'd forget they shouldn't, that nobody does, and they would, fledgling-test their wings and courage in the moment it takes to know they can then up with them and.

She asked if I wanted a small part of her. 'Yes,' I said. Yes. And here.

Where the little beck cut around my ankles. And now the wind. The wind's up. Right up. Taking my balance. But even balance, you can't own.

This wind.

Could carry a voice clean away and she wouldn't have the sense, never did have the sense to stand where I could hear her.

Upwind. Upwind.

Call now and I'll hear you, I'll get you. Hook my arm through yours the way you hooked your arm through mine on Cotters Hill that time, that summer. I'll say. You remember. I'll say.

I'd say.

The wind's OK. The wind's OK. It won't blow you away. We'd be safe in the rhyme of it and our arms would be linked like a chain ready for traction. Not upwind, you are. Moving away from me at forty knots, and carried off in the whip of it, the way your mum was carried off, but looking for you in the dark. The number of places a person like you could be.

This morning I watched a leaf fall the length of the skylight. This is how autumn comes, leaf by leaf.

I'm staying in bed until another one comes.

Kate. Kate was in with us, over us. I jerked back.

'What now?' Abbott said. She was straddling us, her thighs were pale, were mottled, like she'd said. Didn't stop her from bearing down on us. He didn't look up, he'd never looked up. Always. Saves himself from grief. Over and over he saved himself, didn't see, wouldn't look up into her sticky mouth.

'Lick me,' she said. 'Lick right here.'

I opened my mouth. I put out my tongue.

All this. I swallow. All this.

I'm not getting up, but waiting for the second leaf to fall, the next leaf. Every season creeps like this, until the day people say things like all of a sudden.

Everyone says it.

Kate crept down on us.

Didn't creep up. Couldn't be like everyone else.

Old age, this weight, look, they say. It creeps right up. Joan says. Every year at Christmas she says. Every year she looks surprised.

Kate crept down on us, in our bed I mean. She must have crept down, because all of a sudden, there it was, the wet mouth between her mottled thighs. Wasn't clear, no, viscous, too thick to be anything else. Abbott didn't look up. Instead, fumbled. Found himself, he wasn't sleeping, he wasn't looking up, lying with his hand stuck, all three of us stuck.

Did the first leaf fall? Of course, it fell the length of the skylight, I watched it, I saw it fall, I saw it making its way, feather-like leaf like all things light. It'll be on the pavement right now, lying five-fingered, waiting for someone to notice, but you're not supposed to notice creeping.

Can you call me? A.

Ash, give me a call. A.

He doesn't come. Although I waited.

I had a nagging doubt about that leaf. I wasn't sure, but going back over it I know it fell the length of the skylight. I was sitting up in bed and saw it fall towards the pavement. Saw it fall like all things old and light. Fall eventually. Wind or no wind.

'This is Abbott's phone. Please leave a message.'

Please leave.

Leave, leaves, leaf.

Grieve, grieves, grief.

Leaving, grieving, left, grieved, greft. Grieved hangs on far too long, don't you agree? Aggrieved. They won't stop coming once they've started, words, leaves, all of a sudden, all of a.

Please grieve.

Please leave a message.

I won't. Won't leave words anywhere these days. I spat them out over the bridge and into the beck that ran through Nott's Wood. So many times. I spat them when Papa spat. He thumped his palm between my shoulder blades so I could hoik them out. Far too many, coming, spewing, felt better once they were out, got used to it, losing things. Papa said, we'll get used to it, but. Spit and words are like birds.

They keep coming up, coming back.

And Abbott wants them. I won't leave them.

I won't leave words. Turn the phone over. Turn it off.

Call me, she'd say, and I didn't. Didn't like to think of her phone vibrating in her bag whilst she was breathing ujjayi. Whilst she was with the ocean's swell. Couldn't bear to think of it.

'I won't call,' I said.

'Don't you like me then?' she said.

'You like me, don't you?' you said. You turned on your side, so you were facing away. I mention this because I knew.

When you woke the only thing that had changed was the hour.

It couldn't end.

It couldn't end.

It couldn't. Tender like a girl, tender like a boy, and quiet.

All along I'd been all the things you'd said, and still.

You took a breath, a foreboding breath, but your hair was falling around your face, the way it usually fell.

And once I saw your hair, I thought I must have been wrong about the breath, about how a breath could be foreboding, I thought you'd tuck it behind your ears the way you usually tucked it, and things would go on, things would go back. You didn't tuck it, but left it, grazing your cheek, left it so it moved against your jaw every time your mouth opened. You started to explain, that's what you said, you were explaining, and you weren't being anything like you usually were, you were talking, explaining and your hair was grazing your cheek and all your words, strung together the way Joan's words are strung together, and you were talking although you were nothing like you'd ever been and it was hard to understand when the words were coming and you were looking at me, and when you finished, when you'd finally finished, you took another breath. Looked lighter. Looked at me, perhaps to the side. That's where you were looking, but still, there was something in your face, something I hadn't seen before.

Relief, perhaps.

'I'm sorry,' you said. 'Does that make sense?'

I should get out to that leaf.

The second one might have fallen by now.

Something happened at dinner this evening. Charlie, Nelson lying on her feet, put her fork down and looked at me.

Said. 'Ash, if you go to the baths tonight, you might be lucky, you might see the geese flying in.'

She picked up her fork again, bent down, rubbed Nelson's head.

I'd been thinking so much about you. About that breath, the foreboding breath, about your face, the expression on your face, I hadn't thought. Needed Charlie to say, the geese. Ash. Soon the geese will be flying in.

I went under.

I couldn't hear you. I couldn't see anything but the bubbles I was breathing and the shapes the rain made on the surface of the water. I wanted you to have them, the shapes, but you wouldn't come in. Said water wasn't your thing. Didn't like the way your thighs looked. They're mottled, you said, and afterwards you said you'd seen black. Black, right up against the surface, you said.

I went under, blew bubbles. Perhaps you thought I was drowning, perhaps you thought I would never come up.

But.

It's hardly possible to drown here at the baths, hardly possible with these lifeguards, always two of them, one on the tall chair, the other one circuiting. One sits, the other circles, it's always the same type of going round.

Once, I heard one of the circling ones say that you can't be too blasé.

He passed under the tall chair. Said. If it's never happened here it can still happen.

I was in shorts, only in shorts. I stood on the rock, gripping it with my bare feet. I waved to you, brushed the silt at my shins. I wasn't thinking of the boys. The ones Charlie thought she heard. I wasn't thinking.

'Come on in,' I said from out on the rock.

The rain was coming down, but I stood there shouting. You wouldn't come, so I climbed down, stood down in the water. It was deep, it was all the rain, it was so deep it licked up around my neck.

'Kate,' I said, then I went under.

I anchored myself. I stayed under as long as I could, and what were you thinking over there on the bank, watching my bubbles rise up through the black.

'Tell me what you're doing?' you said when I came up.

I laughed. I loved it.

I loved the look on your face, the look of concern, the way you had to ask, couldn't not. I went under again. I went right down, held on, waited.

I'll tell Charlie. The new lifeguard's a girl, that's what I'll say. All those boys, all this time, and now, a girl, a circling girl.

'Do you want something between your legs, Ash? A cock or something?' That's what you said, although I don't know when.

Now look, the girl, the new lifeguard, she's coming over, walking over, walking towards the shallow end.

'Hey, hey,' she says, the girl says.

She's got a streak of red in her hair to match her shorts.

'Hey,' she says, and crouches down, her legs open, my head, my face, my goggles, right there, and what does she want with her legs open like that? You only had to look at someone to know what they wanted. You said.

'Hey,' she says. 'You. Shutting in five minutes. OK?'

'Come on in,' I said, whatever was I thinking? I was asking the same thing over and over, shouting out to you again and again.

Another length or two. Five minutes until my time's run out. The underwater pull is the most powerful part of the stroke.

I've always had it short, yes. My mama would've approved. Cutting off my locks, my locks.

I gripped the rock with my bare feet. There was slime on my shins too.

'Come on in,' I said. I think that's all I wanted. None of it mattered, you know. The black, your thighs, or whatever it was that stopped you. I wanted to know why you couldn't lose yourself with me.

I didn't want anything between my legs. Although what did I say when you asked? I wasn't a boy either, you knew that already. I'd been in, been under and when I came out, after I'd dragged myself up the bank you pulled down my shorts. You took me by surprise, you strode up to me and pulled them down, right down around my ankles, then stepped back. I'd only just got out. You took me by surprise, acting like that, but there I was in front of you, shoulders slack, hair dripping, those shorts around my ankles. That's how I was, and you were fully dressed, the lace on the ends of your sleeves damp and stretched. Your summer hat, your bag. Mascara and disappointment around your eyes. All these things. You knew I wasn't a boy, it wasn't the point, it never had been.

And then what? The sun came out for the first time.

You looked up. The skin on your neck was too loose, as if you'd spent your whole life looking, following the sun from east to west, and never stopping.

'Come on in,' I said again. I had to say something. I was naked, the sun was all over me, calling me out. A girl, yes, although what did we expect, there on the bank that runs down into the lake. We shouldn't have been there. We shouldn't ever have come, but there we were and what was I supposed to think when you pulled off your top and threw it down, and all that lace, that prettiness, was lying in the mud. I mean, you were always so.

'It might not be clean,' I said. Later you said you thought I'd been joking.

You thought, at last, I'd got it.

Why doesn't he sleep? He always sleeps. He turns on his side. He lets out breaths that sound almost like Ujjayi, but aren't. He doesn't know what the Ujjayi breath is. He turns. He breathes, in and out, in, without the sound of the ocean. That's the point of it, the ocean, the swell, that's the point. You said I should try if I wanted to feel calmer. I didn't try. I couldn't. I liked listening to you, I liked the way the world came together.

Now. Abbott can't sleep, he turns on his side, he turns on his back, and it's almost like Ujjayi, the way he breathes, although he doesn't sound like waves, not really. He doesn't sound like waves and neither did you, although I must have said you did.

I'll tell you now, I got used to you.

You were standing on the bank when I went under. Black was coming up from the bottom, you told me later you'd seen it right up against the surface. You wouldn't come in. Come on in, I'd said from the rock, but you wouldn't come, and did you know that ash branches always point towards the sky?

He's lying on his back. Not struggling now, not turning. Nobody ever mistook turn for tern. You didn't ask about my collection, you brushed me off, you were blasé, said everybody collects something. My pebbles, see, you said, and pointed to a pair of wicker baskets on your bedroom windowsill. You promised me you loved beaches, although I never saw you swim.

He's sleeping. Everyone sleeps in the end.

I've never seen him creep. Joan saw me the other day. She hid behind the curtains so she could watch me make my way around the walls of the living room. She hasn't come out yet. Can you believe someone would hide for so long? But she's always been tenacious, that woman. That's what he says, Abbott, although I don't know why. Tenacious old bat, he calls her.

You'd been creeping too, the night before, you came creeping down. And Joan. She saw. Seesaw between my legs, that's what I want. You asked. You knew all along the thing about being a boy was a game. You were on one end, I was on the other, up and down we went and I was the one who ended up creeping. The house martins had gone by one o'clock and the sky was cerulean. It was so clean, you know the way things are when something's missing.

You went down. That's what you called it. Going down, you said. She saw. The next day she leant over the fence. The magnolia was hanging over her, its fleshy heads like mouths. Gamine, she said, and it was a good word. She saw. The magnolia heads fell, their fat heads gorged on daylight. We heard the soft flesh of them hit the ground from our side of the fence. Charlie and I.

You went down and I came. That's what you said. You came, you said. Vulnerable can have three syllables or four, depending on who's saying it.

I could come outside if that's what you want, if that's what you're asking. Yes, now he's sleeping. I could leave him. But you didn't want that, you said at the beginning you didn't want that. You flicked the hair away from your face and said we shouldn't go doing anything stupid like leaving.

I'll come. If you want. If you're asking. Tell me first, if you saw me on the log. I climbed right up onto it and waved, and there you were, your mouth open. Your huge mouth. What do you think to that?

To leaf, a verb too.

To grief, Papa wrote. Did I tell you all this after I came? I meant to. No, you wanted to know what I liked about you. You looked so pleased with yourself, you wanted to know. Tell me, you said, you were asking for adjectives, pressing me for them. That's what they were, those magnolia heads, turgid.

You said I should come out. It isn't the same as come, you said. You hooked your hair around your ear and looked at me as if I'd never considered how a preposition transforms a verb.

And now what? I'll come if you want. I almost always did what you wanted.

I'll come. There isn't any point in lying here with you going on. Tell me first if you saw me creeping. Kate? Kate?

No, you never did what I asked. You never seemed to hear that well.

I'll come. Although I'm tired, and it isn't as warm as it was, but you must know that already, wherever you hide yourself. I guess you saw me creeping. Yes, you probably caught me creeping although now all I want is to curl up. Strange how things come around, with curling up I mean. I'm talking about Charlie, the way she was curled up those first days. She uncurled so slowly we didn't notice it happening, we only noticed she had. All of a sudden. She'd uncurled, she'd uncurled and become Charlie. I called for Abbott. Look, look, I said. I can't think why I was so surprised.

It's cold, yes, but before I come out. Please, whilst I've got you here, I want to tell you.

It was hot, so hot. Charlie had been crying and I didn't know, didn't really think. But let's go back, yes, I'd been swimming out, I'd swum quite far out. I turned and came back as soon as I heard her, started swimming back towards the bank. I swam until my feet touched the bottom and then I waded. I was a long time wading, pushing the water back with my thighs. I could tell by then she was crying, yes, and I was trying to get back, I was wading through the water. I didn't know. I didn't think. Not before we lay down. Yes, we lay down and Nelson was sleeping, I could tell he was, I looked over and his big head hadn't moved.

We lay down and I opened her legs. Kate. That's what I did. And afterwards.

We walked home and the sky was cerulean. It wasn't like me to think in adjectives but that was all I could think. There must've been swifts. I don't remember. I wanted to curl up, but it was hot, so hot.

What do you think to that? Tell me what you think.

'Choose how you feel,' you said.

Tired. I'm telling you now. And cold. Am I allowed to have two?

You said I should come out, and I'm coming. What does coming mean, or can't you speak? You were always ready to tell me. Always wanted to explain.

I'm coming. Out of bed, down to the landing and towards Charlie's room, although I feel like curling up.

Before you swallowed me I meant to tell you things. I meant to tell you about Papa. He'd put the sky in my heart. It was hard for me. I wanted to tell you all that.

'Try this,' you said. 'It's all about downward-flowing energy. I'll show you.'

You squatted. There was no other word for it. You let your feet bury themselves into the carpet.

'Like this,' you said and settled yourself, settled yourself like a mother hen. I reached out, touched you gently, almost tenderly. You looked so grounded, so comfortable, squatting there on the carpet, I almost forgot about the sky. That's why I came up behind you. That's why I put my arms around your waist. I wanted to try.

'You try,' you said, and now I wanted to.

I had to spread my legs, I had to press my body into your back, that's what I had to do if I wanted to get myself around you, and when I did, I mean, when my breasts and body were up against you and you were firmly rooted it happened. All at once, all of a sudden, you'd probably say, yes, our halves came together, they connected. That's what you would've said, they connected, our two halves, and after they did, they weren't halves, no, they couldn't have been halves, but were something bigger. We were big, yes, so big your roots had to dig deeper to hold us.

'Did you feel that?' you said. 'Ash?' you said.

I couldn't say, I wanted to open my mouth, but I was growing roots too, and fast. We needed something, we both knew we needed something, now our halves were one, we needed something more substantial. Black then, just under the surface. We both went in, both blind. I know because you said you couldn't see, and I couldn't see either. I didn't say. Instead, I felt my way into the space between your legs. I knew you by then, but still, I had to press my body, my breasts, yes, right up against your back so I could balance. You swayed as I moved in, I left my hand, left it where it was, and you swayed a bit, got unsteady, said you couldn't see, that's what you said. 'Ash,' you said. 'Ash', and there was something in your voice. Later I thought it might have been panic, the thing in your voice, but what could I do, where could we go. We'd gone too far, we couldn't have taken a single step back towards where we'd come from. Although we knew. We knew about the dangers of coming undone, or was it unravelled, but we weren't unravelling, we were putting down roots, strong roots, we didn't need to worry, so I stayed, stayed where I was with my body and breasts up against your back, with my hand in your space, I stayed until we came.

We came, and we could've kept on coming like that, kept going without saying a thing, but the black had been rising, had risen so high it was pushing up against our surface, and one of us was about to speak, and I don't think it was me, no, although it's difficult to be sure, but one of us said, one of us definitely said, I love you.

I came out, that's what you wanted. I got out of bed, although I felt like curling up.

I got out of bed and walked down to the landing. That's what you wanted, that's what you said.

Charlie's door was on-the-jar, I couldn't see, but could hear her feather-breaths. I crawled in, crawled into the darkness, crawled across the floor, and I must've been quiet because Big Head stayed sleeping. Didn't stir, stayed where it was and I went right up and told him, Nelson, this time, no. And it must have been the first time anyone had told him no, but he understood. Big Head.

I watched Charlie for a moment, all I wanted was to take a moment, although what were you saying, why couldn't you shut up, shut your huge mouth up. I watched her, one moment, two, and before the third I felt under the covers for her arm. Charlie always slept lightly, it wasn't long before she came round, came to, was sitting up and I kept hold of her arm, I pulled on it a bit, said, 'Quietly now, quietly come', and Big Head stayed where it was and Charlie came, walked with me to the door and didn't say. Instead, came with me all the way downstairs and stood in the hallway whilst I got the key.

'It's cold. A bit cold,' I said, and there wasn't much light and the key was rattling in the front door. I was cold, I'd been cold for a while, and Charlie didn't say, just looked like she wanted to curl up, that was all. She didn't look like anything else, didn't even look tired, and all you were saying was come on, come out, that's what you were saying, your huge mouth, opening and shutting and all we wanted was to curl up.

I couldn't get the door open, there wasn't much light, and the key was rattling. Rattling way too much. Charlie was standing and I was bent over, trying not to rattle the key and wondering why, with all this rattling, Abbott hadn't come down.

I got it open, took hold of Charlie's arm, said, 'Come on, move on.' We were getting cold and we needed to move, but we weren't moving. We were standing outside our house, standing on our hill, and what were we supposed to do, out there in the dark with Charlie in her pyjamas. I could tell she was still warm, I could feel the heat coming off her the way you can, although it didn't last long. It wasn't long before she was as cold as I was, and where were you, where had you gone, now, all of a sudden? It was dark out there and too cold to be standing, just standing without moving, and Charlie, Charlie had gone quiet. Gone too quiet. I wanted to curl up, but I knew where you'd be, knew you'd be down there if you weren't here, down at the lake, that's where you'd be and it wouldn't take long, wouldn't take too long if we ran, and anyway, it was too cold to be standing, just standing there, waiting, and I'd spent enough time, waiting. I'd already spent all that time.

I held Charlie's hand. I held it all the way down our hill. I wanted to get moving but Charlie was cold, and what was I supposed to do. I pulled her along a bit, got her trotting along, but she'd gone quiet, gone a bit quiet, didn't say a thing, all the way down the hill. Got her trotting though, down the hill, pulled her a bit, enough to start her off trotting and she didn't say, it was me who did. Said, 'Don't you fancy a swim? A night-time adventure?' I know how to dress it up, but it was cold, and Charlie hadn't said, and she wasn't really moving.

I'd got her trotting, but she looked like she wanted to curl up, that's how she'd looked earlier, standing there in the hallway, so I decided not to look again, made the decision to keep my eyes straight ahead and pull her along.

And she didn't mind, didn't seem to mind being pulled a bit. Didn't mind until we got to the fence at the end of the crescent. She didn't want to go any further, but didn't say. Stood in front of the gap in the fence and didn't say, just went on standing. It was me who said, said, 'Come on, come through.' But she didn't come, didn't want to duck down the way you have to, and what was I supposed to do, we couldn't hang around there in the crescent, it was too cold to be hanging around, but Charlie wasn't moving, was standing in front of the gap in the fence and wouldn't come through. We couldn't stay there, couldn't stand there, so I got her head. I took the back of her head in the palm of my hand and pushed it down, and I didn't let go until the pair of us were on the other side of the fence, and I've got to say I felt a bit stunned, felt a bit out of sorts when I looked towards the lake, looked down at the alder trees. The alder trees, the way their branches were hanging like spectres, over the water.

'Not now,' I said. 'Not now.'

I had to say it out loud if I wanted to stop. I said it. The sound of my voice rang out into the darkness, and that's when I heard you. That's when I knew you were out there on the rock, although we couldn't see the rock. We were still up by the fence that backs onto the crescent. We hadn't come down, hadn't made our way through the scrub, but we heard you laugh and we knew. Knew you were out there, standing out there on the rock.

We should come down, Charlie and I. Come down through the scrub, to the bank. That's what we should do, but those alder trees, their branches. Although I suppose we're a bit out of sorts, standing up here by the fence. It wasn't like me to get hold of Charlie's head but what was I supposed to do. We couldn't stay there, stand there at the end of the crescent, not in the dark, the cold.

And now you, on the rock. I know it's you, calling.

I've got to keep Charlie moving, I've got to pull on her arm a bit to get her to move. She's better once she's going, yes, she seems a bit better once she's moving. We're coming now, down through the scrub, we know it's you, yes, and you'll have to wait, wait out there on the rock, whilst we come down, whilst we make our way through the scrub to the bank. And those alder trees, don't you think, I mean, don't you think. Although we know they aren't, we know they couldn't be, but it's dark, it's almost too dark to see, even down here on the bank now, yes, it's still too dark, but we know it's you on the rock, calling to us. We know it's you. You want us to come out, to swim out. It's calm, you say, we should swim out, yes, there's a little light, enough light, what with the moon, the half-moon behind the clouds, enough light to be able to swim, you say. You say these things from the rock, we're sure it's you, yes, who else would be out there in the dark, calling out to us.

But listen.

We feel like curling up. It's cold, Charlie's getting cold. We want to curl up, although the alders. Look in the water, the alder trees reflected like that in the water, and we shouldn't curl up, not yet, not if there's a little light, if there's enough light to swim, enough light to see across the water, to the far shore even. Yes, we can see across the water and it's calm, although we can't see the rock, can't see if it's you on the rock, although we know it must be. Calling like that. And the water is calm, although we don't say, and Charlie hasn't said, but holds my hand, although she must have seen that it's calm enough to swim. Calmer than the baths, although it's cold. Cold enough to curl up, and we both feel like curling up, although Charlie's gone quiet and hasn't said, and neither have I. So many things I haven't said, but words and birds are like spit, yes, they keep coming up, coming back. You too, came back in the end, didn't you? Couldn't keep your mouth away, although where are you now? We can't see you. It's black out there by the rock, and we can't see, and now, Charlie's feeling it, the cold, she needs to keep moving, but where can we go from here, from the bank, all we can do is swim, that's all we can do if we want to keep moving forward, but Charlie's cold and I didn't bring a jumper. I'd give her mine if I had one, I'd say, here, Charlie, put this on and when we get back, that's what I'd say, but I didn't bring a jumper.

The water might not be that cold, no, the earth cools more quickly than the water in autumn. Yes, it might be warmer in there than we think. It's dark for swimming, although we can see the other side, can see the Toll Estate and we're not going to think about those boys now, the ones who Charlie thought she heard when we were swimming out. We're not going to think about them now. Not here in the dark. Not if we swim, not if we're too far out to get back quickly. It might be warmer in there. And it's light enough, it's calm enough, that's what you said, but we can't see you, haven't seen you, even though we can see the far shore, even though we can see that not everyone in the Toll Estate is sleeping, no, we're not the only ones awake. Charlie, look at the lights over there in the Toll Estate, but Charlie's gone quiet, looks a bit cold, she might be better in the water, she might be a bit warmer, although we feel like curling up, it's calm enough. Calm enough to sail a paper boat, although we never have, not paper. Alder leaves. Yes, that's what we used. Made up little boats with twigs, and they'd be strong enough if the water was calm, as calm as it is now, they wouldn't be pushed and pulled, our little boats, wouldn't sink, wouldn't drown, like that boy, the little boy who drowned in the fjord. But there's no point in thinking about him now, not now it's dark and you're on the rock, calling us to come in, to swim out. No point in thinking about words in a small paperback. It's no big deal really. And it might be better in the water, once we get swimming, might be a bit warmer, takes a large body of water a long time to cool. Weeks longer, Papa said. If we take off our shoes at least, yes, take them off and test the temperature. Here, Charlie. It isn't that bad. It might be warmer once we're in, once we're properly in. And it isn't the kind of night for standing around, no. I'd give you my jumper, I'd say, here, put your arms up, pop your arms up in the air and I'll pull it on. It'll be a bit big, but. That's what I'd say. Still, now we're here, now we're standing on the bank, we might as well swim. You can see right over to the other side, look, Charlie. The Toll Estate, over the other side. And when we get home.

Yes, we know it's you, out there on the rock, although we can't see. Fifteen strokes, that's all. Done it so many times, we know where to come up. We're coming. Coming in, coming out. Charlie's cold, so we're coming in. I've got her arm, got to pull on her arm a bit to get her moving, and it isn't that bad, not that bad, is it, Charlie? Could be worse. Nothing like summer. Nothing like the day I swam right out. The water was soothing, that was the word, I turned on my back under the sky, I was under the sky and the water was warm, was nothing like tonight. I was on my back, my arms spread out, my breasts under the yellow-brown sun water. And after. Nobody came. Nobody ever comes.

Come on, come on in, Charlie. I'll keep hold of you until the bottom falls away, until we feel the bottom falling away from under our feet. And it won't be long, not now, gets deeper quickly, you have to learn to expect it, don't you, Charlie. That's the trick, so many tricks. Papa knew a few, and you'd think it'd be worse. You'd think it'd be colder, but it takes a large body of water a long time to cool. We're coming in, yes, wading in, and Charlie's gone quiet. Always used to go on. On and on. Always been a slip of a fish. Haven't you, Charlie.

Charlie, Charlee, light of my life. Always in my mind's eye, half-submerged, sliding away, an arm, a leg, a torso, a head, appearing then disappearing.

Dear readers,

As well as relying on bookshop sales, And Other Stories relies on sub-
scriptions from people like you for many of our books, whose stories
other publishers often consider too risky to take on.

Our subscribers don't just make the books physically happen. They
also help us approach booksellers, because we can demonstrate that
our books already have readers and fans. And they give us the security
to publish in line with our values, which are collaborative, imaginative
and 'shamelessly literary'.

All of our subscribers:

- receive a first-edition copy of each of the books they subscribe to
- are thanked by name at the end of our subscriber-supported books
- receive little extras from us by way of thank you, for example:
  postcards created by our authors

BECOME A SUBSCRIBER, OR GIVE A SUBSCRIPTION
TO A FRIEND

Visit andotherstories.org/subscriptions to help make our books happen.
You can subscribe to books we're in the process of making. To purchase
books we have already published, we urge you to support your local or
favourite bookshop and order directly from them – the often unsung
heroes of publishing.

OTHER WAYS TO GET INVOLVED

If you'd like to know about upcoming events and reading groups (our
foreign-language reading groups help us choose books to publish, for
example) you can:

- join our mailing list at: andotherstories.org
- follow us on Twitter: @andothertweets
- join us on Facebook: facebook.com/AndOtherStoriesBooks
- admire our books on Instagram: @andotherpics
- follow our blog: andotherstories.org/ampersand

This book was made possible thanks to the support of:

Aaron McEnery · Aaron Peck · Aaron Schneider · Adam Bowman · Adam Butler · Adam Lenson · Adriana Diaz Enciso · Agata Rucinska · Aileen-Elizabeth Taylor · Ailsa Peate · Aisling Reina · Ajay Sharma · Alan Donnelly · Alan Reid · Alan Simpson · Alana Marquis-Farncombe · Alastair Gillespie · Alex Hancock · Alex Ramsey · Alex Robertson · Alexandra Stewart · Alexia Richardson · Ali Casey · Ali Smith · Alice Clarke · Alice Toulmin · Alicia Bishop · Alison Riley · Alison Winston · Alistair McNeil · Alyse Ceirante · Alyssa Tauber · Amado Floresca · Amanda · Amanda Astley · Amanda Silvester · Amber Da · Amelia Dowe · Amy Bojang · Amy Rushton · Amy Slack · Ana Savitzky · Anastasia Carver · Andra Dusu · Andrea Reece · Andrew Kerr-Jarrett · Andrew Lees · Andrew Marston · Andrew McCallum · Andrew Rego · Angus Walker · Ann Moore · Ann Sheasby · Anna Badkhen · Anna Glendenning · Anna Milsom · Anna Pigott · Anne Carus · Anne Goldsmith · Anne Guest · Anne Kangley · Anneliese O'Malley · Anonymous · Anonymous · Anonymous · Anonymous · Anthony Quinn · Antonia Lloyd-Jones · Antonio de Swift · Antony Pearce · Aoife Boyd · Archie Davies · Asako Serizawa · Asher Norris · Audrey Mash · Avril Marren ·

Barbara Black · Barbara Mellor · Barbara Wheatley · Barry John Fletcher · Ben Schofield · Ben Thornton · Benedict Durrant · Benjamin Judge · Beth Sarmiento · Beverly Jackson · Bianca Jackson · Bianca Winter · Briallen Hopper · Brian Anderson · Brian Byrne · Bridget McGeechan · Bridget Starling · Brigita Ptackova · Caitlin Halpern · Caitlin Liebenberg · Caitriona Lally · Cam Scott · Carlos Gonzalez · Carol Christie · Carol Mavor · Carolina Pineiro · Caroline Bennett · Caroline Haufe · Caroline Mager · Caroline Picard · Caroline Waight · Caroline West · Carolyn Johnson · Cassidy Hughes · Catherine Barton · Catherine Lambert · Catherine Rodden · Catherine Rose · Cathy Czauderna · Catie Kosinski · Catriona Gibbs · Cecilia Rossi · Cecilia Uribe · Cecily Maude · Chantal Wright · Charles Fernyhough · Charles Raby · Charles Dee Mitchell · Charlotte Briggs · Charlotte Holtam · Charlotte Middleton · Charlotte Murrie & Stephen Charles · Charlotte Whittle · China Miéville · Chris Gostick · Chris Gribble · Chris Lintott · Chris Maguire · Chris McCann · Chris Nielsen · Chris Stevenson · Chris Young · Chris & Kathleen Repper-Day · Christina Moutsou · Christine Dyer · Christine Elliott · Christine Hudnall · Christine Lewis · Christine Luker ·

Christopher Allen · Christopher Stout · Ciara Ní Riain · Claire Adams · Claire Adams · Claire Brooksby · Claire Malcolm · Claire Tristram · Claire Williams · Claire Wood · Clare Archibald · Clare Young · Clari Marrow · Clarice Borges · Claudia Hoare · Claudia Nannini · Claudio Scotti · Cliona Quigley · Clive Bellingham · Cody Copeland · Colin Denyer · Colin Matthews · Corey Nelson · Courtney Lilly · Craig Barney · Csilla Toldy · Cyrus Massoudi · Dag Bennett · Dan Raphael · Dana Behrman · Daniel Arnold · Daniel Coxon · Daniel Gillespie · Daniel Hahn · Daniel Manning · Daniel Reid · Daniel Sparling · Daniel Sweeney · Daniela Steierberg · Darina Brejtrova · Darius Cuplinskas · Darren Davies · Dave Lander · Davi Rocha · David Anderson · David Cundall · David Hebblethwaite · David Higgins · David Irvine · David Johnson-Davies · David Mantero · David Miller · David Shriver · David Smith · David Steege · David Travis · David F Long · Davis MacMillan · Dean Taucher · Debbie Pinfold · Declan Gardner · Declan O'Driscoll · Deirdre Nic Mhathuna · Denis Larose · Denis Stillewagt & Anca Fronescu · Diana Ball · Diana Digges · Diana Powell · Diana Fox Carney · Dominick Santa Cattarina · Donald Wilson · Dr. Paul Scott ·

Duncan Clubb · Duncan Marks · Eamon Flack · Ed Burness · Ed Tronick · Edward Rathke · Edward Thornton · Ekaterina Beliakova · Elaine Kennedy · Elaine Rassaby · Eleanor Dawson · Eleanor Maier · Elhum Shakerifar · Elie Howe · Elina Zicmane · Elisabeth Cook · Elisabeth Pike · Eliza Apperly · Eliza O'Toole · Elizabeth Draper · Elizabeth Soydas · Ellen Coopersmith · Ellen Wilkinson · Elliot Marcus · Elvira Kreston-Brody · Emily Armitage · Emily Bromfield · Emily Taylor · Emily Yaewon Lee & Gregory Limpens · Emma Barraclough · Emma Bielecki · Emma Page · Emma Parker · Emma Perry · Emma Pope · Emma Strong · Emma Timpany · Emma Louise Grove · Enrico Cioni · Erin Cameron Allen · Ewan Tant · F Gary Knapp · Fabienne Berionni · Fatima Kried · Filiz Emre-Cooke · Finbarr Farragher · Fiona Liddle · Fiona Mozley · Florence Reynolds · Florian Duijsens · Fran Sanderson · Frances de Pontes Peebles · Francesca Brooks · Francis Mathias · Frank van Orsouw · Freda Donoghue · Friederike Knabe · Gabriel Vogt · Gabriela Lucia Garza de Linde · Gabrielle Crockatt · Garan Holcombe · Gary Gorton · Gavin Smith · Gawain Espley · Gaynor Clark · Genaro Palomo Jr · Genia Ogrenchuk · Geoff Thrower · Geoffrey Cohen · Geoffrey Urland · George Christie · George Stanbury · George

Wilkinson · German Cortez-Hernandez · Gill Adey · Gill Boag-Munroe · Gillian Ackroyd · Gillian Grant · Gillian Spencer · Gordon Cameron · Graham Fulcher · Graham R Foster · Grant Rintoul · Greg Bowman · Gregory Ford · Guy Haslam · Hadil Balzan · Hamish Russell · Hank Pryor · Hannah Dougherty · Hannah Harford-Wright · Hannah Lynn · Hans Krensler · Hans Lazda · Hayley Newman · Helen Brady · Helen Conford · Helen Coombes · Helen Gough · Helen Waland · Helen Wormald · Henrike Laehnemann · Henry Patino · Howard Robinson · Hugh Gilmore · Hyoung-Won Park · Ian Barnett · Ian Buchan · Ian McMillan · Ian Mond · Íde Corley · Ieva Panavaite & Mariusz Hubski · Ifer Moore · Ines Fernandes · Ingrid Olsen · Irene Mansfield · Irina Tzanova · Isabel Adey · Isabella Garment · Isabella Weibrecht · Ivona Wolff · J Collins · Jacinta Perez Gavilan Torres · Jack Brown · Jack Fisher · Jacqueline Lademann · Jacqueline Ting Lin · Jadie Lee · James Beck · James Crossley · James Cubbon · James Kinsley · James Lehmann · James Lesniak · James Mewis · James Portlock · James Purdon · James Scudamore · James Tierney · Jamie Cox · Jamie Mollart · Jamie Walsh · Jane Chase · Jane Leuchter · Jane Rawson · Jane Roberts · Jane Roberts · Jane Williams · Jane Woollard · Janet Gilmore · Janette Ryan · Jasmine Gideon · Jayne Watson · Jean-Jacques

Regouffre · Jeannie Stirrup · Jeehan Quijano · Jeff Collins · Jenifer Logie · Jennifer Arnold · Jennifer Bernstein · Jennifer Petersen · Jennifer M Lee · Jenny Booth · Jenny Huth · Jenny Newton · Jenny Nicholls · Jeremy Morton · Jeremy Trombley · Jerry Simcock · Jes Fernie · Jess Howard-Armitage · Jesse Berrett · Jesse Coleman · Jessica Laine · Jessica Loveland · Jessica Martin · Jessica Martin · Jethro Soutar · Jill Twist · Jillian Jones · Jo Conlon · Jo Goodall · Jo Harding · Jo Lateu · Joanna Flower · Joanna Luloff · Joanne Badger · Joanne Marlow · Joao Pedro Bragatti Winckler · JoDee Brandon · Jodie Adams · Jodie Martire · Johanna Anderson · Johannes Holmqvist · John Berube · John Carnahan · John Conway · John Coyne · John Down · John Gent · John Hodgson · John Kelly · John McKee · John Royley · John Shaw · John Steigerwald · John Winkelman · Jon Riches · Jon Talbot · Jonathan Blaney · Jonathan Huston · Jonathan Kiehlmann · Jonathan Ruppin · Jonathan Watkiss · Joseph Camilleri · Joseph Cooney · Joseph Hiller · Joseph Schreiber · Joshua Davis · Joy Paul · Jude Shapiro · Judith Smith · Judyth Emanuel · Julian Duplain · Julie Gibson · Julie Greenwalt · Julie Hutchinson · Julie-Ann Griffiths · Juliet Swann · Justine Mooney · K Elkes · Kaarina Hollo · Kara Kogler Baptista · Karen Jones · Karen Waloschek · Karl Kleinknecht &

Monika Motylinska · Kasim Husain · Kasper Haakansson · Kasper Hartmann · Kate Attwooll · Kate Griffin · Kate McCaughley · Katharina Herzberger · Katharine Freeman · Katharine Robbins · Katherine El-Salahi · Katherine Mackinnon · Kathryn Cave · Kathryn Edwards · Kathryn Williams · Katie Brown · Katie Lewin · Katrina Thomas · Keith Walker · Kenneth Blythe · Kerry Young · Kevin Maxwell · Khairunnisa Ibrahim · Kieron James · Kim Armstrong · Kirsten Hey · Kirsten Major · Kirsty Doole · KL Ee · Klara Rešetič · Kris Ann Trimis · Kristina Rudinskas · Krystine Phelps · Kuaam Animashaun · Kylé Pienaar · Lana Selby · Lander Hawes · Lara Vergnaud · Larraine Gooch · Laura Batatota · Laura Clarke · Laura Lea · Laurence Laluyaux · Laurie Sheck & Jim Peck · Leah Good · Lee Harbour · Leon Frey & Natalie Winwood · Leonie Schwab · Leonie Smith · Leri Price · Lesley Lawn · Lesley Watters · Leslie Wines · Liam Elward · Liliana Lobato · Lily Dunn · Lindsay Brammer · Linette Arthurton Bruno · Lisa Brownstone · Lisa Dillman · Liz Clifford · Liz Ketch · Lizzie Broadbent · Lizzie Stewart · Lorna Bleach · Lorna Scott Fox · Lottie Smith · Louise Foster · Louise Smith · Luc Verstraete · Lucia McNair · Lucia Rotheray · Lucia Whitney · Lucy Goy · Lucy Moffatt · Lucy Wheeler · Luise von Flotow · Luke Williamson · Lula Belle · Lynda & Harry Edwardes-Evans · Lynda Graham · Lynn Martin · Lynne Bryan · Lysann Church · M Manfre · Madeleine Kleinwort · Madeline Teevan · Mads Pihl Rasmussen · Maeve Lambe · Mahan L Ellison & K Ashley Dickson · Malgorzata Rokicka · Mandy Wight · Marcus Joy · Maria Ahnhem Farrar · Maria Hill · Marie Cloutier · Marie Donnelly · Marike Dokter · Marina Castledine · Marina Galanti · Mario Cianci · Mario Sifuentez · Marja S Laaksonen · Mark Sargent · Mark Sztyber · Mark Waters · Mark Whitelaw · Marlene Adkins · Martha Nicholson · Martha Stevns · Martin Brown · Martin Nathan · Martin Vosyka · Martin Whelton · Mary Byrne · Mary Carozza · Mary Heiss · Mary Wang · Mary Ellen Nagle · Matt & Owen Davies · Matt Greene · Matt O'Connor · Matthew Adamson · Matthew Armstrong · Matthew Banash · Matthew Black · Matthew Francis · Matthew Geden · Matthew Lowe · Matthew Smith · Matthew Thomas · Matthew Warshauer · Matthew Woodman · Matty Ross · Maureen Freely · Maureen Pritchard · Max Cairnduff · Max Garrone · Max Longman · Max McCabe · Meaghan Delahunt · Megan Muneeb · Megan Taylor · Megan Wittling · Meike Schwamborn · Meike Ziervogel · Melissa Beck · Melissa Quignon-Finch · Meredith Jones · Mette Kongsted · Michael Bichko · Michael Dodd · Michael Gavin · Michael Holt · Michael Kuhn · Michael Mc Caughley · Michael Schneiderman · Michael James Eastwood · Michelle Falkoff · Michelle Lotherington · Michelle Roberts · Mike Bittner · Mike Timms · Mike Turner · Milo Bettocchi · Miranda Gold · Miranda Persaud · Miriam McBride · Monika Olsen · Moray Teale · Morgan Bruce · Morven Dooner · Myles Nolan · N Tsolak · Namita Chakrabarty · Nan Craig · Nancy Cooley · Nancy Oakes · Nathalie Atkinson · Neferti Tadiar · Neil George · Nicholas Brown · Nicholas Jowett · Nick Chapman · Nick James · Nick Nelson & Rachel Eley · Nick Sidwell · Nick Twemlow · Nicola Hart · Nicola Mira · Nicola Sandiford · Nicole Matteini · Nigel Palmer · Nikolaj Ramsdal Nielsen · Nikos Lykouras · Nina Alexandersen · Nina Moore · Nina Power · Olga Alexandru · Olga Brawanska · Olga Zilberbourg · Olivia Payne · Olivia Tweed · Pamela Stackhouse · Pashmina Murthy · Pat Winslow · Patricia Appleyard · Patricia Webbs · Patrick Cole · Patrick McGuinness · Paul Cray · Paul Daw · Paul Jones · Paul Munday · Paul Robinson · Paula Edwards · Pavlos Stavropoulos · Penelope Hewett Brown · Penny East · Penny Schofield · Penny Simpson · Perlita Payne · Peter McBain · Peter McCambridge · Peter Rowland · Peter Vos · Peter Wells · Philip Carter · Philip Lewis · Philip Lom · Philip

Warren · Philipp Jarke · Philippa Hall · Piet Van Bockstal · Pippa Tolfts · PRAH Foundation · Rachael Williams · Rachel Carter · Rachel Jones · Rachel Lasserson · Rachel Matheson · Rachel Meacock · Rachel Van Riel · Rachel Watkins · Rachell Burton · Rebecca Braun · Rebecca Carter · Rebecca Moss · Rebecca Roadman · Rebecca Rosenthal · Rhiannon Armstrong · Rhodri Jones · Richard Ashcroft · Richard Bauer · Richard Clifford · Richard Gwyn · Richard Harrison · Richard Mansell · Richard McClelland · Richard Priest · Richard Shea · Richard Soundy · Richard Thomson · Richard John Davis · RM Foord · Robert Gillett · Robert Hamilton · Robert Hannah · Robin Taylor · Roger Newton · Ronan Cormacain · Rory Dunlop · Rory Williamson · Rosalind May · Rosalind Ramsay · Rosalind Sanders · Rosanna Foster · Rose Crichton · Rosemary Gilligan · Ross Scott & Jimmy Gilmore · Ross Trenzinger · Rowan Sullivan · Roxanne O'Del Ablett · Roz Simpson · Rozzi Hufton · Ruchama Johnston-Bloom · Rupert Ziziros · Ruth Chitty · Ryan Grossman · S Italiano · Sabrina Uswak · Sally Baker · Sally Thomson · Sam Gordon · Sam Reese · Samantha Murphy · Samantha Smith · Samuel Daly · Sandra Mayer · Santiago Sánchez Cordero · Sara Goldsmith · Sara Sherwood · Sarah Arboleda · Sarah Costello · Sarah Harwood · Sarah Lucas · Sarah Pybus · Sarah Smith · Sarah Watkins · Sasha Bear · Satara Lazar · Sean Kelly · Sean Malone · Sejal Shah · Seonad Plowman · Sez Kiss · SH Makdisi · Shannon Knapp · Shauna Gilligan · Sheridan Marshall · Sherman Alexie · Shimanto · Shira Lob · Sigurjon Sigurdsson · Simon Harley · Simon Pitney · Simon Robertson · SK Grout · Sofia Mostaghimi · Sonia Pelletreau · Sophia Wickham · Sophie Goldsworthy · ST Dabbagh · Stacy Rodgers · Stefanie May IV · Stefano Mula · Stephan Eggum · Stephanie Lacava · Stephen Cunliffe · Stephen Pearsall · Steve Chapman · Steve James · Steven & Gitte Evans · Stuart Wilkinson · Subhasree Basu · Sue & Ed Aldred · Susan Benthall · Susan Ferguson · Susan Higson · Susan Manser · Susanna Fidoe · Susie Roberson · Suzanne Lee · Sylvie Zannier-Betts · Tamar Shlaim · Tamara Larsen · Tammy Watchorn · Tamsin Dewé · Tania Hershman · Taylor ffitch · Teresa Griffiths · Terry Kurgan · Tessa Lang · The Mighty Douche Softball Team · Thea Bradbury · Thomas Baker · Thomas Bell · Thomas Chadwick · Thomas Fritz · Thomas Legendre · Thomas Mitchell · Thomas Rowley · Thomas van den Bout · Tiffany Lehr · Tiffany Stewart · Tim Hopkins · Tim Jones · Tim & Pavlina Morgan · Tim Retzloff · Tim Scott · Tim Theroux · Timothy Nixon · Tina Rotherham-Winqvist · Toby Day · Toby Halsey · Toby Ryan · Tom Atkins · Tom Darby · Tom Dixon · Tom Franklin · Tom Gray · Tom Lake · Tom Stafford · Tom Whatmore · Tom Wilbey · Tony Bastow · Tony Messenger · Torna Russell-Hills · Tory Jeffay · Tracy Bauld · Tracy Lee-Newman · Treasa De Loughry · Trevor Lewis · Trevor Wald · Tricia Durdey · Val Challen · Valerie Sirr · Vanessa Dodd · Vanessa Nolan · Vanessa Rush · Veronica Baruffati · Victor Meadowcroft · Victoria Adams · Victoria Huggins · Victoria Maitland · Victoria Smith · Vijay Pattisapu · Vinod Vijayakumar · Virginia May · Visaly Muthusamy · Volker Welter · Walter Smedley · Wendy Langridge · Will Huxter · William Dennehy · William Richard · William Schwaber · Yoora Yi Tenen · Zachary Hope · Zack Frehlick · Zinnia Ritz · Zoe Taylor · Zoe Thomas · Zoë Brasier · Zuzana Elia

Current & Upcoming Books

AMY ARNOLD was born in Oxford in 1974. She studied Neuropsychology at Birmingham University and has worked in a variety of jobs from packing swedes to teaching and lecturing. She lives in Cumbria, and in 2018 was awarded the inaugural Northern Book Prize for her debut novel, *Slip of a Fish*.